The Island Gang

Legend of Crystal Cove

Book I

Wendy,
Watch for Book 2 in 2007.
Enjoy.

BY: *Larry*

LARRY JOHNS

Tate Publishing, LLC.

Published in the United States of America
by Tate Publishing, LLC
127 East Trade Center Terrace
Mustang, OK 73064
(888) 361–9473

This novel is a work of fiction. Names, descriptions, entities and incidents included in the story are products of the author's imagination. Any resemblance to actual persons, events and entities is entirely coincidental.

ISBN: 1–5988632–1-5

07.19.06

DEDICATION

AND ACKNOWLEDGEMENT

Dedicated to Nate and Drew, without whom there would have been no Island Gang

I would like to acknowledge my nephew, Kyle Smith, for the drawing of the map used on the cover.

I also wish to thank Lindsay Behrens for her contribution to design and layout of both cover and content, and Mark Mingle for his contribution to the editing process. All in the Tate Publishing family have been kind and thoughtful through the process of publishing this work.

Many family members, both immediate and extended, have been supportive and patient through the five years of writing this novel. I owe each one of them my gratitude.

List of Chapters

1

The Power of Light

Chief Aboabo placed the last of the crystals into the hull of the largest boat—then paused to take one last look at the land his family had called home for generations. He could hardly believe what was happening. However, he was beginning to understand why his ancestors had fled their homeland long ago.

His Grandfather, Skyabo, often spoke of the great darkness that entered the hearts of their people. "It began when some began to think they were superior to others," taught Skyabo. "They sought position and authority by becoming popular—popularity generally acquired by breaking their laws. These 'popularity-seekers' became so deeply infiltrated into society, they would offer protection to those in their following. They caused great persecution and suffering for those who sought to live peaceably. By the time their dark works were brought to light, they were too numerous. It was easier to leave them to their ways and seek a new land."

Skyabo had been taught the formula for peace by his father and carefully passed it on to Aboabo. "First, all must live as equals. Some will have greater abilities than others, but even he who has great abilities cannot reach his potential alone. Peace is only maintained when all work toward the common good of the whole. Honest men *must* learn to live as equals. Second, there must be a set of laws defending liberty. He who is found in violation of the law—must be punished. If offenses go unpunished, liberty will not stand."

Aboabo felt the deep convictions of his grandfather,

and taught the formula for peace to his people. All in the village contributed, and families shared equally according to their needs. He looked to the sky in wonder. In spite of his efforts to teach his grandfather's ways, the cycle had begun again.

Under the direction of his great grandfather, his ancestors fled their homeland. They passed through many lands, but of all the places they encountered, the abundance of resources among these islands was most attractive. They were lush with vegetation. Many varieties of evergreen trees and shrubs blanketed the land. Fish and game were plentiful.

At the time of their arrival, days were the longest they'd ever known, and the Skyanabo had worshipped light as far back as records were kept. The long days of the islands were taken as a sign from God that this was to be their new home. Within months their village was established, and they were harvesting crops.

As time passed, days became shorter and the weather more severe. Days became so short there were only a couple of hours of light each day. The Skyanabo began a ritual of fasting and worship, followed by feasting, singing and dancing. This went on for days, even weeks on end, in an effort to please the God of Light.

One evening, a magical display of lights appeared in the sky. The Skyanabo took it as a sign that their offering had been accepted, and soon the days became longer. Each year as days got short, they would repeat their ritual, waiting patiently for the light show in the sky. And each year, the reassurance of longer days came, and the season of light would return. Light and warmth from the sun were what they lived for. It did more than warm their bodies; it drew them in—warming their very souls.

During the season of light, they were industrious—gathering wood, making clothing and blankets from furs, and storing meat, fish and grains. They knew that the season of dark would return, and they worked to be prepared.

Aside from their ritual, each year during the season of darkness they worked tirelessly to create light and heat. Fire provided both. Warmth from fire satisfied, however, firelight did not compensate for the light they craved. It was light equal to the brilliance of the sun that they desired.

During a hunting expedition one season, several members of the tribe came across an unusual cave. Upon exploring the cave, their torches reflected bright light from the cave's walls. With great effort, they broke loose several pieces to take to chief Aboabo. Each break uncovered more and brighter crystals. The cave was full of these curious crystals.

From that point on, crystals from the cave were used throughout the village to remind them of the power of the God of Light. During the season of darkness, large crystals fastened to the end of wooden poles were placed near torches that lit the village. The combination of fire providing heat and crystals reflecting light gave a calming reassurance that the season of light would return.

Crystals were used in art and basketry. They were also ornately fastened to the villagers' fishing boats, which they believed led to safer waters and larger catches. Productivity throughout their village increased as the crystals were prominently displayed, reminding them of their interdependence—and dependence on the giver of light.

Now, after centuries of peace and prosperity, the evil that had driven them to find these islands had once again entered the hearts of their people. Fueled by greed and self-indulgence, affluence had caused some to believe that they were smarter, thus more deserving than others. The days of living as equals and following tribal leadership had been disrupted.

It began with those who worked the sea. Island living depended heavily on sea life for sustenance. Those who were fishers grew aware of that dependence and used their skill to gain favor among the people. They gave extra to those who supported their quest for power. Certain words and signs were given secret meaning so that they could conspire undetected. They went by the name of Skoterga, the same name dissenters had used long ago.

Those who started the division stopped believing in the power of light. They boasted that greater intellect led to their success, and that the long term good of the people depended on a change in leadership. Their ways quickly gained a significant following as they worked to undermine tribal leaders.

Skyabo had gone to great lengths to remove the name Skoterga and its associated practices from the records of the Skyanabo. Some had obviously not forgotten.

The Skoterga made mockery of the crystals, and anything to do with the teachings of the Skyanabo. They desecrated sacred things attempting to prove to onlookers that there was no value in foolish traditions, and that worship of light had no relationship to success and happiness. The Skoterga taught that wealth came to those who were gifted, and that those who were gifted should lead, regardless of ancestral ties. Those who supported Skoterga leaders were promised privilege.

Once aware of their movement, Aboabo attempted to change the hearts of the Skoterga. When that failed, he tried to negotiate a resolution to their differences, believing that there was mutual ground whereupon they could coexist. But the Skoterga were stubborn, and persecution became intolerable to the point that Aboabo requested permission to take his followers and leave in peace. The Skoterga agreed to let them depart, thinking they had won a great victory in keeping the developed village and established industry.

The Skyanabo were permitted to use seven of the tribe's boats. They packed food, supplies, belongings, and as many of the crystals as they could—then looked to Aboabo to lead them on their journey to a new home.

While their next destination was never known, legend speaks of a light worshipping people having settled in the region of the Puget Sound and of a chief who had hidden away a vast collection of crystals near the end of his life.

2

Island Boys

It was Saturday morning in late April and the sun was shining brightly, which was not something you could count on in the little northwest town of Gig Harbor.

As he finished sweeping the entry, Travis checked the thermometer hanging on his porch—it read 75°. His next thought was to check the tide chart, which was located somewhere in his room. He paused just long enough to consider the current state of his room—then realized that it would be easier to simply check the tide from the deck of his neighbor that lived across the street. He dropped the broom and headed to take a look. "High tide! Perfect for bridge jumping! Time to call the guys!"

"Hey Gary, do you know what the temperature is?"

"Looks like a nice day," replied Gary, as he gazed from the window in the bathroom where he was cleaning the tub, "but I haven't had a chance to get outside."

"Then you haven't seen the tide either," Travis fired back at him.

Gary responded with a tone of sarcasm "That's affirmative—why, does it look *special* today?"

"No, *dork*! It's high tide, and my thermometer reads 75 degrees, which translates into perfect conditions for bridge jumping! Can you meet down at the beach?"

"Great idea, but some of us have chores. Ya goin' down now?" asked Gary, anticipating the answer with a nod of his head, and roll of the eyes. Travis was one of those friends that *always* got out of chores.

"My chores can wait, I'm on the way."

"I'll check with mom," replied Gary, "maybe she'll cut me some slack. If not—well, I'll get there as soon as I can. Have you called Justin and Curtis?"

"Not yet. I'll call Curtis. You call Justin. We'll let Curtis call Tyler. See ya when ya get there."

Travis hung up and called Curtis—there was no answer. One of the good things about living on a small island is that whenever you can't get someone on the phone, you can just swing by their house. Nowhere on the island was too far out of the way. Passing Curtis' house wasn't the shortest route to the beach, but it was the only way of finding out if Curtis was home. Travis put on his swim trunks, grabbed a towel, and jumped on his scooter.

Raft Island beach was a favorite hangout, particularly when the weather was good. Along with the park-like environment, the beach had a pier leading to a floating dock. The dock, while important to boaters, was equally important to non-boaters. With no public slips, boaters needed the dock to load passengers and gear. The dock was also the perfect place to lie in the warm sun after a cold swim. The pier leading to the dock and the adjacent bridge, which connected Raft Island to the mainland, were perfect jumping platforms.

Travis had to pass by the Smythe residence on the way to Curtis' house and noticed a moving truck down at the end of the driveway. He remembered having seen a "Sold" sign on the house for the past several weeks, and wondered if the Smythe family was on their way out or if the new family was moving in. There was no sign of people. He was curious, but decided he'd wait and ask the guys if they knew what was going on. He arrived at Curtis' house in time to see Curtis' father carrying the hedge trimmer into the shop. Evidence of the hedge trimmer having been put to use was everywhere. He found Curtis mowing the half-acre of lawn on the back portion of their property. Curtis' mom and older sister were out in the yard, too. "Just as I figured," Travis said to himself, "no wonder no one answered the phone."

Travis waived frantically and yelled as loud as he could, trying to get Curtis' attention over the noise of the mower, "Hey, Curtis!"

Curtis let go of the safety lever, killing the motor. "What's up?"

"Gary and I are meeting down at the beach. This weather calls for some bridge jumping. Can you come?"

"If you haven't noticed, it's yard clean-up day. Dad *might* let me take a break after I finish with the lawn," came the response.

"Well, *hurry*! We'll be down at the beach! Call Tyler?"

Tyler was Curtis' autistic cousin. The guys tried to include him in their activities. He didn't always participate, but he liked hanging out and was usually a good source of humor.

"I'll give him a call as soon as I can," Curtis replied.

Travis hollered, "See ya down there," as he gave his scooter a push, heading toward the beach.

"What is with this?" Curtis asked himself as Travis headed off, "Travis never has to do chores. I am always working—he's always playing. It's just *not* fair." Curtis knew it was no use making the "*it's not fair*" plea with his folks. That would only launch into the "*life's not fair*" lecture that he'd already heard a million times. The best he could hope for was permission to take a break after he finished the lawn.

Gary pled for leniency, and was told that once he finished the bathtub he could join the guys for a couple of hours. His mom was amazed at the surge of energy, and wished she could bottle—whatever it was that got him to move so quickly. Gary assured his mom that he just needed the proper motivation.

As Gary stepped onto the front porch he let out a loud whistle, "Shadow, here boy. C'mon, let's go."

Shadow was Gary's Alaskan malamute. Shadow joined the island boys in most of their activities. He was an amazing dog. People would often remark that he must be half cat. He could walk the upper railing of the wood stake fence surrounding Gary's yard just as well as any feline. In fact, Shadow spent nearly as much time on the roof as he did in the yard, making it impossible to keep him fenced in. It was a source of irritation to some of the neighbors, but Shadow didn't generally get into too much trouble. He stayed pretty close to home unless he was out with the guys.

Within seconds, Shadow was at Gary's side raring to go. "Let's go boy, we're off to the beach." That was all the direction Shadow needed. He led the way, checking over his shoulder now and then to make sure Gary was still with him. Gary stopped at the gated boat ramp just before the bridge. He took a deep breath of salty air as he looked out on the boats moored sporadically in the area used as the marina. "One day," he said quietly to himself as he weighed the pros and cons of the various types of boats before him, "one day we'll have our own boat."

"Hey Gary," shouted Travis as he climbed out of the water onto the dock at the end of the pier. "C'mon down!"

It wasn't long before Curtis' father, Ray, came around the corner on his way from the shop. Ray was a shade tree mechanic, with a shop located behind the house in the lower part of their property.

"Hey Dad!" Curtis hollered, "The guys are meeting

down at the beach. We want to jump off the bridge and go for a swim while the weather is good. Can I go after I finish the lawn?"

"How about the rest of your chores?" his father asked.

"I'll finish when I get back. We *need* to take advantage of the sunshine! Besides, I've been working all morning. I'm ready for a break."

Ray listened patiently, trying to be sympathetic to Curtis' request, and then replied, "You're usually ready for a break—what we *need* is to get this yard cleaned up while the weather holds. I guess you can go down to the beach for a while after the lawn is done, but be home by three o'clock. Your chores *must* be finished before dark."

"I'll get 'em all done, I promise!"

"*Score!*" Curtis said, as he pumped his arm making the gesture you have to make whenever you say, "*Score!*"

With the mower off, now was the opportune time to run in for a glass of water and give Tyler a call.

"Hey Tyler, ask if you can go down to the beach with the guys. Travis and Gary are on their way now. I've got to finish the lawn, and then I'll come by and get you. This weather calls for bridge jumping and a swim!"

"No way!" exclaimed Tyler. "That water is *too* cold"

"You don't have to get wet. Do you want to come or not?" demanded Curtis impatiently.

"Just a minute," Tyler said as he laid the phone down.

Curtis hated it when he laid the phone down. With Tyler, you never knew if he'd actually make it back. Tyler sometimes forgot that he was in the middle of a phone conversation, and just went on to other things.

Soon Tyler did return, "Mom said it's okay,"

"Fine, I'll pick you up in about 25 minutes."

Tyler's family lived just a couple of blocks away, which

made it convenient to include him. Tyler needed someone to keep an eye on him. He sort of lived in his own little world, which could get him in trouble if he wasn't checked on frequently. When he was with the island boys, they did a pretty good job of making sure he stayed out of trouble, and he enjoyed their company.

Curtis hurriedly finished the lawn, making sure to do a thorough job so his dad wouldn't make him do the *entire* lawn over again *just* for practice. He emptied the catcher, put the mower away, changed into his swimming shorts, grabbed his scooter, and headed for Tyler's.

When Curtis arrived, Tyler was waiting out front gazing into the sky with his scooter leaning against the garage door. As Tyler saw Curtis approach, he pointed to the sky and said, "Look, it's a happy day for God!"

Tyler was sure God lived up in the sky. He decided that when the sun was shining God was having a good day, when it was raining God was having a not so good day. He had it all figured out—so he thought.

"Yep, it's a happy day," Curtis replied. "Get your scooter and let's go down to the beach."

Curtis and Tyler arrived as Justin's mom was dropping him off. Gary and Travis had just made their second jump off of the bridge, and along with Shadow, were swimming for the beach.

"Hey guys," Curtis called out, "how's the water?"

"*Freezing!*" Gary answered, "Just like always."

"And just like always, that's the reason I'm *not* going in!" insisted Tyler.

The rest of the guys, including Shadow, spent the next several hours alternating between jumping from the bridge or pier, and then lying on the warm dock to soak up sun. Tyler walked the beach, picking up shells and small pieces of driftwood, placing them neatly in a pile near the pier's ramp.

As the guys lay on the dock, they talked of plans for summer. All at once, Gary got up and headed for the bridge. "Guys, come with me!" Reluctantly they got up from the warm dock and followed Gary down the pier, up the boat launch road, and onto the bridge.

"Look out there and tell me what you see," Gary said pointing out into the marina.

"*Boats*," replied Travis enthusiastically, "all kinds of *cool* boats."

"That's right, *boats!*" said Gary.

"You called us over here to show us boats?" Curtis questioned, pained at having responded to the request. "Boats that we've seen every day of our lives?"

"How are we going to get one?" Gary asked, "It's time we figured it out."

"It would be *so* cool to have our own boat," Justin added, gazing into the marina.

Curtis couldn't believe what he was hearing! Responding to Justin he said, "You're starting to sound like Gary—our resident *dreamer!*"

"Like I've been saying," Gary chimed in, "a boat is the answer to our freedom! Once we have the boat, we'll be free to explore—*everywhere*—*anytime!* Getting our own boat *is* the answer!"

They had already decided that once they had a boat, their first stop would be Dead Man's Island. Stories of the Native American burial ground up on the plateau at the far end of the island peaked their interest. Their folks wouldn't let them explore the island. Instead, they told them stories about people who had been hexed from disturbing the sacred burial ground. There were many tales about how the island got its name, but the fact that it was a Native American burial ground was the only one that held water. The boys had boated around Dead Man's plenty of times, but out of respect for Native Americans, the island was pretty much left alone.

Given the opportunity, they intended to check it out.

As they discussed the upcoming summer and talked about vacation plans, various camps they'd be involved in, etc., they came to the conclusion that even with busy schedules, there would be plenty of time for exploring.

"This is the summer to claim our independence—the answer is *definitely* our own boat. We've talked about it long enough. It's time for action!" Gary concluded.

Travis was simply listening to the conversation about vacations. His mind was on other things.

"Hey Travis," Gary said, "Why are you being so quiet?"

"I just found out that we'll probably be moving sometime this summer," Travis responded. "Mom and dad say the bills are piling up. We may have to sell the house."

Talk about dropping a lead balloon on an otherwise perfectly splendid afternoon. It hadn't been Travis' intent to spoil the good time, but that was his reality. His family might have to leave all this behind. He could feel himself being pulled away from the guys by a situation completely out of his control, and at present he was feeling a little on the outside.

Travis' dad had been working odd jobs since being laid off. The economy was still shaky and unemployment high. Travis' father had learned basic construction skills working with his father from the time he was a young boy. He kept busy doing odd jobs for friends and neighbors, but he wasn't making the money he'd made at the investment firm where he had headed up the I.T. department. Jobs in his field were being outsourced more frequently, making it all the more difficult to find work.

Justin couldn't believe what he was hearing. His family was the only one of the island boys that didn't live on the island, but they had recently bought a lot intending to build. "*Moving*?" Justin questioned. "You can't just—*move*! I haven't even arrived yet!"

"Yeah," Gary chimed in, "Where would you go anyway? Somewhere on the island—right?"

"We don't know any of that yet. It all depends on what we can afford after the bills are paid. Mom and dad said not to count on staying on the island."

The mood turned solemn. With the exception of Justin, their families moved to Raft Island before any of them were born. They'd been best friends all of their lives. The thought of that coming to an end was devastating.

Exasperated at the thought of things that were simply out of their control, Gary exploded, "That does it! We're getting a boat! I don't know how, but by summer we'll have one! This could be our last chance—it just won't wait! Everything could suddenly change—*forever*! We have to *seize* the opportunity!"

"Oh, I see, we'll just like—get ourselves a boat!" Curtis jested.

Gary thought for a moment as he looked out over the water, "If we put our minds to it—we can do it. It'll take hard work, but if we save all the money we can get our hands on, and put it all together, I know we can do it! If we're not too picky—something will come along."

"What do you mean by *something*—don't even think about a rowboat?" scowled Curtis.

"Who said anything about a rowboat?" asked Travis.

Gary responded even more determined, "and why not a rowboat! We're young—and strong! At least we'd be on the water! If we find something better, that'll be great. But a rowboat would work!"

"He's got a point," Justin chimed in, "we ought to be able to get our hands on a boat. We just need to find the right deal."

Travis added, "Count me in. I'll do whatever it takes. This could be my last chance before we have to move.

Which reminds me, does anybody know what's going on at the Smythe's? I saw a moving truck at their house today."

"Mom said they moved out last week," Curtis offered.

"I guess the new family has arrived," said Travis.

"Any kids our age?" asked Gary.

"I didn't see any people, just the truck. They must have all been inside when I passed by. We'll have to check it out."

Gary, determined to keep focused on the boat, spoke up, "We're getting off track—back to the boat. We need to ask for jobs at home, around the island, and wherever else we hear of an opportunity. We have to be committed to saving our money till the right deal comes along."

Shadow's tail was wagging like crazy. He knew what they were talking about, and he liked being on the water as much as they did. Several of their families had boats, so they'd done their share of boating. But it always had to wait until parents were available, and exploration was limited to where the parents wanted to go. They were old enough now for their own boat and a little more freedom.

Curtis got a disconcerted look on his face, "And how much do you guys think boats cost anyway? I happen to know they're expensive. My dad's friend has an old, small, clunker boat—and even that cost him $900!"

Justin interjected, "My family had a small sailboat in Texas. I don't know how much it cost, but we sure had a lot of fun on it. We sold it before we moved here."

"Look," replied Gary, "we can't give up before we even try. We've got to work hard and keep our eyes and ears open. There are boats just sitting in people's yards all over the place—that never get used. If we put our minds to it, we'll find one that suits our needs—and fits our budget! We need to be entrepreneurial—but we can do it!"

Curtis hated it when Gary used big words. He was

sure Gary had no idea what it meant, and it's certain he didn't. With a scowl Curtis asked, "Entre . . . what?"

"Entrepreneurial," repeated Gary. "It means finding creative ways to earn money. Dad taught it to me."

"Whatever," Curtis retorted in disgust. "You're living in a dream world if you think we can get our own boat."

"And a mighty fine world it is!" Gary continued, "If we save allowance, birthday money, and take every opportunity that comes along to earn a little extra—we can do it. It's all in the attitude. Anyway, we have to try!"

"Gary's right! We need to do the best we can and keep our eyes open," added Travis.

"Money's the answer to our problem," Gary added, "Once you've got cash, you can negotiate."

"There he goes with the vocabulary again," retorted Curtis, "So which is really the answer—boat or money?" asked Curtis as he rolled his eyes at the thought of them ever having enough money to get a boat.

"What is it with you, Curtis?" asked Travis, defending Gary.

"That's okay," Gary cut in, "They're both the answer. No matter what your goal is, you have to be willing to work to achieve it. Expecting to achieve something without working at it isn't realistic."

3

The Porch Swing

On the way home from the beach, Travis followed the route that would take him by the Smythe home. Curiosity was eating at him. He had to see if there was any sign of the new family. This time it was very busy. Men and teenagers were unloading boxes, furniture, and all sorts of odds and ends. No sign of kids, so he didn't stop. *I'll get mom to check it out,* Travis thought, *She likes to know everyone.*

Travis didn't find out for several weeks, but the new family did have a kid his age. A young girl named Wendy. As with any move, it took Wendy's family a few days to get settled. Moving had never made Wendy's list of favorite things to do, but her dad's job required it. Wendy's father was a doctor and an officer in the United States Air Force. Needless to say, moving had become a way of life for them. The opportunity to live close to the water combined with the intrigue of island living made this particular move a little more palatable, but nonetheless, Wendy was not excited about the unpleasant task of making new friends.

After several days of unpacking, organizing closets and furniture, and cleaning the mess left in the wake, they located the essentials. Experience taught them that they would be living out of boxes for months to come. The weatherman called for sunshine the following day, so it was decided that it was time for a break. Wendy couldn't wait to become a little more familiar with her new surroundings. She was going to find her way down to the water, gather seashells, and try to meet some kids along the way. Her mom and dad had plans in town.

Wendy awoke early to bright rays of sun piercing through the blinds of her bedroom window. That was the only motivation she needed for an early start. She was up and dressed in no time.

She walked along the street in front of her house, looking for the most direct path to the shore. She could see water through the trees. She just needed a way to get to it. She'd seen the beach on the way in, but that was on the other side of the island. There had to be a path to the water closer to home. But every time there was a clear shot of the water, it was across private property with conspicuously posted signs, "Private Property / No Trespassing."

"The entire shoreline can't be private property," she said aloud. "Certainly some of the waterfront is open to everyone!" But the obvious pathways to the water were driveways. "This is *ridiculous*!" she exclaimed.

She was about to head back to ask her mother for suggestions when she came across a driveway without one of those obnoxious "No Trespassing" signs. With a tone of disgust she said, "Surely this leads to someone's house too!" She looked for signs, but saw none, nor was there a house in view.

Some homes were not obvious from the road, which was the case here. The driveway took a turn to the left about 30 yards from the street, and thick vegetation hid any sign of where it led. Straight ahead of her, across a field of tall grass, was an unobstructed view of the water. And what a view it was!

"No signs! This must be the path I've been looking for," she determined, heading down the drive. As Wendy reached the bend in the drive, the asphalt became a divided concrete driveway that proceeded diagonally to a very nice home. Both drives were lined in dark gray slate with a strip of tall grass down the center. Just in front of the house, a roundabout connected the two drives. In the center of the roundabout was a large fountain surrounded by a low hedge. Off to the left of the house was a large outbuilding. The field of tall grass in front of her was, in fact, someone's front yard. The yard, however, was extremely overgrown.

I wonder if anyone even lives here? was the question running through Wendy's mind. She hesitated for a moment, contemplating the scene, then turned to face the gorgeous view of the water and was reminded of her goal. Ignoring the bend in the drive, she made a beeline through the tall grass toward the water. As long as she kept her distance from the house, what could it hurt? The worst that could happen is that someone would ask her to get *off* of their property.

At the far side of the yard was a fairly steep hill of terraced planters that stretched the entire length of the property. The planters were filled with rhododendrons, azaleas, and roses, many of which were in bloom, boasting an array of colors. Her nose picked up a variety of scents, which prompted her to take a closer look. As with the rest of the yard, the planters were full of weeds. She thought of picking some flowers, but realized she would not be able to carry everything home—her goal today was to collect seashells.

Just beyond the terraced planters, water lapped at the shoreline. The smell of the salty air, birds singing in the trees, the crisp view of snow-capped mountains across the water—it was wonderful! She had been told about the Olympic Mountain Range, but cloud cover had hidden it from view the day they arrived. *My new home is beautiful,* thought Wendy, as a feeling of satisfaction swept over her. *I think a girl could get used to this!*

Along the shore were the remains of various forms of sea life, the majority of which were broken pieces of oyster shells. She had never seen oysters in nature like this. The oysters she had seen previously were at an amusement park; for a price, a worker had pried them open, revealing a pearl in each one. She searched the shore carefully, hoping that among the pieces of shell she might find a pearl or two.

Among the shell clutter were clamshells, mussel shells, and types of seashells that she didn't recognize. There were so many pieces of shells; she could hardly find the sand. It seemed to be layer upon layer of crushed shells lining the shore. She had hoped to take her shoes off and wade in the shallow water, but the broken pieces of seashell were too sharp for bare feet, and dipping her hand in, she determined the water was too cold.

After having gathered a small collection of unbroken shells intended for a display on the dresser in her room, she made her way back up the terraced bank. It wasn't until she climbed onto the last planter that she realized she had used a different path on her return than she had on the way down. She was much nearer to the house.

Immediately catching her eye was a porch swing mounted to the overhang of the house. The wooden porch wrapped around as much of the house as she could see. The swing hung off the side of the house facing the water, allowing who ever occupied it to enjoy a wonderful panoramic view with the Olympic Mountains as a backdrop.

The swing drew her in like a magnet. Before she realized what she was doing, she had climbed the three steps up onto the deck, laid her collection of shells neatly on the railing, and took a seat in the swing. She gave herself a push, taking it all in as she gently glided back and forth. Feeling the tranquility of the moment, she began humming. Her father, the musician in the family, loved to play the guitar and was a sucker for oldies that fared well with the accompaniment of acoustic guitar. He had encouraged Wendy to sing along with him from the time she was just 4 years old. Harmonizing had come natural to her, and she learned to love the tunes her father loved. The warmth and the view got her started with one of his favorites, "Sunshine on My Shoulders," by John Denver. After humming the first few stanzas, she broke out singing as if she were alone in the world.

> Sunshine on my shoulders makes me happy
> Sunshine in my eyes can make me cry
> Sunshine on the water looks so lovely
> Sunshine almost always makes me high
>
> If I had a day that I could give you
> I'd give to you the day just like today
> If I had a song that I could sing for you
> I'd sing a song to make you feel this way
>
> Sunshine on my shoulders makes me happy
> Sunshine in my eyes can make me cry
> Sunshine on the water looks so lovely
> Sunshine almost always makes me high
>
> If I had a tale that I could tell you
> I'd tell a tale sure to make you smile
> If I had a wish that I could wish for you
> I'd make a wish for sunshine all the while
>
> Sunshine on my shoulders makes me happy
> Sunshine in my eyes can make me cry
> Sunshine on the water looks so lovely
> Sunshine almost all the time makes me high

As she finished the song, she suddenly had the impression that she was not alone. She turned to look behind her, and to her great astonishment there was an older man standing in a half open doorway near the far corner of the house. Startled, she jumped from the swing and hurriedly headed for the stairs, nearly tripping over her own feet on the way.

The man called out, "No, please don't leave. You have a beautiful voice. I wish you would stay!"

"I'm really sorry," offered Wendy, still on her way to the shell collection, "I didn't think anyone lived here."

"It is I who apologize," he said. "My yard is in need of attention, but then, if it were neat and tidy I may not have had the pleasure of making your acquaintance. My name is Reg—Reg Grisham."

She remained a safe distance away, "I'm Wendy."

"Wendy. What a beautiful name—for a beautiful girl. Are you visiting the island?"

"No, my family just moved here. We live across the street and down a ways."

Having lived on the island many years, Grisham at least recognized most of the residents. "You must be the new family that moved into the Smythe place."

"Yep, that's us."

"Well then—welcome to the neighborhood. Please, feel free to come use the swing whenever you'd like, and bring that beautiful voice with you!"

"Really?" she asked.

"Absolutely! Unlike some with their 'No Trespassing' signs, I enjoy the company. I'm alone way too much of the time. Please, come whenever you'd like."

"I may have to bring my parents by to meet you—so they're comfortable with the idea."

"That would be great! I'd love to meet them. I know the house is impossible to see from the road, so peek down the drive, and if the car is out front, I'm home. I put the car in the garage today, but usually I leave it out front. Whether I'm home or not, feel free to use the swing—anytime."

Wendy gathered her shells from the porch rail, and

hurried home. She could hardly believe it. Here she had been worried about being chased off for trespassing, and instead she'd made a new friend. Arriving home she told her mom all about her walk on the beach, the porch swing, and Mr. Grisham. Her mother was happy to see her so excited, and agreed to meet Mr. Grisham soon.

Several days later, Wendy decided to take Mr. Grisham up on his generous offer. She and her mother had been over to Mr. Grisham's, and her mother agreed that he was a kind man. Her mother suggested always knocking first whenever she visited, just to let him know she was there. She intended on following her mother's advice, however the car wasn't out front, so she proceeded directly to the swing.

The setting was so serene—it was the perfect place to relax and sing, her favorite pastime. She was swinging and enjoying the view when suddenly something caught her attention. Once again, there was that feeling of not being alone. She quickly turned to look behind her, but saw nobody. There was something though. It was a sound—coming from the back of the house. She attempted to ignore it, but it was persistent. The closer she listened, the more it sounded like something—or someone in distress. It was as if it was calling to her.

She got off of the swing, cautiously making her way around the back corner. The noise became clearer. She continued moving carefully along the backside of the house until she could discern that the sound was definitely coming from inside the house.

Could it be Mr. Grisham? she thought to herself, stopping in her tracks. She listened a while longer, *He's sobbing! What could be so terribly wrong?* She hardly knew Mr. Grisham, but the thought of anyone being so forlorn was disconcerting.

She could hear words, but couldn't begin to understand what was being said. Just ahead of her was a window. She inched her way toward the window, trying to get up enough nerve to have a look inside. She got right to the windows edge and carefully leaned forward just enough to get a peek. There was Mr. Grisham on his knees in front of an easy chair near the dining room. It was as though he was praying—pleading with God about something. Wendy wondered what could be so wrong. She pulled back from the window and just stood there wondering what to do.

All at once tears were streaming down her cheeks. Feeling that Mr. Grisham's heart was breaking had pierced her soul. She could sense his pain, even though she had no idea what was troubling him. She wanted to console him, but this was obviously a private moment and she had no business being there.

She turned to make her way back toward the swing, trying to retrace her steps as best she could. Though she found her way to the window seemingly unnoticed, now her feet were finding every squeaky board in the deck. Finally arriving at the swing, certain that Mr. Grisham had heard the boards, she quickly searched her repertoire of songs for something appropriate for the moment. A song from a favorite old time musical came to mind. She gave herself a push and began to sing.

Unknown to Wendy, Grisham had already arrived at the door behind the swing as she began. He pulled the door part way open leaving the screen door closed, and stood and listened as she reverently sang Edelweiss.

At the conclusion of her song, Grisham pushed the screen open, "I was hoping it was you," he said to Wendy, walking out onto the deck.

Wendy was nervous. His words indicated that he heard the noisy boards.

"How is it you always know just the right time to come—and just the right song to sing?"

Wendy hadn't realized that there had been anything to the timing of her visits.

"Edelweiss is one of my all time favorites," came Wendy's response. "Is everything okay?" Before she realized what she was saying, she'd given away the fact that she knew something was wrong. She bit the side of her cheek awaiting his reply.

Feeling a little embarrassed, Grisham responded, "Oh—I'm sorry—you must have heard me."

Realizing that the squeaky boards didn't necessarily indicate that she'd been anywhere near the back of the house, and in an effort to undo the damage of her previous statement Wendy replied, "Heard what? It's just—you look a little sad."

"I'm doing okay now. Some days are just harder than others. My wife passed away several months ago—sometimes I still get sad."

Wendy remembered the last time she was there he commented that too much of his time was spent alone. She wasn't sure what to say. "I'm sorry to hear—was there an accident?"

"No, Lucille battled Multiple Sclerosis for many years, and it finally got her. She was a trooper, and fought her way through many tough years. Sometimes I just miss that old gal more than I can stand."

Wendy could hear the loneliness in his voice. "Don't you have any family?"

"No one close by," came the reply. "We only have one son, and he's an east coaster. After completing college, a firm out of Boston recruited him. With his young family, and having only been at his job a short time, he doesn't get much time off. Makes it hard for him to get away."

"Do you get to visit them?"

"We made a couple of trips back east while Lucille was able, but traveling was so hard on her the last few years—we—I mean—I, haven't seen them since Lucille's memorial."

Wendy had an idea. "I have a similar problem."

Somewhat confused, Grisham asked, "You do?"

"Yeah, we move every few years—my dad's in the Air Force. When he retires, we plan to move close to my grandparents, but in the meantime, I rarely get to see them. One of the lessons we covered in school this past year was the role of surrogates."

"Are you suggesting . . ."

Before Grisham could finish, Wendy interjected, "Exactly! Mr. Grisham, would you be my surrogate grandpa?"

"I'd be honored," Grisham replied. "And you'll be my surrogate granddaughter?" he asked.

"I'll do my very best," said Wendy, as she threw her arms open to give him a hug.

Grisham could feel his emotions surfacing. His vision blurred a little as he fought back the tears welling up in his eyes. This friendship with Wendy might be just what he needed.

4

Legend of Crystal Cove

"Hey guys, look—the door's open!"

The boys had knocked on Grisham's door, but apparently there was nobody home. Travis spotted the open door to the adjacent building as they turned to leave.

"I wonder what he keeps in there?" Travis asked.

"You know we can't leave without having a peek," Gary replied, as he broke into a sprint.

The others were right behind him, except for Curtis, who hesitated. The last time he was this close to Grisham's place, he had been sent to chase the ball during a game of street ball. That ball managed to make the turn in Grisham's driveway, rolling into the bushes right up by the fountain. About the time he reached to pick it up, the deepest bark he'd ever heard came from the garage. All he could think of as he dug the ball out of the bushes was headlines in the morning paper, "Raft Island Boy—Eaten by Dog." He grabbed that ball and ran for his life, vowing never to go near Grisham's place again. Now these knuckleheads were talking about trespassing.

Curtis tried to take comfort in the fact that he was in the company of the bravest guys he knew, but sometimes their idea of bravery had a strange resemblance to stupidity. In an attempt to get them to rethink their intentions, Curtis, who was trailing behind, shouted, "We can't just nose around in Mr. Grisham's property without asking."

"C'mon," replied Gary, "What are you afraid of? Aren't you even a little curious?"

"Go ahead if you want, but I'm waiting outside," Curtis blurted out—intending on firmly standing his ground.

"Are you sure we want to do this?" Justin asked.

"Sure," Gary said. "We aren't going to hurt anything. We're just going to have a look around. After all, the door *is* open. Maybe there's *already* an intruder, and we'll be the heroes for chasing them off."

"Right," replied Curtis, "you do have an imagination."

It wasn't a very convincing argument, but Gary was determined to have a look. He had a fascination with the content of old buildings. The rest of the guys could join him or wait outside. It didn't really matter either way.

Gary persisted, "So you guys coming or not?"

Travis was right behind him.

Tyler was ready to follow, no questions asked. His sense of reasoning was based strictly on experience. As yet, he hadn't had the experience of entering the old shed. No experience—no fear.

Justin wasn't about to risk being ridiculed, "Count me in."

Curtis couldn't believe what he was allowing himself to get into. "So this is peer pressure," he said under his breath, "ignoring your gut when it's telling you—*'get out of there!'*" Then loud enough for everyone to hear he added, "I want it on record that this is against my better judgment."

Although they had been talking rather gregariously the last several minutes, the second Gary pushed the door open, rusty hinges let out a moan to wake the dead! They ran for cover!

From where they had ducked down behind the thick brush, Gary whispered loud enough for the others to hear, "For crying out loud! Have you ever heard a door moan like that before?"

There was consensus in the ranks. That was a *big*

noise. The salt air had a way of getting to everything made of metal. They were sort of used to that, but something about being where you weren't sure you should be had a way of augmenting suspense, and unexpected noises didn't help.

Just being at Grisham's place was eerie enough. Grisham had been sort of a loner as long as they could remember. All they knew about him was that he did *"top secret"* government work—whatever that meant. And he had never been around much, which built upon the aura of mysterious. He and his wife had lived on the island forever, but lately things had been even more strange than normal. It seemed they were never home. Almost everything about Grisham's place gave the impression that it was abandoned.

They waited in the bushes for a minute to see if neighbors were going to gather to see what all of the ruckus was. When it appeared the coast was clear, Gary urged the guys onward, "C'mon guys, how are we ever going to become famous adventurers if we're afraid of a little noise?"

Curtis' gut was really talking now. "*Cut and run while you still can!*"

"I'll lead the way," Gary said, motioning them onward.

"Right behind you," replied Travis.

"What's everybody so nervous about?" asked Tyler, who in spite of his disability had a fairly keen sense to others' concerns.

"Yeah, really," Travis added, "Why is everyone so jumpy?"

Curtis gave them a curious stare and thought, *How quickly they forget that I wasn't the only one that ran for cover!*

They gathered at the door for the second attempt.

"This door is in serious need of lubrication!" said Gary, swinging the door all the way open.

Grisham's house and outbuilding were located at the back of his lot. The large outbuilding backed right up against a tall stand of firs. At the moment overcast skies blocked most of the sunlight, however, buffered light through a side window exposed a vague outline of the contents of the building. The room appeared to be full of something—though they weren't sure exactly what.

"We need some light," whispered Travis.

"Must be a switch here close to the door. I'll check this side, you check over there," replied Gary, motioning to Travis to feel his way along the wall.

The two of them proceeded cautiously, when all of a sudden—the room lit up like Christmas—exposing the most dangerous animals of the known world!

"*Look out!*" Tyler yelled as he turned to run.

Reaching out to grab Tyler by the back of his shirt before he broke his neck trying get through the clutter, Gary said rather matter-of-factly, "Tyler—they're *dead!*"

Upon closer examination, Tyler agreed, "Oh yeah, I guess they are dead. But, aren't they still scary?"

His autism sometimes made it difficult for him to separate his imagination from reality.

"No," Curtis replied sharply, trying to compensate for the jitters causing his knees to shake, "They're not scary!" Then a bit more timid he added, "But I still have this feeling . . ."

Their entering the building had triggered a motion sensor that Grisham used for a light switch. The first thing that came into view were trophy animals mounted on the wall just above them—deer, elk, moose, caribou, big horned sheep, buffalo, and one each grizzly, polar, and black bear.

After a good look at the collection, Gary exclaimed, "Can you believe this! I've only seen pictures of most of these guys!"

He had a point. The zoo had polar and black bear exhibits, and elk hunting was common to the northwest, so they'd seen their share of elk, but grizzly, moose, big horn sheep, buffalo—this was definitely a first!

Travis walked from animal to animal, looking into their eyes, and studying their features. He paused in front of the bears as his imagination went to work. He could just picture Mr. Grisham out in the wild bringing them down. Half under his breath he muttered, "Can you imagine running into these guys out in the wild?"

"You've got to be kidding!" exclaimed Curtis. "They'd be looking at us thinking, 'dinner' and that would be the end of it!"

Once they got past the animals and boxes stacked near the front, they spread out and began making their way through the rest of the clutter. Outbuildings were common in this part of the country, but this one had no end! There was at least one of every type of yard equipment they'd ever seen. And so many shop tools—it was amazing. There was even a wooden airplane—looked to be a glider—hanging from the ceiling off to one corner. Projects in the works were everywhere!

As Justin made his way to the back of the building, there was an old backhoe, a bulldozer—and, the best find of all—a boat trailer. "Guys—look!" shouted Justin. "Could be for the boat down at the beach!"

"This place is sure bigger than it looks from the outside," said Gary. Can you believe all the junk in here? This guy needs a garage sale!"

"He could run his own rental business with all of this equipment," added Travis.

"Yeah, and I'll bet my whole house would fit under this roof," said Justin, "if, it weren't for all the—stuff!"

The middle of the building must have been at least 25 feet high. Right about the center of the building, there was a wrought iron spiral staircase that led to an enclosed room built on a couple of cross beams. The rest of the high area was open vaulted ceiling. There were three sets of double-wide roll up doors on either end of the building, all equipped with automatic openers.

"I wonder what's up there?" asked Gary inquisitively, pointing to the top of the staircase.

Travis was standing closest to the stairs, but just as he was about to venture up, he heard Justin let out a loud gasp from across the room, "*Score*! Look over here! Boat supplies!"

Quickly, they made their way over to where Justin was. Sure enough, there, hanging on a wall, were two large aluminum oars, 5 life vests, a life saving ring, and other boat paraphernalia.

Tyler, pointing to a wall adjacent to the one they were all gawking at, asked, "Is that a sail?"

"Look! It is a sail," said Justin, verifying Tyler's find. "And look—a tiller and drop keel. I'll bet this stuff is used to convert that boat down on the beach to a sailboat!"

Curtis saw something across the way that got his interest. It looked like a motor on a stand. A similar scene had adorned his father's shed more than once. He walked over and lifted the corner of the tarp, uncovering a 20-horse outboard. "Now this is what that boat needs!" The easy way—was his way.

"Unbelievable! This is great," exclaimed Travis. "Mr. Grisham not only has the boat we need, but he has all of the gear! We're just gonna have to make him a deal he can't refuse."

Wendy had been on her way to the porch swing when she heard the commotion coming from Grisham's shed. She made her way to the open door, standing there unnoticed as the boys gloated over their find. "*Excuse me*!" she shouted, "What are you guys doing in Mr. Grisham's shed?"

Stunned at the young female voice they didn't recognize, they each turned to see who was addressing them. Standing there in the doorway through which they had entered was a girl none of them had ever seen before! She was fairly tall, which initially gave them the impression that she might be older. Her red hair was pulled back and braided into pigtails. She had on a long sleeve blue and yellow striped shirt and blue jeans. The way she had barked at them—it was as if she had some authority where Mr. Grisham's property was concerned.

"Who are you?" questioned Gary.

"Who I am is *none* of your business!" she answered somewhat sarcastically. "What are *you* doing in Mr. Grisham's shed?"

"Shed? This is some shed," replied Travis. "Looks more like a museum."

Gary piped up, "Anyway, we came to see Mr. Grisham, and he wasn't home. The door was open, so we decided to have a look around. I'm sure he wouldn't mind."

The words she had used kept running through Travis' head. She asked what they were doing in *Mr. Grisham's* shed. She hadn't asked what they were doing in her uncle or grandpa's shed. Reason dictated that she wasn't a relative. Unable to focus on anything else until he knew who she was, Travis took a stab at one of the few possibilities he could imagine, "Are you from the island?"

"Yep," she responded.

"You must belong to the family that moved into the Smythe place."

"What of it?" she questioned.

"Well, why don't you just tell us who you are so we can quit playing this guessing game?" questioned Curtis in frustration.

"*My* name is Wendy," came the reply, most matter-of-factly.

Being that she was new to the island, Travis was trying to figure out how she was chummy enough with Grisham to question their being in his shed. He thought he'd call her bluff.

"Mr. Grisham allows us to come over whenever we want."

That sounded rather odd to Wendy. Mr. Grisham clearly said visitors had been scarce. "*Well*, I'll just have to ask him about that when he gets home," replied Wendy.

"So—how do you know Mr. Grisham?" stammered Travis, trying to determine whether or not it was time to start back peddling.

"He and I have become *close* friends," Wendy replied.

Girl talk, thought Gary, *Guys become good friends. But not girls, they become close friends.*

"*Close friends*, huh," chuckled Curtis, raising his eyebrows up and down, "How close is *close*?"

"Very funny," snapped Wendy. "I don't think Mr. Grisham would appreciate that comment, and I certainly do *not*! I thought *you* were his friends!"

"Wait a minute here," Gary said, feeling their boat deal being jeopardized. If, in fact, she were as chummy with Grisham as she professed, they'd do better to become her friend than her enemy. Playing the politician, he interjected, "We're not getting off to a very good start here. Curtis, you owe Wendy an apology."

"*Sorry*," said Curtis half-heartedly, "I was *just* kidding."

"We haven't introduced ourselves," Gary continued, "I'm Gary."

Gary stood about five feet tall, had brown hair, crewcut style, brown eyes, olive complexion and a carefree air about him.

"Hey—I'm Travis."

Travis was a little shorter than Gary, with brown disheveled hair, blue eyes, freckles, and a fair complexion.

"I'm Justin."

Justin was the best mannered of the bunch. He had

sandy blond hair, gelled against his head with the exception of his bangs, which stood straight up. He had blue eyes and a slight overbite.

"I'm Tyler, and this is my *rude* cousin Curtis." Some things got by Tyler—but apparently not everything.

Tyler had dishwater blonde hair, also in the popular crew-cut style, hazel eyes, and was large in every direction. Wendy could tell he was a bit different by the way his eyes wandered as he addressed her, but she wasn't sure what to make of it. In his awkward way he had apologized for his cousin.

Curtis was the shortest of the bunch. He had very curly sandy blond hair, brown eyes, a fair complexion, and was quick with sarcasm.

Wendy softened a little after the introductions and began making her way across the shed. Gary decided it was time for an explanation. "We have been saving our money in hopes of getting a boat. There's this boat down at the beach that looks abandoned. We think it belongs to Mr. Grisham. We came by to ask him about it. When no one was home, we turned to leave, but like I said, we saw the door ajar and couldn't resist taking a look."

In a condescending tone, and an effort to get even, Wendy asked, "So, you *boys* think you are old enough for your *own* boat?"

"Sure do," Travis replied. "We've been around boats all of our lives. Problem is, the boats we currently have access to require adults. We intend to get our own boat so we can explore whenever and wherever we want."

"Explore?" Wendy questioned. "Just what kind of *exploring* do you have in mind?"

"Water exploring," replied Gary. "All of the really cool places around here are water access only."

"Are your parents in on this?" Wendy asked.

In a hushed tone, indicating that he was sharing

strictly classified information, Travis replied, "We don't intend to tell them about it until we actually have the boat."

Talk of exploring got Gary thinking about a story his uncle told him the previous evening, the story of the *Legend of Crystal Cove*. Gary's uncle, nicknamed Buzz, was just ten years older than Gary, so he was still trustworthy. Gary told Buzz about the plans to get a boat and explore the Puget Sound, after which his uncle told him about these hidden crystals. Gary spent all night imagining himself and the Island Boys searching Henderson Bay for a secret cove. The moment seemed right to share the story. "Has anyone ever heard about the *Legend of Crystal Cove?*"

"*Ooh*—a legend," sighed Curtis as he rolled his eyes in disbelief.

All eyes were on Gary. "My uncle Buzz was over last night. I told him about our plans to get a boat, and he told me about this legend. Somewhere out in Henderson Bay there's supposed to be a secret cove with these exotic crystals stashed in it. My uncle does work on reservation land, and has made friends with a lot of natives. Several of them—even from different tribes—have shared bits and pieces of the legend. They say the crystals could actually be diamonds."

"*Diamonds?*" questioned Curtis. "You mean to tell me that you think there are a bunch of diamonds just *sitting* in a cove somewhere—that *nobody's* ever found? I've heard *everything* now!"

Travis was getting a little out of patience, "Curtis—give it a rest!"

"Yeah Curtis—shut up already," Tyler added.

Sometimes Curtis' negative attitude got on their nerves.

"As the story goes," Gary continued, "years ago there was this boat called the Diamond Knot. It was an ornate fishing boat that got its name from these crystals that were imbedded into the wood of various parts of the boat. Some tribe from up near Alaska discovered these crystals and thought that they brought good luck. They placed crystals throughout their village, on their fishing boats, and used them in tribal art. They believed the crystals had some great power. One day the chief was overthrown and he and his followers took provisions and the crystals, loaded them on board the Diamond Knot and headed south, settling somewhere in the Puget Sound. Buzz says the Diamond Knot is a charted wreck out in the Strait of Juan de Fuca!"

Everyone except Curtis was in awe. Curtis just looked around at the faces of the rest of the group with this expression of disbelief; *you guys really believe this stuff?*

"So what's this about a cove?" Travis asked.

"According to legend, when the chief became very old he stashed his crystals in a secluded cove. Some believe the cove is right here in Henderson Bay!"

Travis' mind was racing! What he could do with a stack of diamonds. Maybe his family would be able to stay on Raft Island after all. "Is that it?" Travis demanded. "Is that *all* your uncle knows?"

"That's all anyone knows," Gary replied. "If he or anyone else knew more, they'd have the crystals."

Justin spoke up, "And how do we know the crystals haven't been found?"

"No one knows for sure. But Buzz says that if they had been found, it would have made the news. Everyone would know it."

"*Hocus pocus!*" Curtis cried out. "That sounds like an old wives' tale if I ever heard one."

"That's why it's called *a legend*," replied Gary. Then he looked straight at Wendy, "This could be just the beginning of what's out there, which is why we've got to get a boat—*before* Travis has to move!"

Wendy was fascinated. She was prone to fantasize, and this played right into her overactive imagination. "A search for *hidden* treasure," she said with a glimmer in her eye, "now you're talking!" She then turned to Travis, "What's this about moving?"

"Dad's been out of work for awhile. The bills are piling up."

Gary looked to Travis, "I know it's a stretch, but what if we actually found the crystals! If they are diamonds, we could solve *lots* of problems, including yours!"

"There you go *dreaming* again," said Curtis. Then, looking to Wendy he added, "Gary's our resident dreamer. He thinks '*Im*possible' means '*Is* possible.'"

"Yeah! I guess I am a bit of a dreamer," defended Gary, "but it makes life more interesting."

"It can't hurt to dream a little," added Wendy, "As long as you can live in reality while pursuing your dream."

"*Exactly*!" replied Gary nodding his head. He appreciated the show of support.

Justin decided it was time to bring this conversation full circle, "Since the boat down at the beach basically looks abandoned, we figured Mr. Grisham might make us a deal on her."

"I want to see it," Wendy said, with determination.

"C'mon guys," Gary replied, "Let's take Wendy down to the beach."

As they got to the top of Grisham's driveway and turned toward the beach, Gary spotted Shadow marking his territory on the neighbor's bush. "Shadow," Gary yelled out, "Here boy!" Shadow came running.

"That's a good looking malamute," Wendy stated, showing her knowledge of dogs.

"Thanks," replied Gary, leaning down to give Shadow a rub around the collar. "Let's go to the beach boy, c'mon!"

5

Little Imp

They were showing Wendy the boat when Grisham's white Caddy started across the bridge. They stopped what they were doing and headed up the hill. They didn't want to let this chance to catch him home pass them by.

As they rounded the bend in Grisham's driveway, there he was—standing alongside of his Cadillac with an armful of bags he'd just retrieved from the backseat. For what seemed like minutes, they froze in their steps—him staring at them—them staring at him.

Grisham had a full head of white hair. Surprisingly, he stood tall and straight for an old man. Every time they recalled seeing him prior to then, he had been sitting behind the wheel of his car. They had no idea he was so tall. He wore a heavy mustache with the ends rolled in the handlebar style, and a cap on his head. He looked more like an old salt than a mountain man. But proof of his hunting escapades was hanging in the shed. There was a kind smile on his face—he appeared almost happy to see them.

Finally, it was Grisham who broke the silence, "Hey Wendy, who have you got with you?"

"Now that's odd," Curtis let out under his breath, knowing that with the exception of Justin, the boys were lifelong residents, yet his greeting was to Wendy.

Either way, that was their cue to keep walking.

"These are some guys from the island."

"Oh yes," he replied, "I recognize some of you now. You're all getting so big! What can I do for you?"

Grisham knew they were up to something. It had been years since he'd seen kids anywhere near his property, but then he hadn't been home all that much. His wife's illness had kept him on the go, and the last couple of years he sequestered her at *Le Chateau*, a fairly new retirement village located along the waterfront of Tacoma. It was closer to hospitals and doctors and took the uncertainty of bridge traffic out of the equation.

"Come to use the porch swing, have you?"

Wendy led out, "Well—we may do that also, but the main reason we've come over is to talk to you about *Little Imp*." She'd seen the name stenciled near the stern of the boat.

Now Grisham was curious. He knew *Little Imp* had sat unattended down at the beach for sometime. "What about *Little Imp*?"

Travis decided to cut to the chase, "We want to buy it."

"Yeah," Tyler chimed in. "We've been saving—we have $300,"

Shadow put his nose to work, while they negotiated with Grisham.

Grisham eyed each of them closely for what seemed like an eternity. He could only imagine the condition *Little Imp* was in after having sat on the beach for more than two years. "And what would you do with her?"

Gary spoke up, "We have *big* plans!" Shadow let out a bark, as if to confirm Gary's statement. "We're going to explore every inch of Henderson Bay." Wanting to avoid any mention of their plans to go in search of *Crystal Cove,* Gary threw out a decoy, "We'll find the best fishing and crabbing spots, the best place to watch for seals, and . . ."

Travis cut him off before he could finish, " . . . And we're going to become famous explorers—like Lewis and Clark—only we're "The Island Gang!"

Gary tossed a glance his way as if to threaten, '*Don't you dare divulge Crystal Cove!*'

Travis took the hint, "Henderson Bay is first on our list. But one day, we're headed to the San Juan's and beyond. We're going to explore *all* of the waters of the Northwest!"

Nice dodge, thought Gary.

They were itching to get to Dead Man's, but knowing that adults would frown on the idea, that little fact remained unmentioned.

Wendy liked hearing the words, *The Island Gang*. Prior to then, they'd always referred to themselves as *The Island Boys*. It was looking like she was in!

Grisham, intrigued with their enthusiasm replied, "Three hundred dollars, huh? And you want to buy *Little Imp*? Are you sure you've got the right boat?" asked Grisham, rubbing his hand on his chin, "I don't know if Little Imp is up to all that serious adventure."

"She'll suit our needs just fine," Gary chimed in. We'll take real good care of her too—you'll see!"

"The Island Gang, huh? Sounds exciting! Got room for an old timer?"

"Why, sure . . ."

" . . . Just kidding," Grisham interrupted. "I'm afraid I'd just slow you kids down. But I have a proposal for you. I've got several projects around here that I could sure use some help with." Placing his hand on Wendy's shoulder, he said, "If you boys and this young lady will do some chores for me, I'll pay you with the boat, that way you can hang on to your $300. *And* as part of the deal, I'll get her all fixed up so that she'll serve you well. Do we have a deal?"

They could hardly believe their ears. It was like Santa made a guest appearance in spring!

"*Deal*." Gary shouted as he extended his hand for the shake that seals all deals. He wasn't about to let this one slip away. His dad, the salesman, always said, "Once you shake on something—both parties are obliged." Gary intended to close this deal before Mr. Grisham had a change of mind!

"This is *awesome!*" exclaimed Travis, giving the thumbs up sign with both hands.

Grisham got the boat up to the shed, and over the next several weeks he worked on *Little Imp*, getting her outfitted. Though *Little Imp* had been mainly used as ship to shore transportation to and from *Sea Imp*, Grisham's 52' sailing yacht, she was capable of much more than a dinghy. Grisham had all the accessories to convert her into a fine sailboat. She was even capable of sporting a small outboard. Removable slatted floors added comfort on longer outings, and created several shallow hatches for storage. Many memories resurfaced as he worked on *Little Imp*. She had been a lot of fun for Lucille and him. Whenever they wanted to explore a piece of coastline up close, they had anchored *Sea Imp* and taken *Little Imp*. Oh, how he missed the water.

The Island Gang worked hard to fulfill their part of the deal. They got Grisham's yard whipped into shape. They mowed, edged, weeded, pruned, and even painted the white picket fence that lined the bank at the head of the terraced planters. Days that were too rainy, Grisham put them to work in the shed. That was their favorite. Each box they sorted through uncovered new and interesting things. Working in the shed was almost *like* hunting for treasure. Whenever they came across something that they thought would make a good addition to *Little Imp*, they would set it aside and ask Grisham about including the item as part of the deal. He would generally find an additional chore they could do to earn the item.

It was the middle of May when The Island Gang showed up one Saturday morning to find Grisham waiting for them. He stood there in the opening of the shed with his chest out and arms folded across his stomach. With a big smile on his face he yelled out, "*Hurry*! Come in out of the rain." He was excited about something.

"Have a look at *this*!" he said. "I heard you talking about wanting a boat that didn't require adults, so *voila*— here you go. It's my newest invention—a *boat dolly*. You can get the boat to the launch and back all by yourselves."

Grisham had designed a contraption that turned the boat into—a big *wheelbarrow*! The dolly was just large enough to cradle the hull at the very front of the boat, and was made of heavy aluminum tubing. He had secured pads to the tubing where the hull rested and installed handles up near the bow of the boat. With one of them on either side, they could lift the bow and place it onto the dolly. A pair of leather straps buckled across the top of the bow, holding it securely in place. The dolly rode on a pair of bicycle wheels attached with quick disconnects. Grisham had rigged the oars so that they mounted on the upper rail of the boat along each side, paddle end forward. Aluminum extensions slid out of the oar handles. Snap buttons held the extensions at the desired length. The extensions were long enough to allow for two kids on each handle. *Little Imp* maneuvered just like a *giant* wheelbarrow. No trailer—no adults.

"In—de—pendence!" shouted Travis with a tone of confidence and satisfaction, "That's what I'm talking about!"

"What's this for?" asked Curtis, pointing to the back of the boat.

"That's your cold storage," Grisham answered. "Here, let me show you how it works."

The large black tub mounted on a bracket that had two positions. It locked in the raised position for maneuvering on land and in the lower position while on the water.

"This lower position," explained Grisham, "will hold enough of the tub below the waterline to keep your food items and fresh catch nice and cold."

"What are these snaps for?" asked Travis, noticing a

row of snaps along the perimeter of the entire boat.

"Those are for the tent," replied Grisham. "If you can talk your folks into a sleepover on the boat you can rig the boat tent—just in case it should decide to rain in the night. The tent fits in the front floor hatch. These PVC pipes are the inner support for the tent, and when I'm finished, they will mount right here along the inner walls to keep out of the way when not in use.

"*Awesome!*" said Gary. "Mr. Grisham thought of everything! We are ready for *adventure!*"

Justin stood there shaking his head.

"Unbelievable," Curtis kept mumbling in disbelief.

"Yeah, *unbelievable*," added Tyler!

Anxious to give the contraption a try, they ignored the light rain. Justin and Travis got on one oar, and Curtis and Gary got on the other. As soon as Shadow saw that they were headed out of the shed, he let out a bark and jumped up into *Little Imp*. He wasn't about to be left out.

"Hey guys, wait," shouted Tyler, "I'm getting in with Shadow!"

"Negative, Tyler," came the reply from cousin Curtis, "You're pushing like the rest of us. Your spot is right here in the middle, we'll steer."

Tyler got to slack off now and then, but when he was capable of making a meaningful contribution, he was expected to help.

The wheelbarrow idea worked great, except for the fact that it was a little hard to see what was coming at the front of the boat, especially when they got to the end of the driveway.

Grisham, walking alongside admiring his handy work, noticed their plight. Wendy had remained under cover of the open garage door. "Wendy," Grisham called out, "here's your spot!"

Wendy pulled the hood of her fleece up over her head

and ran to catch up.

"You'll have to be their eyes or they'll *never* get to the launch and back in one piece."

Wendy took her place out front, watching for traffic as they made their way out onto the street.

"Make sure you have a good grip on the handles when you get to the downhill or you'll run right over the top of her," cautioned Grisham.

"Not a bad idea," mumbled Curtis under his breath.

"I heard that," said Gary, "were you referring to our portable boat, or running Wendy over?"

Curtis just smiled and nodded without adding any clarification.

It wasn't time to take *Little Imp* down to the water yet. They turned her around and headed for the shed, again thanking Grisham for his ingenious idea.

With a tone of victory, Gary shouted, "We're *ready* to explore!"

They took turns thanking Grisham and expressing how glad they were to have him as a friend.

"I feel the same about you," Grisham replied. "How many guys my age are lucky enough to have a group of friends like The Island Gang? And, you're some of the hardest work-ers I've known. My yard hasn't looked this good in—years! On top of that, you're honest, loyal, and true friends to each other," as he winked and gave a nod in Tyler's direction.

Grisham was impressed with the way that The Island Gang took Tyler in. He had told each of them on various occasions how great he thought it was that Tyler felt like one of the gang. Many boys and girls in today's world would make fun of Tyler's disability, and wouldn't take the time to include him the way they had. To them it was no big deal. Tyler had been one of them as long as they could remember, and he was usually a lot fun to have around. It was sometimes difficult to get him to focus on the task at hand, but Tyler was never expected to do as much as the rest of them. He did what he could, and they were generally happy to make up the difference. Tyler made his own unique contribution to The Island Gang in the form of comic relief.

"Can we see her fully outfitted?" asked Travis.

"I don't see why not," replied Grisham.

They placed *Little Imp* on her stand near the center of the shed, where there was plenty of height to accommodate the mast. Grisham helped them mount the mast and raise the sail. They mounted the tiller, and he showed them where the drop keel went. They couldn't put the keel in place because the stand didn't get *Little Imp* far enough off of the ground. Then they lowered the sail and set the tent up, snapping it down all the way around with the exception of the flap at the stern.

"She's *lookin* good!" exclaimed Travis. "Let's get her on the water!"

"Isn't there a three day holiday this weekend?" asked Grisham. "We should plan her maiden voyage so you can get her checked out. A trip out to Dead Man's Island and back would give you a chance to make sure that everything is working just the way you think it should."

"*Great idea!*" Gary shouted.

Though The Island Gang hadn't actually spoken with Grisham about their little plan to explore Dead Man's, he overheard them talking about it on a couple of occasions and didn't see much harm in it. In a roundabout way, he let them know that he knew what they were up to; however, he wasn't sure they caught on. "You'll be respectful of the burial ground, right?"

They assured him they would.

Grisham went in the house, leaving The Island Gang alone to make plans. They were so anxious to get *Little Imp* out on the water, they weren't sure they'd make it to the weekend.

The forecast called for questionable weather starting sometime on Friday. You never knew what to think of the forecast, though. Sometimes you could flip a coin and come up with as good a forecast as the weathermen. The day that was most likely to have good weather was Thursday. Since Thursday was a half-day at school, they talked their parents into letting them take their maiden voyage as soon as school let out.

They knew their parents wouldn't be keen on them spending any amount of time on Dead Man's, but a careful plan would leave them temporarily marooned due to the changing tide. Their parents would never expect them to row back against the tide. That would leave them enough time to have a look around.

6

The Underground

Gary's uncle wasn't the only one that paid attention to stories about the *Legend of Crystal Cove*. Stories surrounding the legend caught the attention of many. People who spent any amount of time working with natives of the region had gleaned bits and pieces, and while most considered it just that—a legend—ranking right up there with folk lore and fairy tales—there were some who took the stories more seriously. It didn't seem likely that firewater and peace pipes could be credited as the sole source for stories with so many similarities—amongst so many different groups of natives.

According to legend, the crystals had been carried down from the far north by a sun worshipping people. Answers as to why they had come to the Puget Sound region were said to be hidden away with the crystals. To be sure, natives of the region had migrated from somewhere. The story behind the legend seemed as good a reason as any as to why Native Americans were in the Puget Sound. If the story ended up *not* being true, the origin of the light-worshipping natives inhabiting the Puget Sound would remain a mystery.

While some people were genuinely interested in learning more about Native American history, others were interested in just one thing—*treasure*. If the stories had any truth to them, there was a pile of these crystals hidden away out there somewhere, and they were worth a lot of money.

A group of businessmen from the community had a common hobby—treasure seeking. They'd dived every charted wreck they could find record of and were credited with charting others they discovered along the way. They also spent significant time and resources searching out information that might lead them to places of Native American antiquity, hoping to uncover treasures from any of a half dozen legends they had dug up information on through the years. However, their key focus was the mysterious *"Crystal Cove."*

One of these men, Kat Kane, having acquired substantial wealth, quietly formed a foundation he named TMG (The Manhattan Group), whose secret mission was to find the crystals. The foundation's charter was based on research and preservation of Northwest First Nation culture. To give the foundation legitimacy, several natives were recruited to positions on the foundation's board and led the research among their people, always steering conversation to the *Legend of Crystal Cove*, attempting to uncover new information that would lead them closer to the treasure.

Kat was into all aspects of land use and development and had many parcels of land under his control. However, some of the land he sought access to was under the control of tribes of the region, leaving him with no legal way of gaining access. Forming the foundation put him right where he wanted to be—in regular contact with local natives, who were beneficial in helping him accomplish his designs.

Research among the natives uncovered an array of legends whose stories had been preserved in tribal culture. Those that had made their list were the *"Legend of the Mask," "Legend of the Cave," "Power of Light," "Legend of the Orcas," "Walking Stick,"* and—the *"Legend of Crystal Cove."* If the collection of crystals was as large as natives described—and if they were, in fact, *diamonds*—there was a fortune out there!

Similarities in names of legends led researchers to believe that several of them could have taken their origin from a single event—possibly the same story, told and retold so many times that over the years had taken on different names. The prevailing idea was that at some point, ancestors of these tribes had found a way to produce brilliant light using some sort of crystal. The idea that these crystals had come from a cave and had been put back into a cave or a cove was also a repeated theme.

Through the years, tens of thousands of dollars had been put into the search for *Crystal Cove*, which thus far had left them empty-handed. Though all in the treasure hunting group occasionally spoke of the legend, Kat had successfully kept the foundation from his associates. He didn't want undue attention that might bring serious competition.

What began as an innocent venture, almost overnight became not so innocent. Kat ran gravel quarries, mining operations, and construction companies. One of his construction companies had won a bid to participate in the development of a large retirement community called *Le Chateau*, a development that sprawled over 350 acres. It included expansive gardens both indoors and out, as well as tennis courts, health clubs, spas, and 27 holes of golf. *Le Chateau* had everything from luxury condos to an assisted living center, all on one campus.

The most prestigious of the luxury condos, *Le Perle*, was built at the far end of the property on a precipice overlooking the water just south of The Narrows. While reviewing plat maps and drawings for the development, Kat realized that *Le Perle* was located just a quarter mile south of one of his inactive mines, *The Sedgwick*. He was reminded of the final shaft they had blasted in an effort to keep the mine open—a shaft that was never charted—that ran nearly the full distance to *Le Perle*—albeit the shaft was seventy-five feet below.

While blasting for the footings of *Le Perle*, Kat had his contractor drill at a slight angle, deep into the granite. They successfully reached the shaft, piping water and power into the old mine! The only known opening to *The Sedgwick* sat nearly at sea level just east of the train tracks that paralleled the water. For safety reasons, the opening had long since been barricaded, sealing off the mine. It was perfect! No one would ever suspect the mine! It was in *The Sedgwick* that Kat's dark works began. With untraceable access to water and power, and rail access just outside the mine, he had the perfect set up!

On another construction project, an upgrade of the rail terminal in the Tacoma flats, TMG gained access to rail communications. Kat had his men tap into the system, and in time had a reader board installed at *The Sedgwick*. He then had terminal communications wired from the Tacoma Terminal directly into *The Sedgwick*. He now knew schedules and movement of every train passing through the Tacoma station! Kat had created the ideal situation to produce and distribute that which poisons the mind and exploits mankind. Illegal drugs!

It was an industry literally immune to economic downturn, with users that were generally twenty to forty year customers. Those who become trapped in the culture are so wrapped up in their habit, they often become involved with distribution in order to afford to use. Many reach their 50's and 60's before realizing that life has passed them by, while they have helped to provide untold wealth to those who would never think of using.

Most druggies come from one of two completely different walks of life. There are the privileged that seem to run out of legitimate ways to get a thrill and turn to drugs to experience new highs, and then there are the poor who use drugs seeking an escape from their reality. It seems odd that such a steady stream of money could funnel in from the impoverished of the world, and while not all in this second category come from the roles of welfare recipients, a large percentage of these users have worked themselves into a situation where they are not reliable employees, ending up on the dole. However, employed or not, drug addicts are among the most tenacious at finding ways to come up with money. They know they must have money to use, and they must never short pay their suppliers—that would only bring harm, if not death. So, they rob, steal and participate in all sorts of plunder in order to pay the piper.

Kat became so consumed with greed that what started as the search for a mysterious source of light, evolved into a pact with darkness, perpetuating that industry which erodes the very fabric of life—taking prisoner all who become lured into its grasp.

7

Grisham's Attic

It was the day before their maiden voyage. The Island Gang met at Grisham's for final preparations. Grisham wasn't around, but the shed was unlocked as always. For some reason, Shadow headed straight up the stairs to the loft room. Seeing Shadow's determination, Gary followed him up the stairs. His nose was going crazy—something was up. Even when there's no other evidence, a dog's nose can pick up on the fact that changes have taken place.

Seeing Gary follow Shadow up the stairs, Travis asked, "Where you going?"

"Just following Shadow," Gary replied. "He's on to something."

"The attic is always locked," came the reply.

"I know, but look, Shadow's got a scent or . . ."

Just as Gary reached the top of the stairs, Shadow pushed the door wide open.

"Hey guys—look! It's open!"

They were up the stairs in no time. The upstairs room was small. Light from the shed exposed clutter—it looked similar to what had been in every corner of the shed when they began. Along one wall, boxes appeared to be stacked to the ceiling from the doorway all the way to the far corner. The outline of a desk and a couple of filing cabinets were off to the back. They were reminded of when they first entered Grisham's shed as they felt along the wall for a light switch.

All at once Travis, who had wandered toward center of the room, felt something in his face, "Ugh! A spider web," he said, brushing his hand through the dark to clear the way. That's when he realized it was a string, not a web. He pulled it, and a light came on.

"Holy smoke," Gary said. "More boxes!"

Boxes were everywhere. But these weren't like the boxes that had been down stairs. These looked more like business files.

Travis had seen similar boxes in his parents' attic. "Probably tax records," Travis offered. "My folks have boxes like these. There are certain papers adults have to hang on to."

"Hey, look over here," said Curtis as he stooped down to pick up an old metal box leaning against the desk. "It has a combination lock." Still in a half-crouched position, he pushed the button on the combination pad—the box opened! Curtis stood straight up, dropping the box onto his toe. "Ouch!"

Gary chuckled at Curtis' response, "Little jumpy there, eh, Curtis—expecting a ghost to jump out at ya?"

"Very funny," Curtis retaliated as he hopped around the room holding his toe. "We shouldn't be up here in Mr. Grisham's private stuff—it gives me the creeps!"

"Oooooh," Gary replied, making the best eerie sound he was capable of.

The box lay there on the ground—the file folders having spilled onto the floor.

"Mr. Grisham must have forgotten to change the numbers after he closed it last," said Travis, reaching for the box.

It sort of reminded Travis of the metal case his father carried, only with this one, the top portion of the box was hinged, leaving an area just the right size to house the file folders, which were now all on the floor. Travis reached to gather the files. "This thing is heavy!" he said, scooting the case to one side. The fact that these files had been stored in a lock box increased their curiosity. As he gathered them into one pile he asked, "What do you suppose they are?" He read the labels as he straightened the pile. "AI, MI, FI, VI, BI, SJI, GI, VI, QCI, ALI . . ."

"They all end in I," Gary stated.

One of the folders had fallen further from the rest. "And, DMI," stated Justin, reading the label on the folder that sat near his feet. "Why does that sound familiar?"

"That's a map!" stated Gary, seeing a document that had come part way out of the folder. "Let me see it!"

Justin picked the map up and handed it to Gary.

"It's Dead Man's!" exclaimed Gary, recognizing the location and shape of the island.

Surprised, Justin, who was standing right next to Gary, read the heading on the map aloud, "Dead Man's Island! Do you suppose all of these files are about islands?"

Travis flipped through the folders. The first thing inside each folder was a map.

"These must be places Grisham went sailing or hunting! What else is in there?" asked Justin.

"You'd better put those folders back before you get them all mixed up," warned Curtis.

That seemed like odd advice from the one responsible for opening the box in the first place.

Travis stacked them neatly alongside the box. He opened the last folder as he placed it on the stack. "Aleutian Islands! For crying out loud! Do you know how far away that is? We're talking Alaska!"

Remembering the animals hanging on the wall downstairs, Gary added, "That's probably where he got those bears!"

Curtis was getting more nervous by the second. "Don't you think we should put all of this away? What if Grisham comes home? These are obviously his private things or he wouldn't lock the door—and the box!"

"Curtis buddy, you need to relax a little," Gary replied. "You're way too uptight."

"I don't have a good feeling about this," Curtis persisted.

Gary was busy looking through the DMI folder when, all of a sudden he let out, "*Holy Smoke*! Look here! You guys aren't going to believe this!" Gary read the inscription, "*Legend of Crystal Cove.*"

Interest in the other folders immediately faded. They gathered around Gary for a closer look. They hadn't stopped thinking about *Crystal Cove* since Gary told them the story. Now here it was again!

Doubtingly, Curtis asked, "Do you really think this is the same *Crystal Cove*?"

"And just how many *Crystal Coves* do you think there are around here anyway?" was Gary's reply. It was clear by the tone in his voice that he was happy to have a document validating the story. "Mr. Grisham must believe that Dead Man's has something to do with *Crystal Cove*!"

"I *knew* there was something more to Dead Man's than just a burial ground," said Travis, slapping his hand on the floor.

"No way," Curtis blurted out in a tone of disgust. "If *Crystal Cove* were at Dead Man's, someone would have found it by now. Give me a break already!"

They continued to study the papers from the folder.

"He's right—it can't be that easy," replied Justin, reaching for the DMI folder. "Even though Dead Man's is more or less off limits, if anyone believed for a minute that *Crystal Cove* was out there, they would have torn the island apart looking for it. The island is so small, there's no place to hide a cove!"

Near the back of the folder, neatly folded, was an old piece of parchment. It was worn and larger than the rest of the papers, which explained why it was folded. Justin unfolded it. It was a very old map with strange markings.

"Do you suppose it's the map to *Crystal Cove?*" asked Wendy.

"Can't be," replied Gary, "or Grisham would have the crystals."

"Maybe he did find them and just hasn't told anyone," said Travis. "He could have stashed them somewhere—cashing them as he needs money. Look at all of the stuff he has, and all of the exotic hunting trips—that all takes money—and lots of it!"

"Good point," said Justin. "I hadn't thought about that."

"You guys are too much," Wendy said, coming to Grisham's defense. "There's no way he would have taken the crystals and not told anyone—he's not that type!"

"Who would he have to tell?" asked Gary, "It's not like they belong to someone."

They were deep in thought as Gary pointed to images on the map. "Looks like a trail, leading to—a web of some sort."

"It's directions," Justin butted in, pointing to three sets of number letter combinations in the center of the web. "Look, N–E7–W3—must be north, east and west!"

Curtis' interest was peaked. He flipped through some of the other folders while the rest of them studied the *Crystal Cove* map. Inside the San Juan Islands folder, he halfheartedly read aloud, "Legend of Walking Stick." He flipped through the Gulf Islands folder, "Legend of the Masks," and then the Queen Charlotte Islands folder, "Legend of the Orca."

No one paid the least attention to the words he was uttering. They were all too focused on the maps of Dead Man's Island.

"I wonder why he would keep these locked up?" Curtis asked under his breath, taking the box into his hands for a closer look. The top portion of the box was deeper than was necessary for the height of the folders. Feeling along the inside edges, Curtis found a recessed lever. As he moved the lever, a secret compartment opened.

"Hey guys!" The tone and volume of Curtis' voice got their attention. He moved the false bottom out of the way exposing passports, various other papers, and a handgun secured in a leather holster.

"Now that explains why it was *locked*!" exclaimed Justin.

"Only it *wasn't* locked," replied Travis.

"I'm sure he *meant* for it to be locked," scowled Curtis.

They examined the documents. Several passports belonged to Grisham—only one belonged to his wife. "Why would Grisham have more than one passport?" asked Curtis. He read the stamps on various pages, learning that Grisham had been to Canada, Mexico, Guatemala, Costa Rica, Argentina, Brazil, Chile, Japan and Russia. His wife's passport had only been stamped for Mexico and Canada. "He's an international traveler!" exclaimed Curtis. "Maybe he does have the crystals."

"That looks like a cop gun," offered Gary, taking the holster in his hand. "He must be a secret agent or something."

"Leave it alone," said Curtis, "it might be loaded."

"It wouldn't do anybody any good if it weren't," Gary responded, taking the gun from the holster." Gary knew something about guns from the collection his dad had. "Safety's on," he said, as he looked the gun over, trying to figure out how to check to see if it was loaded. He'd never seen a gun exactly like this one. "This is definitely one of those police guns, you can tell by the way . . ."

Just then, Gary accidentally found the switch that released the magazine. Curtis about jumped out of his skin as the magazine sprang loose. "Put it away—before you kill somebody!"

"I'm not gonna kill anyone," replied Gary. "But, it is

loaded."

"Okay, that's real good," continued Curtis. "Now put it back!"

Gary replaced the magazine, put the gun back in the holster and tucked it back into the secret compartment with the other papers.

Justin reached for the Dead Man's map, "Compare this drawing with the one on the old map of Dead Man's. I think they're similar."

The upper edge of the old map was extremely worn. In fact, the upper left hand corner of the worn map was completely missing. There had been a title, but all they could make out now were portions of words that had not been worn completely away.

" . . r . . s t . .1 C. . v e—*Crystal Cove!*" Justin blurted out. It's right in front of us!" Pointing to similarities in shape at the far end of the island on both maps, "This old map is of Dead Man's too—*look!*"

"Maybe we should ask Mr. Grisham about this," suggested Wendy.

"And let him know we were in his locked room!" Travis replied. "Are you crazy?"

"Travis is right," agreed Gary. "We can't afford to lose his trust. We'll just take it with us to Dead Man's when we go for our maiden voyage. We can check it out then. It might make better sense once we're over there."

"What if we lose it? Maybe we should trace it onto another paper," said Justin, as he stood to look for something to write with.

Gary nodded in agreement, "You're probably right."

Curtis interjected as if he'd just solved the mystery, "Maybe it's supposed to be *Crystal Cave* instead of *Crystal Cove*."

"Anything is possible," Travis seconded.

Justin hurried back. He had a pencil, but was unable

to find paper thin enough to trace with. Gary tried to draw the map the best he could on a cardboard flap he tore from one of the boxes. After erasing and starting over several times, he folded both maps, and put them into his pocket. "I'll take responsibility. It makes no sense to go to Dead Man's without these," he said patting his pocket. "Before you close that metal box, write down the combination. It might be locked when we go to put them back."

Travis flipped the top over. The combination was set on 4, 1, 3, 2. "Tyler, memorize that just in case."

"4, 1, 3, 2—got it. Right here in the old memory bank," Tyler said, pointing to his head.

They searched the entire upper room before leaving, still wondering if Grisham had, in fact, found the crystals and had them locked up there out of sight. But—no luck. They determined the crystals must still be out there—somewhere.

8

Maiden Voyage

The Island Gang gathered at Grisham's as soon as the school bus dropped them off. *Little Imp* was still outfitted with the tent and mast from a couple of days earlier. They didn't dare try sailing until after Grisham's lessons, which would have to wait for a later trip. They were determined to make the maiden voyage on their own. They had big plans for Dead Man's and didn't need any adults getting in the way. They took the tent down, removed the mast and all of the sailing gear, and hung it all neatly on the wall. The window of opportunity to take advantage of the tide was upon them. They took their positions on the boat dolly and headed for the launch.

"I can't get over how ingenious this dolly is," said Justin. "I'll bet Mr. Grisham could get a patent on this thing."

"Sure works for us," Gary replied. "No trailer, no adults . . ."

" . . . And *no worries*," Tyler hollered out, repeating a statement he'd heard the others use many times.

Wendy led the way watching for traffic, and Shadow rode right up at the bow as they pushed *Little Imp* down to the beach. Being that this was their first time taking the boat out on their own, several parents and Mr. Grisham had gathered at the beach where they could be a part of the experience. Curtis' dad had launched the family boat and tied it up to the dock so that he'd be ready if the kids ran into any trouble.

Leaving at the right time, they would catch the

ebb tide carrying them toward Dead Man's. Their parents wouldn't want them back in the water until the tide subsided. With a little pleading, they were sure they could convince their parents to allow them to wait for ebb tide before making the return trip. That would give them several hours on Dead Man's.

They ran through the checklist one last time before pushing off. Supplies were in place—lunch was packed—they were ready. As they put their life vests on, Gary took on the role of captain, "Travis, let's get the bow on the water. Curtis, you and Justin get in first. Get to the front of the boat and remove the wheels from the dolly." Gary and Travis pushed *Little Imp* a little further into the water. Shadow jumped on board and turned to watch the others. "Okay, Wendy and Tyler, you're next." Gary waited a minute for them to get settled, and then looking to Travis, he said, "On three, ready? One—Two—Three."

On the three count they pushed off, jumping onto the cold storage. It took a little maneuvering, but soon all were in place. The oars were unlocked from the top rail and set into the oarlocks. Anxious to be the first to row, Gary climbed onto the main rowing bench. Travis and Justin were busy making sure everything on the boat was secure. Wendy got comfortable next to Tyler up toward the bow. With the tide in their favor, they were heading almost effortlessly toward the Raft Island Bridge. Since their main objective was to show their parents that they were competent on the water, Gary was certain to be seen rowing whether it was necessary or not.

They could hardly believe it! They were on the water, headed for their first adventure. At this point, it didn't much matter what they found at Dead Man's. The fact that they were on the water in their very own custom boat was as much as they could have hoped for. Sensations of freedom and accomplishment were very satisfying. At that very moment, anticipation of what they might uncover at Dead Man's was secondary.

Grisham hooked them up with two-way radios so that they could stay in touch. Once on the island they would radio their folks, making them aware of their plight and the need to wait for a change in tide. Their parents would have to agree. It would be too late to do anything about it.

As Gary rowed, Justin and Travis watched the currents. Tyler laid his head back and gazed into the sky, thinking how good God had it up there with the big puffy clouds. Wendy imagined what *Crystal Cove* would look like.

It was only minutes until they crossed under the Raft Island Bridge where their parents and Grisham had gathered to watch. From the bridge, the northern tip of Dead Man's was in sight so onlookers would know that The Island Gang reached Dead Man's without any problem.

"Another happy day for God," said Tyler. "When I get rich, I'm going to have a room full of pillows just like those," he said, pointing toward the sky. "I'll bet they're the most comfortable pillows in the world."

Soon after they crossed under the bridge, it was time to switch oarsman. In the short time it took for Justin to get seated and grab hold of the oars, *Little Imp* became caught in a current that was pulling them toward the open bay.

"Row hard, Justin," encouraged Gary. "We need to get out of this current."

Within a couple of strokes Justin had them back on course. It wasn't long till it was time to switch again. "Your turn, Curtis," said Travis, motioning for Curtis to get in position to take his place.

Wendy gestured rather indignantly, "Wait just a minute here—I get a turn like everybody else!"

They were a little surprised that she actually wanted to row, but then she always insisted on pulling her weight. She didn't want to ever be accused of not contributing, and seeing that they were getting close to Dead Man's, she was afraid of being left out of the rotation.

Tyler lay comfortably up against the bow of the boat with his arms folded across his chest, and added, "Yeah, you guys aren't letting Wendy have a turn." He was all too anxious to support her position, but made no issue out of the fact that he hadn't had a turn.

Looking to Wendy, still assuming the role of captain, Gary responded, "You'll get your turn, we still have the return trip ahead of us. Depending on how long we explore the island, we might not have the tide to our advantage on the return trip. Then it could take all of us to get back. We'll even give you a turn, Tyler," he said as he smiled and winked at Curtis.

"That's okay," Tyler said, locking his hands together behind his head looking up to the sky. "I'll be a gentleman and give my turn to Wendy."

Tyler's response was anticipated. Once Tyler had the opportunity to become confident in his ability, away from the pressure of changing currents and watchful eyes, he'd be more inclined to take a turn. But he avoided uncomfortable situations.

Curtis had been the one outspoken against a rowboat. It was clear now that his aversion to rowing was due to experience. Curtis was the smallest of the guys, but obviously size wasn't everything. Form had a lot to do with it. In no time, his long steady strokes carried them within yards of the island.

As they approached the shore, the bow of the boat was being pulled to the right. They knew about eddies and back eddies, and were now experiencing one firsthand—without the usual help of a motor.

"Stroke hard," Justin shouted, "Do you need me to take one of the oars?"

It was Curtis' turn to be poised, "*Relax*, it's just an

eddy—no need to *freak out*!" He calmly gave a couple of hard strokes, pulling them through the eddy and onto the beach.

Tyler shouted, "*We're here—Land ho!*"

Even though they had been in sight of land the entire 35 minutes, in Tyler's mind they were in the middle of the ocean about to explore an uncharted island—with the very real chance of running across the Loch Ness monster. Tyler was the only person they knew who could explore exotic places without ever leaving his room. It must be cool to have an imagination like that.

Shadow was first off the boat. There are some definite advantages to having four legs—like the world is your toilet, no bedtime, and it's much easier to keep your balance when getting into and out of a boat that is on the water.

Gary was next to make his way over the bow of the boat. "Pass the wheels forward. We'll need to pull the boat up past the drift line. We don't want *Little Imp* leaving without us."

It was nearing low tide, but knowing the tide would change by the time they departed, they locked the wheels in place, brought the stern around and pulled her up where they knew she'd be safe. It was time to radio their folks.

Travis got the radio out of his backpack, "Ship to shore. The Island Gang has arrived safely—over?"

"That's a big 10—4," came the reply, "I've got you in my crosshairs—over."

"Crosshairs?" Travis questioned. "Is that you Mr. Grisham?"

"You got it," he replied. "I brought one of my high powered scopes down to the bridge. I'm watching you tie *Little Imp* up as we speak—over."

"Hey guys, its Grisham! He's on the radio—watching us from the bridge through a telescope!"

"Tell our folks we're stranded here until the tide changes—over."

"I'll let them know," came the reply.

Grisham wasn't about to spoil their adventure by making their folks aware that they had planned this in advance. "Leave your radio on in case we need to get in touch. If we don't talk between now and then, be sure to radio us before leaving the island—over."

"10—4. By the way, the boat worked swell! Over and out."

The Island Gang was prepared. Top of the list was food—sandwiches, powdered donuts, and milk. They were prepared with flashlights, rope, and pocketknives. Travis even packed his machete, just in case they needed to cut their way through some berries. Familiar with the northwest, they knew they could easily run into serious vegetation problems. During the growing season, wild berries grew so fast you almost could watch it happening.

"Off with the life vests—on with the packs," Gary called out, still playing the role of captain, "Let's get the map out and try to find that trail."

The south side was the highest point of the island. It came to a plateau right up on top, and then dropped off about seventy feet to a beach area that was only exposed at low tide. Northwest winter storms had carved a virtual cliff along the south shore. They knew from the map that the trail led to the high point of the island. All they had to do was find the trailhead.

"It must start over here," said Travis.

"I think he's right," agreed Gary. "See this?" pointing to the map, "This marking must be that old cedar."

"The cedar looks old enough," replied Travis, "It could easily have been there when this map was made."

"C'mon mateys! Enough standing around chit chatting," Tyler called out, "we'll never find treasure standing here!"

They turned to see that Tyler sported a patch over

one eye, a hook on his left hand, and a Pirate hat.

"What ya got there, Tyler?" asked Justin.

"*I'm ready to hunt for buried treasure,*" Tyler replied in his best pirate voice.

"Buried treasure, huh?" replied Curtis.

"*Yep, now let's get on with it!*"

Tyler had obviously packed his Halloween costume from the previous year. Now that he was appropriately attired, he was ready for the hunt.

They had a quick laugh and hoisted their packs onto their backs, heading for the cedar.

Shadow led the way. It was obvious the lower portion of the trail had not sat completely unused. Made them wonder how many folks had come searching for clues of *Crystal Cove.*

"Over this way," said Gary, once again indicating that he'd found another match to the markings on the map. "According to the map, we've got to pass to the right of that boulder over there."

They stopped at the boulder to look at the map again. "Here is the bend in the trail," Travis pointed out, "now we need to head for that ridge."

"Right up to the plateau," Justin added.

The closer they came to the top, the thicker the vegetation.

"This calls for the machete." Travis drew his machete from its sheath that was strapped to the side of his pack, and began hacking through overgrowth like he was blazing a trail through the wilds of the Amazon. With the exception of Tyler, who was last on the trail, each of the guys insisted on having a turn. The idea of cutting their way through the vegetation on their way to the unknown produced more than enough adrenaline to get the job done. After all, this is what adventure was all about.

The end of the trail took them right to the entrance

of the old burial ground. It was covered with tall grass. Mixed in with the grass were large stones and random sections of tree trunks lying here and there.

"Think these are all grave markers?" questioned Curtis.

There was a sudden rustling as the wind danced through the grass.

"Did you hear that?" asked Curtis. "This Indian burial ground is probably protected by spirits. Maybe we shouldn't be poking around up here."

"Don't be silly!" Gary said. Then looking to the others, he raised his eyebrows up and down and asked, "*Is anybody here afraid of spirits?*"

Two hands shot up. Curtis and Tyler.

Exasperated, Travis threw both hands down to his side. "We can't afford to be afraid of spirits right now! We have to stay focused on finding *Crystal Cove*. As long as we stay together, everything will be fine."

Gary chimed in, "He's right! We have to follow every clue! We've got to learn whether or not any of this *Crystal Cove* stuff is real! Finding those crystals would change everything!"

Now Gary was speaking a language that Tyler could understand. Fickle as usual, Tyler shouted, "*Yeah! We go for the crystals!*" All of a sudden, spirits were no big deal.

Curtis dropped his arm. It wouldn't do any good to be the only one in protest. He had the same feeling he'd had when they trespassed into Grisham's shed, and he had to admit, that had turned out okay.

"This is confusing," said Gary, "According to our map, this web formation should be right here. I wonder if there is a drawing on one of these rocks or a carving on one of the trunks?"

"Let's split up," said Travis, "it must be here somewhere.

Curtis, still a little concerned about spirits, added,

"Be careful not to disturb any of the graves."

"You're far to worried about spirits," chided Gary.

Just then, the wind caught the grass once again, grabbing their attention. Carefully, they began searching rocks and logs, looking for any clues that matched the strange drawing on the map. The rest of the map had made sense—the trail, the old cedar, the ridge—there just had to be a web somewhere.

"Why do you suppose all of these logs are laying out here in the grass like this?" Curtis asked. "They can't be grave markers—all random like this."

Shadow was having a hey day. So many new smells—so many places to christen.

Exasperated, Gary blurted out, "We're missing something! Everything leads us here. The next clue has to be here somewhere!"

"Maybe there was some kind of woven artifact that has since been removed, or rotted away," said Curtis, ready to concede. "I think we're wasting our time."

"These people knew northwest weather," replied Travis, "They lived here! They would have taken the elements into consideration."

Pointing across to the other end of the plateau Gary said, "Is that tree on the map?"

They gathered around for another look. There must be a clue they hadn't picked up on.

Frustrated, Gary said, "I'm going to climb the old maple."

Once Gary was up in the tree he looked out across Henderson Bay, daydreaming of adventures that lie ahead. *There's a whole world waiting out there,* he thought. *Now that we have a boat, it's all within our reach. The Island Gang—famous explorers—I can feel it.*

The maple's location offered panoramic views in every direction. The Olympic Mountains on the horizon, Henderson Bay in the forefront, and coves and inlets everywhere. *That's where our cove is,* was the thought going through his mind, *out there—across the bay.*

As he turned to see what the others were up to there was a voice in the wind. *Dream catcher . . . dream catcher.*

"Dream catcher?" Gary repeated out loud. "*Hey, did you guys here that*?" he yelled down to the others.

"*Hear what*?" Curtis yelled back.

"*That voice—sounded like it said—dream catcher*!"

"Dream catcher?" asked Curtis.

Gary stood there on a bough near the top of the tree, looking down on the guys, when suddenly a pattern came into clear view. The harder he focused, the clearer the pattern. The overgrowth just sort of melted away, leaving only the pattern of a huge dream catcher in the layout of the burial ground.

"*Guys—get over here! Hurry! You've got to see this!*" Gary hollered, compensating for the distance and the breeze.

They hustled over to the tree.

"*What is it*?" Travis yelled from the base of the tree. "*Did you find the web*?"

"*You'll never believe it until you see it for yourself! Get up here, quick*!"

"I don't climb trees," whined Tyler.

"Just wait here at the bottom," Curtis said in a reassuring tone. "Shadow doesn't climb trees either. He'll keep you company."

Shadow let out a whine and nervously meandered around as the gang took turns getting onto the lowest branch and climbing toward Gary. Shadow pawed at the tree and then sat down next to Tyler, anxiously looking up at the others and then begging Tyler for attention.

The rest of The Island Gang hustled up the maple as fast as they could, thinking Gary had spotted *Crystal Cove.* Once they were all up in the tree, Gary said, "Look down at the cemetery and tell me what you see."

As they looked down, they saw what he was talking about. The rocks and logs were in some kind of formation.

"There's our web," stated Gary, "it's a dream catcher! See the pattern?"

"He's right!" Justin exclaimed. "It's been right in front of us the whole time! I read where the natives believe that dream catchers are symbolic of the weavings of your life. All of your good ideas, thoughts, and actions get woven into the web—to strengthen it. Bad stuff passes through the hole in the middle and goes away. Having your own dream catcher is supposed to keep evil spirits away . . ."

" . . . And bring good luck," concluded Gary.

"In that case, we should all have one," said Wendy. "We can use all of the luck we can get!"

"This would be the ideal place for a final dream catcher," said Gary. "Right here in their burial ground."

Curtis piped up, "Oh no, here we go again. Our resident dreamer is now a philosopher. *Heaven forbid!*"

"C'mon," Travis said, urging them out of the tree, "Let's go check this dream catcher out. Maybe those numbers on the map will make more sense!"

Wendy read the sequence of letters and numbers from the map, "N—E7—W3. Maybe these are directions, like Justin suggested."

In the center of the dream catcher drawn on the map was a drawing of an old style key.

"Is that a key—right there in the center?" asked Wendy

Gary stood up and walked out to the center of the pattern. "The key must be out here in the middle," he said with a puzzled tone in his voice.

"That has to be it!" Travis seconded, joining Gary in the center of the burial ground, "But how is it the key?"

"What if these are numbers—like coordinates?"

asked Justin.

"Oh, so now you're saying these guys knew geometry," Curtis blurted out, rolling his eyes.

"Let's plot it out," stated Wendy, "you never know."

They tried to figure out how to chart the coordinates, using the center as the starting point. But it wasn't making much sense. They stood in the center of the formation, compass in hand, facing north, pacing 7 steps to the east, and 3 steps to the West. Nothing made sense.

"For crying out loud," Gary said, "How on earth is the center the key?"

"You guys look ridiculous," objected Curtis. "How is all of your pacing around going to lead to a cove?"

"*That's it!*" Gary cried out. "We need to be looking for a cove! The only chance for a cove—would be out there," pointing toward the bay.

Travis had an idea, "Let me see the compass."

"Sure," came the reply.

Travis took the compass, positioned himself right in the center of the burial site, and faced due north. "Justin, go stand at the very north end of the formation, directly in front of me. Curtis, you stand right behind Justin, and take 7 paces to the east. Keep your paces on the perimeter of the formation."

"Like we're supposed to know what size pace these guys used," retorted Curtis in his normal doubting attitude. "We know nothing about these natives!"

"For crying out loud, Curtis!" Gary cried out in frustration. "Keep your sorry attitude to yourself. Travis has an idea—let's give it a try!"

Travis continued, "Justin. Since Curtis can't handle the pressure, would you take 7 normal size paces east?"

Justin began at the due north position and walked off seven paces.

"Wendy, start right behind Justin and take 3 paces

back toward the West," instructed Travis. "Okay, now everyone hold your positions."

Gary referred to the map while Travis studied their positions. Then he saw something he hadn't noticed before. At the worn end of the map, outside of the southern most portion of the diagram of the dream catcher, were the remains of what appeared to have been a large dot!

"Hold it!" Gary cried out. "That's it! How many lines can you draw between two points?

Travis got that "you're a genius" look on his face, and said, "Wendy, look directly across the cemetery and tell us what you see."

"That tall rock on the opposite side of the burial ground."

Gary walked over and stood right behind Wendy, looking over her shoulder.

"She's right! The only thing that stands out is that large rock at the far end."

"Well of course I'm right," Wendy stated indignantly.

"I didn't mean it like that," defended Gary, as he laid the map in front of them. "Look at this worn edge of the map! I hadn't noticed it before, but I'll bet this marking is supposed to be that rock!"

Wendy and Gary hurried over to the rock. Justin had already climbed to the top and was looking out over the water.

"What landmarks do you see?" asked Gary.

"Landmarks? I see a long rugged coastline. You guys tell me when I'm facing the right way, and I'll see if there are any landmarks that line up."

Gary was sold on the rock being part of the equation, but the idea of paces leading them to exactly the right point on the perimeter of the dream catcher was disconcerting. "Wait just a minute. Justin, you wait there. The rest of you come with me." Gary got everyone in position once again. Instead of paces, let's try something else." He looked to the compass and located due north. Then he counted the lines on the compass 7 degrees to the east of north, and 3 degrees to the west of north. Gary stood there silently.

Suddenly, as he was studying the compass, it hit him! "We're making it too hard. It's basic math!" he shouted loud enough for everyone to hear. Gary found the line that was just 4 degrees to the east of due north. "Stand right there!" he shouted, pointing to the spot until Wendy had positioned herself in just the right place. "That's it!"

"Now let's see where the line from that spot to the rock hits the shore on the other side of Henderson!"

Shouting across the burial ground, Wendy coached Travis as to the direction he should be facing, "Turn a little to your right! Okay, stop! Right there!"

Gary was a little confused at the fact that the center spot where he stood was outside of the line between Wendy's position and the rock. Then he realized that the center point of the burial ground was not meant to be part of the line, but was, in fact, the key to locating the point from which to find the line. "This is it! I know it!" he shouted

Justin found a landmark, but he needed to get a better look. "Tyler, come here—hurry!"

Tyler sensed the excitement and hustled over to Justin.

"I need the binoculars out of your backpack!"

Travis arrived at the large rock the same time Tyler did and helped locate the binoculars. Justin took them and found his landmark and then slowly dropped his view to the water. "There it is!"

Justin no sooner had his eye fixed on the water across the bay when a call came across the radio, "Island Gang— over."

It was Curtis' dad checking in. The Island Gang all

gathered at the rock.

"This is Travis—over."

"Hey, is everybody okay over there?—over."

"Yeah, we're great—over."

"Staying out of trouble I trust?—over."

"No trouble over here. We're just exploring a little—over."

"I hope you're not disturbing that graveyard. You know it's protected by the government—over."

"They would absolutely kill us if they knew we'd been trampling all over these graves," whispered Curtis, just loud enough for those nearby to hear.

"We haven't trampled on any graves," replied Wendy, "we have actually been very careful."

Travis pressed the button on the radio, "We know. We're staying out of trouble—over."

"The tide changed a while ago, you guys getting ready to head back?"

"Yeah, we should be back to the boat in about half an hour—over."

"Okay. We'll keep a watch for you—over and out.

"Out," replied Travis.

"Half an hour!" Curtis cried out. "What are you thinking? We'll never get to the boat that quick!"

"Curtis!" Gary hollered. "Focus for a minute. All we have to do is memorize a couple of landmarks—then we'll make tracks for the boat!"

Gary and Travis joined Justin on top of the rock. Shadow sensed the excitement, and stood at the base barking. Gary took a turn with the binoculars and as he raised them to his eyes, Shadow faced out across the water pointing with his right paw.

"What do you know, boy?" Justin asked as he watched Shadow.

With Justin's help, Gary scanned the waterline spotting the cove. "Anyone have a camera?" he asked. "We need some pictures!"

"*I do,*" Wendy replied.

"Watch it! *Those* words imply *commitment*!" muttered Curtis.

Wendy smirked at Curtis and retrieved the camera from her pack. "How about a hand up?" she said, reaching her hand out for assistance. "It's my new digital—it will probably be easier for me to take the pictures than to explain how it works."

There was room for one more. Gary stepped to the halfway point and extended his hand. Once on the rock, she took her camera out of the case, "Point me in the right direction and I'll take some shots."

Gary helped Wendy identify the location through the binoculars, "See the tops of rocks sticking out of the water just off shore? That could be our cove."

Wendy got a good look with the binoculars, found the spot through the telephoto lens of her camera, and took several pictures.

"Got it," said Wendy. "We'd better head for the boat!"

They hustled back to *Little Imp*, loaded their things as fast as they could, and pushed off. It was time to paddle hard for Raft Island.

"How and when?" asked Travis, referring to their getting to the cove.

"We've got to go while it's all fresh," said Gary as he stared across water. "What if this is it? Can you even imagine?"

Now Curtis, the eternal pessimist's mind was racing. *If this—Crystal Cove turns out to be something; maybe those other legends are for real!* He didn't say anything quite yet. He was holding judgment to see if *Crystal Cove* panned out. But Curtis was slowly becoming converted to the whole Legend thing.

They made it back in about 45 minutes. Having missed the ebb tide, they *really* had to paddle their way back, but slack tide and no wind was like rowing across a still pond.

They greeted family and then got the boat out of the water and back to Grisham's. All they could think about was getting to the cove.

9

Henderson Bay

The next day, Gary was out walking Shadow when he ran into Wendy, who was on her way to get the mail. "So, how'd you sleep last night?"

"I couldn't stop thinking about the cove," she replied.

"Boy, can I relate! We're going tonight!

"What do you mean tonight?"

"I mean we're going. We have it all planned out. The guys are all going to tell parents that we're staying the night at Curtis' house. After dinner, we're going to tell his parents that we've decided to go to Travis' house instead—they never check. Then we're headed to the beach. We'll get the boat to the water before dinner."

"You're not going without me," insisted Wendy.

"Like your parents are going to let you spend the night with a bunch of guys."

"I'll worry about that. What time are you guys pushing off?"

"We're meeting at dusk."

"Don't leave without me! I'll be there! Wouldn't it be something if we were the first to figure out the dream catcher?"

They talked for several minutes concocting plans, when Wendy's mother stuck her head out the front door, "Did the mail come?"

"Yep, I've got it mom. Be right there."

They said goodbye, and Gary and Shadow continued their walk. He walked Shadow toward the beach and out across the Raft Island Bridge on his usual route, once again stopping to gawk at all of the boats. He had dreams of something bigger and faster than *Little Imp*, but she would do fine for now. He and Shadow crossed the bridge, and then turned to head back.

From the far end of the bridge he noticed a slightly overweight man headed toward him on a bicycle. He knew most of the families on the island—this guy didn't look familiar. About 30 yards before they were going to cross paths, Gary could see one of those holstered cell phones dangling from the guy's side. Gary's mind began processing. He had just seen a spot on TV where a pickpocket had snagged a cell phone from an unsuspecting passer by in a situation exactly like this.

Gary was always imitating stunts he'd seen on TV. He could roll a top hat off the back of his hand right onto his head just like Fred Astaire, draw a six shooter as fast as Clint Eastwood, and just as he was about to pass this guy, he wondered if he could duplicate that cell phone heist. The idea of not trying it with the perfect situation right in front of him was tormenting. Thinking aloud he said, "How often do you get the opportunity to try something on an unsuspecting passerby, particularly with a guy who couldn't catch you even if you do have to run for your life? *It couldn't be more perfect than this!*"

They were on the same side of the bridge. Just as they were about to cross paths, Gary raised his hand to wave. Then, when he and the bicyclist were right next to each other, he pretended to stumble over Shadow and the leash—allowing brief contact. On contact, he bumped the phone right at the base of the holster, and it popped up and out—he caught it mid-air. "It worked," he said under his breath as he turned to face the cyclist.

Gary had bumped the guy a little harder than he

intended. The man regained his balance, stopped and turned to make sure Gary was okay—just in time to see Gary holding the phone. Glancing down at his holster, he realized his phone had just been jacked—at which point he let the bike fall to the ground!

Gary immediately got into position like he was playing shortstop, setting up a pickle, and said to the guy, "Don't worry, I'm not after your phone—I just thought I'd point out the vulnerability of that holster. Someone not as nice as me could grab your phone and be gone with it—just like that."

The man got a puzzled look on his face, like—*'Who does this kid think he is?'* Then he reached around his back under his oversized un-tucked t-shirt and pulled out a handgun. "Let me introduce you to your vulnerabilities," he said as he pointed the gun in Gary's direction.

"Uh oh—what did I get myself into?" he said out loud. Gary was just playing around, and now a complete stranger was holding a gun on him. Shadow was in a half-crouched attack position, teeth showing, and putting on a mean growl. He could always sense danger.

Gary tried to calm Shadow, and then threw his hands up in the air, shouting, "You win! My vulnerabilities are *definitely* more vulnerable than yours!" He reached to hand the stranger his phone.

Still puzzled at the exchange of events, the stranger said, "You want to walk over here nice and slow like and hand me that phone?"

"That was the next thing on my mind," Gary replied, hands held high. In an effort to bring some humor into the situation and get this man to relax a little, he said, "You can put that gun away now. I won't hurt you—I promise."

Comic statements were Gary's natural defense when struck by fear, and it seemed like a better idea than wetting his pants, which was next on his list if the guy didn't lower the gun.

Shadow was running out of patience. He was about to lunge and take the guy's hand off.

Sensing that Gary wasn't really a threat and realizing that he had just reacted out of habit, the man tucked the gun back into his pants. "What were you thinking, kid?" came the question.

"I guess I wasn't thinking," Gary replied. "I saw that stunt on TV awhile back, and ever since, I thought about trying it if the right situation came along. Then, there you were."

"That was a stupid stunt," the guy said. "Don't you know you're not supposed to attempt the crazy things you see on TV?"

Gary agreed it wasn't the brightest idea he'd ever had. Shadow was finally calming down, though he wasn't at all sure what to make of this guy. Gary handed over the phone. "It's okay, Shadow, he's not going to hurt anyone."

As Gary handed him the phone, the man let out a curious chuckle and asked, "What's your name, kid?"

"My name is Gary. What's yours?"

"Folks call me Streets."

"Streets? What kind of name is that?"

"They say it's because I'm always out and about. I like being outside—walking, riding my bike, whatever—just checking things out—observing my environment I guess. Outside's better than inside. When you're in the city—outside always meant that I was on the streets. There's not much of country roads like these where I come from."

"Streets, huh—okay, I get it. Where do you come from?" It was clear from his accent that he wasn't native to the Northwest.

"I was raised in Chicago," he replied. "I have lived a few places since then, but the accent seems to follow me around."

"Chicago! That would explain the gun."

"What do you mean by that?"

"You know, Chicago—gangs—mafia—and all that stuff."

Streets just chuckled and shook his head, "Ever left the Northwest, kid?"

"Name's Gary—remember?"

"Oh yeah. Well, Gary, you don't really believe everything you see on TV now do you?"

"Not everything—I guess."

"Well not everyone in Chicago is part of the Mafia, and they don't all carry guns," Streets assured him.

"You're probably right, but I'll bet most guys with a gun tucked into their belt are up to no good. What ya doing with that anyway?"

"I carry it for defense against kids trying to steal my cell phone," Streets replied, again chuckling.

"Really—why do you carry a gun?"

"I used to do some P.I. work down in California. I had to carry it then, and I just kind of got used to having it on me."

"Wow, you're a private investigator?" Gary asked.

"Well now, just how private do you think it would be if I ran around telling everyone? Maybe I am, maybe I'm not—who's to tell?"

"How long have you been in the Northwest?" asked Gary.

"Just a few months. I had a couple of setbacks. But I'm getting a new start on life. I had this opportunity to use my background, and I needed a change of scenery, so here I am. How about you?"

"Lived here all my life."

"Lucky you," Streets replied, looking around at the tall evergreens that surrounded them, and taking a deep breath of fresh, clean air. "It's like living in a national park."

"I guess," answered Gary, "it's all I've ever known. So,

you ride this way often?"

"First time across the bridge, but I come up Rosedale and out around the Ray Nash loop several times a week, usually in the morning. Got to stay active so I don't get any more excess than I already have," replied Streets, belly in hand.

Gary wasn't sure what to say next. It was Street's physique that gave him the nerve to try the stunt. "I'll watch for you. Maybe we'll talk again sometime."

"And I'll look for you when I pass Raft Island. You know, there are easier ways to make a friend than lifting a cell phone. You're lucky that I'm easy going."

They talked awhile longer then went their ways.

―――――――――――――――――――――

Late that afternoon, the guys met over at Curtis' house.

Gary told the guys about running into Wendy that morning. "Wendy says she's coming—said she'd meet us down at the beach and not to leave without her. I'm not sure how she's planning to work it out, but I think she'll be there."

"Time will tell," replied Curtis, "but at dusk, we leave—with or without her."

"Everyone told their folks we'd be at Curtis' house tonight—right?" asked Justin.

"Right," answered Gary, "then after dinner we tell Curtis' mom that we've decided to go to Travis' house instead."

"Then we're footloose and fancy free," said Travis, "they'll never even check!"

"Everybody bring a sleeping bag and food. We'll meet at Grisham's at 6:30."

―――――――――――――――――――――

It was 6:30 on the nose when the guys met up at Grisham's. No one was home—it was perfect.

"Okay guys, let's make sure we have all the gear," Gary said. "Travis, you got the list?

"Got it!"

"Call out the items, we'll make sure there on board."

"Oars."

"Got 'em!"

"Fishing gear."

"Got it!"

"Crab pots."

"Right here!"

"Dome tent."

"It's here!"

"Boat tent!"

"On board!"

"Sleeping bags."

"Six accounted for!"

"Life vests."

"They're all here!"

"Life Ring."

"It's here!"

"First aid kit."

"Got it!"

"Flashlights."

"Got 'em!"

"Lantern."

"Got it!"

"Compass."

"Right Here!"

"Flare gun."

"Here."

"Everyone got their 10 essentials?" Curtis asked.

"Yeah, yeah, be prepared," added Gary.

"That's the motto," Travis offered. "It's what our

scout training is all about."

"I know, I know . . ." replied Gary.

" . . . And it only takes one person to ruin things for everybody," Travis continued, "Speaking of which, has anyone helped Tyler get checked out?"

"Got it covered," replied Curtis, which meant he'd take care of it right then. He laid his pack down and walked over to Tyler.

"My pack is fine," Tyler replied.

"C'mon Tyler, take it off and let's go through it. What are you reading anyway?"

Tyler had been listening in on the conversation, but was intently studying something at the same time. Whenever he had the chance, he would read. He loved to learn, and seemed to retain everything.

Curtis grabbed the booklet from his hand. "Tide tables! You're reading the tide tables? That's the sign of a sick mind." Sometimes Curtis was gentle with Tyler—other times he was just out of patience. Truth was, Tyler's feelings didn't hurt very easily.

"Give me that back," Tyler insisted. "It's Mr. Grisham's. I got it from the bench."

Curtis handed it back to him. "Fine, but you have to help check your pack."

"I already did. Everything's there."

Curtis double-checked, even though he knew if Tyler said he had everything—he probably did. Tyler could do a lot of annoying things, but lying wasn't one of them. His mind just didn't work that way.

Wendy showed up late and had been watching the boys from the side door. Only Shadow had been aware of her presence, and had joined Wendy at the doorway. The boys were too engrossed readying *Little Imp*. "Looks like we're ready," she stated, walking across the shed.

"Hey, Wendy. How long have you been there?" asked

Travis.

"Long enough," she replied. "Are we taking the boat down to the water now?"

Shadow barked and then ran and jumped into the boat as if to say, "You're not going without me!"

Acknowledging Shadow's plea for attention, Gary said, "Yeah, we'll pack some food and doggy snacks for you too. We wouldn't leave you behind."

"We were just headed to the water," replied Travis. "You're just in time. You and Tyler take this radio. Once we clear the driveway, you two go ahead and act as lookouts."

They got the boat off of the stand and onto the dolly. "We need to get there inconspicuously," said Gary. "The last thing we need is for someone see us and spoil our plans."

They managed to get the boat down to the beach without drawing unnecessary attention. It was time to head to Curtis' house for dinner.

"See you back here at dusk," said Gary.

"I'll be here," Wendy replied.

Following dinner, the guys went down to the daylight basement. That's where Curtis' bedroom and the game room were located.

"Ready to go?" asked Travis.

"Yeah, let's get to the boat," answered Justin.

Curtis ran back upstairs to tell his mom the change of plans. "Mom, we've decided to sleep at Travis' house tonight."

"Does Travis' mother know?"

"Yep. Travis already cleared it."

"Okay," she replied, "See you tomorrow."

That was almost too easy, thought Curtis as he went back down the stairs. "C'mon, let's head for the boat!"

When they arrived at the beach, Wendy was waiting for them. "About time!" she said.

"What'd you tell your folks?" asked Gary.

"Nothing," came the reply. "I simply retired to bed early—then snuck out the back."

"Your dad will kill you—and all of us if he finds out!" exclaimed Gary.

"What are your parents going to do if you get caught?" she asked.

"We'll all be grounded for life," replied Travis.

"There you go," replied Wendy, "There's times in life when you have to take a little risk. And, there's no way you're going to *Crystal Cove* without me!"

They boarded *Little Imp*. Gary and Travis pushed them off and climbed aboard. In no time they had crossed under the bridge and were out of danger of being spotted. They had to work the oars pretty hard the first little while in order to maintain a straight course, but they were so excited about getting to the cove, and so busy with the binoculars they didn't notice the fact that they were fighting the tail end of an ebb tide.

They were only half way across Henderson Bay when it became dark. The tide slackened and rowing was easier— they were making pretty good time. They were firmly fixed on the outline of landmarks on the horizon that they had identified the day before.

"We'd better light the lantern," Curtis said. "We'd be in trouble if another boat happened along and couldn't see us."

"I know where it is," offered Justin. "I'll get it."

Soon the only thing they could make out across the bay was a single light, and it was quite a bit north of their intended destination. They decided to head for the light and then make their way south along the bank until they came upon the cove. They were sure to hit the rocks jutting above the water's surface as long as they stayed close to shore.

"This is taking longer than I thought it would," said Justin.

Curtis seconded the comment, "Yeah, are you sure we haven't passed it?"

"Positive," replied Gary as he leaned across the bow, shining the light on the water. "There's no way we'll miss the rocks at the entrance."

"I'll know it when I see it," added Wendy, "even in the dark."

"Here we are now!" Gary said, pointing to the rocks. "That should be our cove."

Travis was at the oars. Slowly they made their way through the rocks and into the cove. The terrain along the shore was rugged.

"Right there!" alerted Justin. "There's some sand! Let's get her beached!"

"Look—*there*!" insisted Curtis, "Right back over there—see it?"

"See what?" Gary questioned.

"That dark area, I think it's the secret entrance!"

Travis gave a couple of hard strokes, landing the bow in the sand.

"Get your flashlights," ordered Gary, "Let's go ashore and check it out!"

Shadow was a bit hesitant, which wasn't normal. "Hey Shadow," Gary said reassuringly, "What's the matter, boy? Aren't you coming? C'mon, there's nothing to worry about."

Wendy knew that if something was bothering Shadow, there was reason to be cautious. "I think I'll wait on the boat and keep Shadow company," she said. "There will be plenty of time to look around tomorrow, when we can actually see."

"I'm with her," stated Tyler.

The others were too excited to consider Shadow's reaction.

Justin took hold of the guide rope and tied the boat off. Once the boat was secure, the four boys hiked around looking for signs of an opening into a secluded cove. The rocky shoreline extended right out into the water. Rocks as big as they were, and bigger, were everywhere. Whatever Curtis thought he had seen must have just been shadows. They were bound to end up wet if they spent too much time climbing around in the dark. They decided to call it a night and headed for the boat.

"We should push out a little and drop anchor," said Gary, encouraging support for the idea, "It will be safer sleeping on the boat."

Being as serious as he could, with eyes as big as saucers, Tyler said, "Yeah, we don't want any wild animals joining us while we're asleep!"

Everyone agreed. The boys were suddenly keen to Shadow's uneasiness. After pushing out past the rocks, Travis set the anchor. Gary, Justin, and Wendy got the tent out, while Curtis shuffled the dolly wheels around trying to find space for them out of the way, "These wheels are going to have to go on the dolly. They're taking up valuable sleeping space in the boat."

"Mr. Grisham said to keep them out of the salt water," said Gary, "Otherwise the bearings won't last. Tie them to the top of the cold storage."

It was going to be a cozy evening with six of them on the floor of the boat, but it would help to keep them warm. They lifted the hatch doors and stowed as much as they could.

With the poles in place, they all worked together getting the tent snapped down. They talked into the night about their plans for the crystals. The motion of the boat gently bobbing up and down soon rocked them into a deep sleep.

10

Sedgwick

Tyler was first to wake the next morning. Feeling as though they were moving across the water, he unbuttoned the flap at the stern and stuck his head out to see what was going on. "Hey, *where's the cove?*"

"What do you mean 'where's the cove'?" replied Curtis, unzipping the opening to his mummy bag. Curtis crawled to where Tyler was. "*You guys, wake up!*" Curtis yelled at the top of his lungs. "*Where in the heck are we? There's no cove!*"

"The cove's gone?" Justin asked as he sat up clearing sleep from his eyes.

"*Absafloginlutly!*" Tyler shouted.

Gary, thinking that the boat had simply pivoted on the anchor, got a kick out of Travis, who was shuffling around trying to respond, but couldn't get his voice to work. "What's the matter Travis—got a frog?"

"Very funny," replied Travis, "I've always made a conscious effort to keep reptiles out of my throat, thank you very much. I don't get where that phrase comes from anyway."

Wind and light rain caused them to stay under cover of the tent. At Gary's suggestion, Justin stuck one arm in the water and began paddling, spinning *Little Imp* in a circle, hoping to see the cove.

"Pull the flap open so we can see what's going on," instructed Gary.

Justin ignored him and kept paddling. "You're wrong Gary," Justin said as *Little Imp* came around, "there's no cove. We've drifted."

Everyone headed for the small opening at once.

"*Whoa there!*" screamed Curtis. "You guys are going to *capsize* the boat!"

"Everyone calm down," interjected Wendy, who was trying to keep from being trampled. "We need to get the bedding put away before everything gets wet. Then we'll put the tent down and figure out where we are."

Travis checked his watch; it was 7:05 a.m. "We didn't even get to sleep in!"

They acted quickly, getting their bags into stuff sacks and then into plastic. Travis made his way to the bow to check on the anchor. As he leaned out and tugged on the rope, he realized the problem, "The anchor isn't hitting the bottom."

"Did anyone think to check the tide last night?" Gary asked.

"Oh, crud!" replied Travis.

Gary continued, "Must have been low tide when you set anchor."

Tyler got this look on his face like a clairvoyant taking a reading from a crystal ball, "May 30, high tide 10:37 p.m.; May 31, first low tide 3:34 a.m.; first high tide 8:32 a.m."

Tyler's mind was amazing. He had instant recall of anything he'd ever read.

The rising tide pulled the anchor loose, and they had been adrift through the night.

Gary got the maps out while Travis checked the compass for a reading. Curtis unlocked the oars getting ready to row, hesitating just long enough for Gary to tell him which direction to go.

"I knew his photographic memory would come in handy for something," said Justin.

"That's great! I wonder if his photographic memory can tell us where we are!" chided Curtis, as he began to row.

"I hope we aren't near the Narrows. Without a motor, we won't be able to fight the currents!" Curtis headed for the rocky shore to their starboard side. The more excited he got, the harder he rowed.

"Like panicking is going to help," Gary said. "We'll figure out where we are soon enough. You guys see any familiar landmarks?"

Frustrated, Curtis continued his sputtering, "Dad's gonna kill me! And if there's anything left—uncle Tim will finish the job."

The thought of being near the Narrows was on Tyler's mind. He, too, had been warned about its stiff currents. "No, no, no, no, no, *stop it*!" he yelled, "we can't be near the Narrows—*we'll drown!*"

Tyler was killing them with his lines from "*Hook*." They vacillated between wanting to drop everything to have a good laugh—and being scared to death. They were trying to get their bearings, but with land and water in every direction, it was difficult. They were now less than a hundred feet from shore. It was tempting to go all the way in, but it made no sense to get tangled up in the rock—especially if it was the wrong shore.

Curtis noticed a dock just ahead. "We should tie off there while we figure out where we are."

"*Seize the day!*" hollered Tyler. "*Let's tie up!*"

"That's probably a good idea," said Gary. "Head for the dock."

As they got closer, Gary noticed something. "It isn't a dock, it's a pier! Must be high tide!"

"It is a pier," agreed Travis. "Which means we can't tie up for long. We've had enough bad experience with tides for one day."

Other than the fact that they were missing the opportunity to explore the cove, Gary couldn't have been more excited. This was adventure at its best! "We're facing sort of northwest," he said, reading the compass that Grisham had mounted to the upper rail of the boat.

Gary held the boat secure while everyone climbed onto the pier. "Let's see if we can pull *Little Imp* up on the pier," he suggested, "that way we won't have to keep such a close eye on her."

Tyler mused as he watched them struggle to get *Little Imp* out of the water, "*Ha, Ha, Ha, Ha, good form!*" he hollered.

It took all five of them pulling as hard as they could to get *Little Imp* on the pier. Those that hadn't found their rain gear while panicking on the water were now searching frantically. The key to staying warm was to remain as dry as possible. Gary untied the wheels from the cold storage and mounted them on the dolly. Once everyone had dressed for the weather, they made sure everything was put away. The wind had picked up, prompting them to secure everything. Finally they were free to resume trying to identify their location.

"Where's the map?" asked Travis.

"Right here," replied Gary, "but where are we going to look at it? If we open it here, it will get wet and soggy!"

Curtis, Justin and Wendy huddled together, stretching their rain gear out, providing a makeshift shelter so that Gary and Travis could look at the map. The compass showed that they were facing west as they looked straight out from the end of the pier. West from where was the question. There are so many pieces of land in the region, they could be facing west from any number of places. The map wouldn't be much help until they knew their location.

"We need more information!" said Travis. "If we only knew where we are, we could figure out how to get back!"

"Let's check it out," Gary said, pointing up to the opposite end of the pier. "Maybe we'll find someone to ask for directions. There has to be something that will at least give us some clues as to our location."

"Count me in," added Travis.

Tyler's frustration was beginning to show. He had a way of getting uneasy when he sensed that things weren't exactly as they should be. In familiar surroundings like Raft Island, he could wander for hours without the least concern. But tension was so thick you could cut it with a knife, which was causing him to feel out of sorts, and when he was out of sorts, he had a habit of acting out. Suddenly, he stood straight up, clenched both fists, threw his arms straight down to his side, turned beet red and yelled, "*Where are we?*"

Curtis, realizing Tyler was a bit stressed, gathered his composure enough to console his cousin, "Calm down, Tyler. It'll be okay. We'll figure this out."

"This pier is awful old," said Gary as they walked toward land.

The pier was in need of repair. Clearly it had not been used for some time. The shoreline was a bank of large rock, as was common throughout the Narrows. Trees lined the area just back from the water. Under the trees was a blanket of thick vegetation that extended within a couple of yards of several sets of railroad track. Beyond the track was a high wall of granite. The granite was a shear cliff for the first fifteen to twenty feet, after which it tapered off slightly. They had no intention of attempting to climb it. Besides which, other than improving their view, it showed no sign of providing an answer as to their location. They were in the middle of nowhere! Shadow was attracted to a large barricade made of railroad ties built right into the granite wall.

"Looks like the blocked off entrance to an old mine," offered Gary.

The wall of granite paralleled the waterfront as far as they could see in either direction. The only thing that varied was the elevation in the wall. In some places it was *high*—everywhere else it was *higher*. It was the *perfect* place to be if you didn't want to be found.

Shaking his head as if in denial, Justin uttered, "We've crossed The Narrows. Think about it! Where else would there be railroad tracks along the water?"

They talked about it for a while, but other than coming to agreement that they must have crossed The Narrows, they were perplexed as to what to do next.

Curtis, aching to get under the skin of the others, said rather snidely, "Well, the *famed* Island Gang has done it now! We've discovered—*nothing*! And—we're gonna get our rear ends kicked and lose our boat to boot!"

"*Time to discover food!*" yelled Tyler at the top of his lungs.

"If there's anyone in earshot—Tyler just announced our arrival," muttered Curtis, trying to keep his remarks about his cousin to himself so as not to offend.

Tyler wasn't the only one that was starving. It was now 9:00 a.m., and they hadn't eaten a thing. That might be okay if they were still asleep, but they'd been awake for nearly two hours—working up an appetite the entire time. It was time to get back to the boat and get some food.

"What do we have here, anyway?" was the question Gary posed to himself as he dug into the cold storage. "Ah yes, chocolate *and* powdered donuts. The stuff that sustains life!"

"*Powdered donuts!*" exclaimed Tyler. "*Yuck! Don't we have any real food? I'm hungry!*"

Shadow let out a bark. He was hungry too.

"Okay boy. I'll get your food," Gary replied. "Just a minute while I find it. Here are the cookies! Want a cookie boy—huh—want a cookie?"

Whenever Shadow heard the word 'cookie' he went nuts. Anyone who thought dogs don't understand words hadn't met Shadow. He was practically fluent in English.

While Gary was taking care of Shadow, Curtis was

looking for something to satisfy Tyler. "Let's see here, we have apples, oranges, beef jerky, trail mix . . ."

" . . . and roast beef sandwiches," added Justin, holding up a large zip lock bag containing several sandwiches. He had been home alone while preparing for the outing and raided the fridge. Two pounds of sliced roast beef and a package of individually wrapped slices of cheddar cheese had been enough to make a handful of sandwiches.

"Sounds like *real* food to me," replied Curtis, patting Tyler on the shoulder. "Does any of that sound good?"

Enthusiastically Tyler replied, "I'll take an orange, a roast beef sandwich, and milk."

"I've got the drinks," Wendy offered.

"I'll bet that milk stayed nice and cold," remarked Gary. "It's just what I need to wash these donuts down."

"The milk is freezing! This cold storage idea works great!" commented Wendy after taking a sip. "Here you go Tyler, I poured you a glass too."

"Hey, how about me?" asked Gary.

"Hold your horses," she replied.

"Where's the binoculars?" asked Curtis.

"Right here," answered Travis.

"We're going to be in so much trouble," Tyler kept saying as he wolfed his food down.

The rain had let up, but there was still a fair amount of wind.

Now that they were sure they'd crossed The Narrows, the map might make a little more sense.

"Looks to me like a group of buildings surrounded by a high chain link fence, out there in front of us," Curtis said, pointing out across the water. He lowered the binoculars and looked at the map again. "*I'll bet that's McNeil.*"

McNeil Island had been turned into a state penitentiary years ago. They were all familiar with it.

Travis took a turn with the binoculars. "That would

make this Eagle Island right off to the left—I think he's right!" Travis panned the horizon, until he was facing the direction from which they had come. High on a precipice on their same side of the water was another group of buildings, also surrounded by a fence—only these buildings were surely residences. "Too bad we can't get there. Someone there could surely help."

"Help how?" demanded Curtis. "Do you know how far we are from Henderson Bay? We must have been drifting all night! We'll *never* get back over to Raft Island, at least not in time to save our *necks!*"

Once again, Gary couldn't be bothered with consequences that might await them. This was true adventure, and he intended to make the best of it. He turned back toward the wall of granite. Off in the distance through the trees, he could see a truck driving down the railroad tracks. "What in the world? Look at that truck! It's driving on the railroad tracks!"

The truck came to a stop. They took off in a run, thinking they had finally found someone that could help. As they got part way down the pier, their run turned into a timid walk as they watched the truck drive off of the track and across the dirt toward the barricade. Suddenly the barricade of railroad ties just—opened up! They sensed it was time to use caution. Something didn't quite feel right. They *were* after all in the middle of nowhere and these were complete strangers. They crouched down behind the heavy undergrowth that stood between them and the railroad tracks.

"Must be railroad employees," offered Travis. "We have a friend who works for the railroad. One time he took us for a ride in one of his engines. I remember seeing trucks like that at the rail yard."

They got a little closer just in time to see the truck drive into the opening.

"Something's not right," whispered Wendy. "That

truck should say Burlington Northern, Union Pacific, or something on it!"

"It is a little fishy," said Justin. "No name on the truck—no signs—this whole abandoned—whatever it is . . ."

" . . . I agree with Gary, looks like an old mine," said Travis.

Shadow was curious and anxious. "You have to stay down, Shadow," Gary whispered as he pulled him down by the collar.

"What would that truck be doing in an old abandoned mine?" asked Curtis.

"Exactly!" stated Wendy. "If this were an active mine, there'd be people and equipment."

Gary got a puzzled look on his face, "We should check it out!"

"What are you, *nuts*?" asked Curtis, "There's no way we're going anywhere near it!" His gut was sending the same uneasy signal.

In a shaky, unsure voice, Tyler repeated, *"Let's—get—out—of—here."*

"We've got to check it out," insisted Gary. "What if something is going on, and we're the only ones that know about it?"

Almost pleading, Curtis said, "*Let's just get out of here!* When we get home, we can tell our parents. They'll send the police to check it out."

"Who said anything about needing the police?" asked Travis. "I'm with Gary. We should at least get a closer look. Maybe it's nothing, in which case, we ask the best way to get back and be on our way."

At first, Wendy's mouth was wide open. She couldn't believe they would actually consider going into the mine. But the thought of exploring an old mine did intrigue her. Somewhat hesitating, she added, "Uh, I agree. Let's go for a closer look."

The guys driving the truck hadn't shown their faces since entering the mine. The Island Gang couldn't see the truck, but they suspected that it was hidden in the shadows just inside the opening.

They crept through the brush until they were well to the side of the opening. Gary gave some instruction, "Curtis, you and Justin stay here and keep an eye on Tyler. Keep your radio on, but don't contact us. We'll radio you. C'mon—let's go," said Gary, taking on the role of expedition leader.

Gary, Travis, and Wendy made a dash across the railroad tracks for the wall of rock. They slowly crept along the bank toward the opening.

At the opening, Gary got down on his knees and peered carefully around the corner, "I can see the truck!" he whispered as he turned back toward the others, "It's right in the shadows like we thought. I'm going in! Travis, you coming?"

"Right behind ya!"

"Me too," Wendy chimed in. She was out to prove that she was as brave as they were.

Not realizing he was holding the talk button down, Curtis turned to Justin, "Their brains have all dried up! They're crazy to go in there! Who do they think is going go rescue them when they get in trouble?"

Gary hit the button that sent a beep through to the other radio. Curtis realized his finger was on the talk button, and let up in time to hear Gary order in a whisper, "Just keep your ears on. And keep your finger *off* of the talk button or we'll have to turn our radio off! We'll let you know if we run into a situation."

Cautiously, Gary, Wendy, Travis, and Shadow made their way in alongside the truck. They waited for a couple of minutes—listening and letting their eyes adjust.

"Crying out loud," said Travis, "look how far back it goes!"

They made their way past the truck and around a corner, where they could see a faint glow of light coming from an opening ahead. Gary and Wendy approached the opening, which made an immediate left, and then turned back to the right. The turns in the tunnel dimmed the light, but it appeared there was plenty of light back in there. They could hear voices in the distance.

Travis lagged behind. He had his mini flashlight out, and was having a look around. "*Look*," he whispered, pointing to a large wooden sign mounted above their heads. In it were engraved the words, *The Sedgwick*. *Must be the name of the mine.* Travis continued sweeping the area with the flashlight. "*Over here*," he called quietly to the others, "*Let's go up there!*" A shaft led up an incline and appeared to be a safer route to explore than charging directly into where the voices were.

Gary, Wendy, and Shadow joined him.

Not far along, Travis said, "Hold on a second. Let's see what happens when I extinguish the light." He slowly rotated the barrel, dimming the light until it went out. They could see a faint glow coming from the end of the incline. "I wonder if the light ahead could be coming from the same source as what was down there!"

"*Lead on*," replied Gary

They followed the tunnel further than they thought they should have to go. The farther they went, the brighter the light became.

They came to a juncture where the tunnel branched off into several directions. At the end of the closest alternative, the light was bright.

"*There it is!*" exclaimed Wendy.

Travis paused as if he were trying to decide which choice to follow first.

"Over here, guys," Wendy insisted, as she headed for the opening, "We've *got* to see what the lights are all about first!"

The opening had a ledge about waist high from which they looked right down on the area where the voices were. It didn't provide a full view of the room, but what they did see shocked them.

"*A nursery?*" questioned Travis.

"Look at all of the planters!" whispered Gary.

"And all of the *lights*," Travis added. "There's enough to light the little league field!"

It reminded Wendy of a documentary she'd seen on TV. "*Its drugs!*" she replied. "I'm sure of it! All secluded back here in this old mine—what else would it be? I saw a show on TV about using lights to grow marijuana."

Just then they heard a voice coming over a radio. Thinking it was theirs, they quickly shrank back from the opening, trying to muffle the sound. There was a sigh of relief as they realized it wasn't them.

Travis whispered, "That was close!"

Gary and Wendy acknowledged with a nod of their heads.

The voice over the radio was feeding a steady stream of information, with no pause for response.

"What is it?" asked Travis.

"Listen! It's like—a schedule or something," Wendy replied.

They listened closely, and heard, "11:30 a.m. on track #1, four engines pulling 73 cars leaves Tacoma for Olympia; 12:15 p.m. on track #2, five engines pulling 116 cars arriving Tacoma from Portland; 5:35 on track #1, 3 engines pulling 50 cars arriving Tacoma from Olympia; 6:15 p.m. on track #2, work crews with one engine and 4 sleepers heading south from the yard; no further track activity until 6:30 a.m. tomorrow."

"Its track information," said Wendy. "That's how they get away with running that truck on the tracks!"

"That leaves us less than an hour to sweep our tracks and close up," said one of the men.

"You're right!" replied Gary. They use the track when they know it's clear!"

Wendy was nervous now. She was hoping for crystals—not drugs. "C'mon guys, we've seen enough, time to split."

"Hey Streets," a voice called out, "give me a hand. Let's unload the truck and close up.

Gary froze when he heard the name.

"Uh oh, we're too late. They're headed for the door," whispered Travis as he grabbed Wendy, pulling her toward the tunnel. "Now what are we going to do?"

They knew they'd never make their way down the narrow tunnel to the opening.

Gary hadn't moved. He just stood there staring into the opening. He was stunned, but it wasn't at the possibility of being trapped in the cave. "Did you hear that guy? He called one of the men 'Streets!'"

"Yeah. So what?" replied Travis

The encounter Gary had on the bridge the previous day was running through his mind. The man had introduced himself as "Streets."

"You're never going to believe this, but I might know this guy 'Streets.'"

"You *what*?" questioned Wendy.

"I sort of ran into him yesterday on the Raft Island Bridge. We had a brief conversation and introduced ourselves to each other. He said he was new to the northwest. He's like, a detective from Chicago—said he was getting back on his feet!"

Wendy and Travis made their way back to the ledge, where Gary was trying to get a look at the man.

"Did you see him?" asked Wendy, "Is it the same guy?"

"What do you mean you ran into a man named Streets at Raft Island? What was he doing there?" asked Travis.

"I don't know! I was out walking Shadow, and he was riding his bike. We met each other—that was that." Gary couldn't bring himself to relate the entire incident quite yet.

Shadow sensed that they were uneasy and let out a whine. Gary grabbed Shadow by the muzzle and they all fell back from the opening. "Shhhh! You've got to stay quiet, boy!" he whispered.

They lay there perfectly still, hoping the men hadn't heard the whine. Gary was comforting Shadow, clamping his mouth shut at the same time.

"You guys hear something?" asked one of the guys, looking up toward the opening.

"No. Why?" asked one of the others.

The men stopped what they were doing and stared toward the elevated opening, "Not sure—it was probably nothing."

Gary, Travis, and Wendy quickly followed the tunnel back to where they could see the truck. A couple of guys were unloading bags. One of them stopped, set his bag down, opened a control panel and pushed a button. The barricade began to close.

"Did you see that?" exclaimed Travis. "It's like—a garage door opener—only it moves sideways."

Taking a turn at sarcasm, Wendy replied, "Yeah, that's really *cool*. Now we're *stuck*!"

"Good point," replied Gary.

One of the guys in the mine called out to the others, "We might as well get tonight's delivery on the truck."

"Tonight?" repeated Wendy. "We can't be sitting around here till tonight! We've got to get home!"

"We'll just have to find another way out," replied Gary, quite matter of factly.

They could hear the men returning to the truck.

They decided their best bet was to head back up the tunnel. Maybe one of the trails that branched off up above would lead them out.

"C'mon, Shadow. Let's find a way out of here," said Gary.

Travis had his flashlight out. He spotted something as they made their way back to the juncture. "Look there," he whispered pointing the flashlight. "See that pipe?"

Just overhead was a pipe that led down one of the tunnels.

"We should follow it," suggested Wendy. "Maybe it will lead out."

They were suddenly startled by a noise. As they stopped to listen, they recognized it was the sound of water running through the pipe.

"*A water pipe*!" indicated Gary, as he climbed to where he could put his hand on the pipe. "This is how they get their water. Wendy's right, the pipe has to lead out."

A little way down the tunnel, the pipe branched off, this time into a large open area that had a terrible odor.

"What is that *smell*?" asked Wendy.

"Probably more drugs," replied Travis.

There were a series of dimly lit red lights along one wall. They could see several sinks and a long counter that had jugs of various sizes, all sorts of beakers, and a large caldron. The place had the appearance of a science project gone bad!

"Must be a lab," added Gary, recalling his experience of having once visited the high school science lab with his brother. "But the red lights—make it look like a darkroom."

They made their way back to the main pipe and continued to follow it, which eventually found them on their bellies squeezing through a small opening. While Gary coaxed Shadow through, Travis used the flashlight to look around. "There's a second pipe! Right behind the water line. We just couldn't see it before."

"Probably power," replied Gary.

"Holy smoke!" exclaimed Travis. "This shaft goes forever!"

"This better be our way out," replied Gary.

"It's awful dark to be a way out," added Wendy.

They followed the tunnel to a dead end, at which point the two pipes took a turn straight up—right through the top of the mine.

"*Now* what do we do?" asked Wendy.

Gary replied, "Well, this isn't the way out. We'll have to head back!"

They paused for a moment trying to figure out where the two pipes led.

"We must be out of ear shot of the men—we should try the radio," suggested Travis

They were rather isolated. Gary agreed. "*Nothing,*" he said after several attempts. "We must be out of range—probably too deep into the mine."

Travis pushed a button on the side of his watch lighting the faceplate. "It's been more than an hour. Curtis and the guys must be in a complete panic!"

Suddenly the ground began to rumble beneath their feet.

"*Earthquake,*" said Wendy in a shaky voice, "*Quick,* take cover!"

They knew the drill, but there was nothing to get under. They huddled together against the side of the tunnel to wait it out. Nearly a minute went by. The intensity of the shaking hadn't changed—the ground was still rumbling.

"It's the 11:30 train," Gary said with a sigh of relief, "Remember—the guy on the radio?"

"He's right," confirmed Travis, "it's just a train. C'mon, we have to find a way out!"

As much as they didn't want to go all the way back by the operation, they knew there had to be another way out. The men obviously only used the main entrance for the truck.

"One of the other choices back there must lead out," Wendy said.

On the way back, they were more observant and saw several additional shafts that branched out from the main tunnel. They had missed them earlier—intent on following the water pipe. Travis shone his light down each one. They were curious, but worried about becoming lost, and, anxious to get out, they pressed on.

They no sooner arrived back at the main juncture than Shadow took off.

"Shadow," Gary called out as softly as he could, "where you going, boy?"

They followed Shadow and within minutes came to a set of steel stairs. "Do you suppose they lead out?" Wendy asked.

"Shadow seems to think so!" replied Gary as he carefully followed Shadow up the stairs.

At the top of the stairs was a cover. "Must be our exit," stated Gary. "There's one way to find out!" Gary carefully made his way past Shadow and pushed the cover open a couple of inches, checking in every direction. "Daylight! Coast looks clear!" He pushed the cover all the way open and exited. They were near the top of the wall of rock. There was a trail leading further up through some brush, and nothing below but a steep drop to the bottom.

Wendy spotted Curtis, Tyler and Justin. "*Look*! Down there in the bushes across the tracks," she said pointing.

They waived, but the guys down below hadn't noticed them. They resisted the urge to yell. They didn't need any unwanted attention.

"Let's see where this trail goes," said Gary.

"What?" questioned Travis. "How is following that trail up—going to get us down there? We've *got* to get to the boat!"

Gary knew the trail wouldn't lead them to the others, but it was going to take some mental preparation before scaling the rock wall, and he was all but certain that would end up being their only option.

At the end of the precariously narrow trail they paused. The buildings off on the precipice were now in clear sight.

Wendy looked longingly, "There has to be help there!"

The terrain between them and the buildings was rugged.

"We'll never make it," insisted Travis, "and if we did, look how tall the fence is!"

They had seen the buildings from the pier, but from this vantage point, it was clear that the fence was intended to keep animals and unwanted guests *out*!

"We're better off taking our chances with the rock wall," Travis added. "Besides which, we need to stay together—no matter what!"

The trail they were on continued through some brush. Gary saw what he suspected was the end of the trail. "I'll be right back. You guys check back along the ledge down by the hatch and see if you can find the safest route down."

Gary hadn't followed the trail far when it opened onto a gravel road where an older car and pickup were parked. He looked around for a minute and headed back to find Wendy and Travis. Noticing they had left the hatch door open, Gary thought it best to leave it the way they'd found it. As he closed the hatch, he noticed it was on hinges. He'd been so anxious to get out, he hadn't paid any attention when he pushed it open. He opened and closed the hatch several times examining the hinges.

"*Who's there?*" came a yell from inside.

"*Time to split*," said Gary, as he dropped the hatch

and hurriedly made his way down to the others. "*Hope you guys found the way down! We've got company*—they're on their way up the stairs!"

"*Hurry*," called Travis, "This way!"

Travis had found the area with what appeared to be the shortest drop. Even then, it looked long and painful. They quickly made their way to the lowest spot, which still looked to be fifteen to twenty feet from the ground. They looked up to see two men watching them. They hesitated, wondering if there was someone else waiting for them down near the barricade. Shadow jumped, and as they watched, they could see a train coming from the south.

"The next train," yelled Gary. "We're safe! They won't open the barricade with a train there. We've got to get down—now!"

He was right. All they had to do was get across the tracks ahead of the train, then get the boat in the water before the train passed. The rest of the gang had spotted them. Shadow was at the bottom, barking as if cheering them on.

"Follow me!" Gary said. He sat with his legs hanging over the edge, turned, let himself down as far as he could, and started a count, "One—two—ready—drop!" Gary yelled.

They all three pushed off at once. *Thump*! They were a little shaken up, and had a few scratches from scurrying down the rock—but their legs seemed to be in working order.

"Hurry guys!" shouted Gary as he stood to run across the tracks, "We've got to cross ahead of the train!"

The rest of the gang was waving them forward, frantically pointing at the approaching train. They turned from the wall and ran hard, getting across the tracks just in time.

Curtis hollered, "The men are coming!"

"The train will hold them off," Gary replied. "Quick, head for the pier!"

As they ran for the pier, Tyler tripped and fell. Gary

ran back to give him a hand, "Tyler buddy, are you okay?" His hands were both bleeding, and he just sat there looking at them. "C'mon," said Gary, helping Tyler up, "There's no time—we've got to hurry!"

They reached the boat at the end of the pier to find that the tide was out. There was a pretty good drop to the water.

Gary had a plan. "Everyone get your life vest on! Curtis, help Tyler—*quick*! You guys are going to have jump into the water. Travis and I will push the boat off of the end of the pier, and then we'll jump in right behind the boat. We'll have to climb aboard as we float in the current."

They all looked at him like he'd lost his mind—but they could see the end of the train not far off and realized there was no choice.

"That water is freezing!" exclaimed Tyler.

"No different than swimming down at the beach. You've got to jump!" Gary called out. "Would you rather be freezing or dead? Ready! *One—two—three—jump!*"

On three, Curtis and Justin each took hold of one of Tyler's hands, and ran to the edge of the pier, pulling Tyler with them.

"*This is really going to hurt!*" yelled Tyler as they approached the end of the pier, "*Geronimo!*"

Wendy jumped right behind them.

Gary and Travis grabbed the oar handles that were firmly locked in place, lifted the back of the boat, and Gary began another count. "On three! *One—two—three!*"

On three, they took off running. At the end of the pier they pushed out and down on the oars, trying to prevent *Little Imp* from falling nose first! As they watched the nose of the boat drop, it appeared for a moment they were doomed. Then, all at once, the hull bounced off of the water, and *Little Imp* settled into the current.

"*Hurry—jump!*" Gary hollered.

Shadow had waited till last—probably his protective instinct. Now they were all floating down the Narrows—the one place they'd been warned never to swim.

11

Tacoma Narrows

"C'mon guys—we've got to get out of the water!" shouted Gary, encouraging everyone to swim to the boat as quickly as possible. "We'll get hypothermia—hurry!"

It was one thing to swim in the shallow waters of Raft Island, which warmed substantially on a sunny day. It was another to be in the deep, cold waters of The Narrows—on *any* day! The average summertime water temperature for that area of the Narrows was just 52°F.

Gary was the first to climb up across the cold storage and into the boat. He began pulling the others aboard. It was a bit of a balancing act getting them safely on board, but the ballast provided by the cold storage made *Little Imp* fairly stable on the water. Shadow was last to get pulled aboard. As soon as he was out of the water he had a good shake—sending drops of water flying in every direction. Good thing everyone was already wet!

Travis grabbed the oars and started rowing. They had to get across The Narrows if they were going to make Hale Passage. And, Hale Passage was their last chance to get back into Henderson Bay. If they missed, they would have to wait for the tide to change and row back, or figure out a new plan.

As Travis rowed, the others got out bedding and whatever else they could find that was dry to provide warmth. They took off as much wet clothing as they could and wrapped up.

"We could use two sets of oars about now!" said Travis as he paddled for all he was worth.

"Forget oars," said Wendy, who was shivering so badly her teeth were chattering, "We need motor power! When we get home we'll have to cut a deal with Mr. Grisham."

"*If* we get home!" replied Curtis.

"Yeah! *If we get home!*" yelled Tyler.

"That motor *would* come in handy about now," added Gary.

According to the compass, the current was carrying them in a Northeasterly direction. They rowed as westerly as they could, doing their best to cut across the current.

Worn out, Travis offered up the rowing bench. "Who's next?" he shouted, "I've had it!"

Gary made a move in that direction, but Curtis was closer and got into position first. "I've got it, but no guarantees!"

Curtis started with his long, steady strokes, putting his whole body into the motion. They were making good time, but the current was moving too rapidly! It became obvious they'd never make the passage.

Curtis, frustrated by the lack of success yelled, "*Someone else's turn*! *I'm beat*!"

While Curtis was rowing, Gary had positioned himself so that he could be next, "I'll take a turn."

Gary paddled for the shore, hoping for an eddy that would get them back to Hale Passage. But they were quite a distance beyond where they needed to be. The water was shallow—they'd be dragging bottom if they got any closer to shore, and there was no sense getting any nearer to shore, as they were up against high bank shoreline as far as they could see! If there was an eddy, it wasn't enough!

"No sense in going ashore here," Gary gestured. "We'll have to keep going." Gary pushed the oar to the ocean floor, pushing the boat further from shore and continued rowing.

"Look—the Bridge!" exclaimed Justin, who was first

to see it.

All Curtis could think about was consequences. "When my uncle learns about this . . ."

"We know—you're a dead man. You already told us," assured Gary.

"Completely dead," repeated Curtis again, making sure he'd driven the point home.

"I didn't know there were different levels of dead," Travis commented, trying to bring a little humor to the situation.

"Anyway, the harbor is our last chance. We've *got* to make it. At least then we'll be out of this current!" stated Justin.

"We'll make the harbor," assured Gary, "then we'll have to get someone to pick us up."

"Miss the harbor—we might as well just keep on going—we can start a new life in Canada as the 'The Renegade Gang.'" announced Justin.

Wendy was beginning to internalize the consequences she would be facing once her folks learned what she had been a part of. The harmless night at the secluded cove hadn't at all worked out.

The afternoon sun broke through the clouds, providing welcome warmth after being soaked to the bone.

"I can't go any longer," said Gary, "Who's up?"

"I'll take over," Wendy offered. She took hold of the oars, and pulled as hard as she could, trying to stay close to shore. Fickle currents kicked them further from shore as they crossed under the bridge. She fought the current the best she could, giving it all she had! "I didn't know ocean current could be this strong! It's like being in a river!"

They'd gone through a full rotation at the oars by the time they approached the mouth of the harbor. Travis was back at the oars facing a major dilemma. With the tide headed out, the current at the mouth of the harbor was coming right at them! "*I can't do it*!" he cried out. He was rowing as hard as he could, but *Little Imp* just stood still at the mouth of the harbor.

"*Forget it*!" yelled Gary. "*We'll never make it until slack tide*! *Head for the beach*!"

Right beyond the mouth of the harbor was a beach that was home to Gig Harbor's lighthouse. If they could only make the beach, they could wait out the tide.

Travis pulled the oars for all he was worth, maneuvering *Little Imp* across the mouth of the harbor. As soon as the water was shallow enough, Gary jumped in and pulled them up onto the beach.

"Can you even believe it?" Travis said as they collapsed on the shore. "That current is something else."

"*That was scary*!" yelled Tyler at the top of his lungs, releasing the emotion he'd bottled up as he watched the frantic efforts to get to safe ground. "*You guys tried to kill us*? *I thought we were all gonna drown*!"

A swim had been the last thing on their minds when they left Raft Island the previous evening, proven by the fact that none of them had considered swimsuits or a change of clothing. It was just supposed to be a little jaunt across Henderson Bay to check out a cove.

Curtis, responding to his cousin, said, "The fact is, we hadn't planned on being anywhere near the Narrows, much less *in* it! What the heck was in that mine, anyway?"

Justin added to the inquisition, "Yeah, we thought you guys were dead for sure after that barricade closed. We didn't know what to do. Who were those men?"

Everyone was talking at once. Justin was firing off questions about the mine, Wendy was mad about not making it to the cove, Travis was offering solutions for getting back to Raft Island—all at once Curtis hollered, "*Time out*! One person at a time! What was going on in there anyway?"

"No crystals," replied Wendy.

"At least not the kind of crystal we're looking for," said Gary.

"What do you mean?" asked Justin.

"Drugs!" responded Gary, "It's a drug operation!"

"I've never seen so many lights!" added Travis, "Big lights—like at the little league field."

"*Why did they have lights?*" Tyler yelled. Once he became excited, his frustration was expressed by making all of his communications at *high* volume.

"They were growing plants," replied Travis, "Lots of them. We're sure it's drugs. There was a man on a radio relaying train schedules to them. They use that truck to transport their drugs on the railroad track."

Wendy wrinkled her brow and interjected, "And Gary knows one of the guys."

"Gary?" questioned Justin, "You know a drug dealer?"

"Like I started to tell these guys while we were back at the mine before everything got crazy, I was out walking Shadow yesterday morning when I passed this guy on a bike on the Raft Island Bridge. He was overweight, a little frumpy looking, and he had a cell phone dangling at his waist in one of those holster things. I instantly remembered seeing a special on TV where this pickpocket was showing how he could take watches, wallets, and all kinds of things from people without them even knowing. They showed this guy take a cell phone out of one of those holster things—the guy he took it from was clueless! I always thought if the situation arose, I was going to give it a try. Then there it was—the perfect opportunity, staring me in the face—so I gave it a shot."

"You jacked a cell phone from a *complete* stranger?" asked Wendy.

"Yep," Gary replied, proud of his accomplishment. "I pretended to trip over Shadow just as I was right along side of him, and then bumped up against him, hitting the cell phone in just the right spot—exactly like the guy on TV. It jumped right out of the holster, and I caught it in mid air—I wasn't quite as smooth as the guy on TV, but I did it!"

They all knew that Gary liked to live on the edge, but they couldn't believe he had actually tried that stunt on a stranger.

"Then what happened?" Wendy questioned.

"I never intended to take his phone; I just had to try the stunt. Anyway, I sort of knocked him off balance when I bumped him. In the process of juggling his phone, trying not to let it hit the ground, I turned to face him just as he looked over his shoulder to make sure I was all right. There I was holding his phone. He looked down at the holster, let the bike drop out from under him, reached back under his shirt, and pulled a gun."

"A gun?" asked Travis. "The guy pulled a gun on you?"

"Yeah—can you believe it? I told him that I was simply showing him his vulnerability, and he said, 'I'll show you vulnerability' and pulled a gun!"

"Then what did you do?" asked Wendy, trying to hold back her laughter at the stupidity of pulling such a stunt.

"I introduced myself, gave him his phone, and we had a nice chat."

"You had a nice chat?" questioned Curtis. "You jacked a cell phone from a drug dealer—then had a nice chat with him? Something's missing in this story."

"Look—he said he was a private investigator. He was raised in Chicago and he has the accent to prove it, but now he lives in California. He said he was down on his luck and came to the northwest to get a new start."

"So that was the guy in the mine?" questioned Travis.

"Could be!" replied Gary. "The fact is, I never saw

the guys in the mine—until we were hanging from the edge of the wall of granite. I just heard them call out the name 'Streets,' same as you. I've never known another Streets. Could be the same guy. He seemed like a pretty nice man when I met him."

"A nice guy that pulled a gun on you!" reminded Curtis.

"I hope he's working undercover, and not involved with the drugs," said Gary.

Justin interjected, "If that's really a drug operation, we've got to go tell someone!"

"It has to be," replied Gary. "Wendy saw a TV special where they caught some drug growers. They were growing marijuana in an old warehouse. They had a bunch of lights, exactly like what we saw in there."

Wendy cut in, getting back to their experience in the mine, "While we were trapped inside, we saw them unload some bags from the back of the truck, and then they loaded some boxes onto the truck. We think the bags were fertilizer. The boxes must have been—drugs—because they referred to it as their 'payload.' We knew we had to get out of there, but they closed the barricade before we could. We hiked all over looking for a way out."

Gary continued, "We followed this tunnel to a place that looked down on the area where all of the plants were. That's where we heard these train schedules and heard them say they were going to close the barricade. We hurried back toward the barricade, but like Wendy said, there was no way for us to get there in time. Then we followed the trail that led us up. We hiked all over the inside of that mine, but all we found was this room that had really a bad smell—looked a lot like a science lab—probably crystal meth—drugs for sure!"

Not wanting to be left out, Travis chipped in, "We found these pipes that supply water and power to the operation. We followed the pipes, thinking they would lead to a way out, but they only led to a dead end. When we backtracked, Shadow took off down a shaft that led to some metal stairs—that was our exit!"

"We saw you guys at the top of the rocks," Justin said, "we called for you, but the wind was blowing right at us, so you couldn't hear."

"We saw you guys too," added Wendy, "but you weren't looking up at the time. We didn't call down to you because we didn't want to be heard."

"I hiked out to where their cars were parked," added Gary, "trying to see if there was some option to the cliff—no luck. *The Sedgwick* is as rural as it gets in these parts."

"*The Sedgwick?*" asked Justin.

"Yep, that's the name of the mine. There's a big sign right inside the entrance."

"As far as we could tell there are only two ways in and out," added Travis, "the barricade and the hatch door up top. If anyone knew that barricade opened—they'd be busted!"

They talked about what a disaster the day had been as they soaked up sunshine, waiting for the tide to change. They'd set out to discover *Crystal Cove*. Now they were in a load of trouble and didn't know any more about *Crystal Cove* than they had the day before.

"We've got to get back to that Cove," Travis said.

"First things first," said Curtis. "We've got to get *Little Imp* back to Raft Island, try to save our necks, and turn the bad guys in."

Gary lay there on the beach with his hands clasped under the back of his head. As he thought back on the adrenaline rush of the day, he could only imagine the adventures awaiting them. If the past couple of days were an indication of what was to come, he could hardly wait! He couldn't bother fretting over consequences. Whatever was going to happen—was going to happen. And whatever it was would *not* deter him from his goal—*adventure*! Then, like a light bulb turning on in his head, he exclaimed, "*I have the new name for our boat! Lost Change!*"

"*Lost Change?*" Travis questioned. "Where in the heck did that come from?"

"First of all, when we set out to get the money for a boat, what was one of the things we did?"

No one answered.

"We searched high and low for *lost change!*" replied Gary. "Secondly, we just spent a good part of the day *lost*, which means we're going to have to *change* the way we go about this adventure thing or our parents are going to end up getting in the way. Plus—being out here with *no* change of clothes, *no* way to communicate with anyone, and *not* enough food—our whole approach has to change! We should be counting crystals; instead we're laying here on the beach, nowhere near Henderson Bay."

"How about your little slogan—'easier to ask forgiveness than permission'—maybe we ought to rethink that too," added Curtis. "At least if someone knew what we were up to, they'd know where to start looking for our bodies . . ."

Gary cut him off, "Oh, look! I found them! Our bodies are right here!"

"Funny!" snapped Curtis, "You know what I mean!"

Though what Curtis had to say made some sense, Gary didn't have any confidence in the outcome of asking permission to head out across Henderson Bay in search of crystals. They were lacking a bit in planning, but they had a *great* start on adventure!

"I think that name sounds kind of catchy," Wendy said in support of changing the name of their vessel to *Lost Change*. "It has *character*." They had been intent on renaming *Little Imp* and discussed many options. But until now, nothing quite fit. "The name *Lost Change* tells a story," she added, "our story!"

They put it to a vote—it was unanimous. "From now on, you're *Lost Change*," said Gary, patting the side of the boat.

Being a deeper thinker than most of the gang, Justin stated, "And all of this happened just because the anchor wasn't securely set."

Travis spoke up, "Sorry—I'll never let it happen again. I forgot about the tide."

"I wasn't pointing a finger of blame," Justin replied, "none of us remembered either. We were so focused on exploring that cove—we didn't take the appropriate precautions. Even though some good might yet come of today's activities, we'd be a lot better off if we'd have set the anchor the way we'd been trained. Sort of applies to other areas of life too."

Justin had them all thinking quietly.

After a time, Gary broke the silence, "When are we going back? We've got to get back to the cove—soon! We'll never know if we've solved the puzzle until we do! There could be a fortune waiting for us!"

"You do have a one track mind," said Curtis. "We haven't even recovered from nearly drowning in the Narrows, and you're already looking for more trouble."

"No trouble," responded Gary. "*Crystals*—I'm all about looking for *crystals*!"

"Gary's right! We have to get back," said Travis. "What if we are the first to uncover the whole dream catcher thing?"

"We just have to figure out when and how," added Wendy, "Chances are we won't be able to use the same strategy a second time."

"Exactly," answered Curtis. "Once our parents figure out that we snuck out last night, they'll confiscate the boat and ground us for life!"

It wasn't much longer before the tide let up. They

began rowing toward Gig Harbor's public dock at Jerisich Park. Wendy was in awe at the setting as they made their way across the harbor. It was the first time she'd seen the harbor from the water. She sat in the bow, looking back toward the mouth of the harbor. The change in weather brought clear skies, exposing the snow-covered peak of Mt. Rainier off on the horizon. "This is gorgeous," she said. "Water, mountains, islands—the more time I spend with you guys, the more I see why you were so focused on getting the boat. God made some beautiful places!"

On the way to the dock, they tried to put together a story that would be believable and leave them in possession of the boat. They knew full well that even though they had earned her, their folks could take her away. Their plan needed to be *bulletproof*! And somehow, they had to get the police out to *The Sedgwick*.

Wendy cut in, "If we can get everyone's attention on the mine—maybe that will take us *out* of the limelight!"

They talked through all kinds of scenarios, but the deeper the stories got, the more unbelievable they were. Rather than make matters worse, they decided that the best answer was to call home and tell the truth.

Travis was the first to call. "Hey, mom—what's up?" he asked as nonchalantly as he could?

"Oh not much dear, how about you? Are you guys having a fun day?"

"Fun—oh—yeah—we're having great time," Travis replied. Then holding his hand over the mouthpiece, he turned to the others, "She hasn't even missed us!"

"What are you guys up to?" she asked.

"We're hanging out down in the harbor."

"When ya coming home?"

"In a couple of hours or so—just thought I'd call and check in."

"Okay, thanks for calling. Hey, that reminds me, is

Wendy with you guys?"

"Yeah—why?"

"Her mom called looking for her. She said she never even heard Wendy leave the house this morning. I told her I was sure she was with you guys, but you'd better have her call home."

"I'll tell her to call right now."

"You guys have fun, and be good."

"We will." Travis immediately handed the phone to Wendy, "You've got to call next. Your mom called my place looking for you. We should all check in before we panic. Mom didn't suspect a thing, and if any of our parents were really upset, they'd all be on a rampage!"

Wendy was next, "Hey mom, what's up?"

"Where are you, girl? I've been a little worried."

"I'm with the guys. We got an early start on the day. We're down in the harbor—just hanging out."

"What time are you planning on being home?"

"Not sure—why?"

"I want you home for dinner."

"Okay. See you then—love you."

They each had a similar response. Their folks were so accustomed to them spending the entire day running around together, they hadn't even been missed!

In disbelief, Curtis said "*Score*! We're not dead after all. *But* what happened to telling the *truth*?"

"We may not have told the whole truth, but we didn't *lie*," said Gary. "Now all we have to do is get *Lost Change* back to Raft Island," he said, slapping his hand on his leg.

"We'll still have to explain about the mine," Justin interjected. "We have to report those guys! There's no way we can just let it go!"

"I've got it!" exclaimed Wendy, "Let's call Mr. Grisham! If he's home, he'll bring the trailer. And he'll know what to do about the mine. He's pretty smart—for an adult."

Things would definitely go over much better if the boat were home before the whole story got out.

"We're dead after all," said Curtis. "We can't tell about the mine without revealing the fact that we were in The Narrows. Life as we know it is over!"

"Maybe, but we've got to get *Lost Change* back to Raft Island. Who's going to make the call?" asked Justin.

"Wendy should make the call," responded Curtis.

"That's it—make me do the dirty work!" she scowled.

"You have been the spokesperson with Grisham all along," replied Gary, supporting the idea, "it only makes sense that you call."

None of them knew Grisham's phone number—luckily it was listed in the phone book.

"Hello, Mr. Grisham?" Wendy asked.

"That's me."

"It's Wendy."

"Well hello, Wendy. How are you?"

"I'm fine thanks, but—I'm with the guys—and we sort of have a situation. To make a long story short, we are down in the harbor and need a ride home."

Grisham thought that sounded a little odd. He'd known these kids to walk or ride bikes into town often. And on a nice sunny afternoon like this—he was a little curious, but replied, "No problem, I've just been puttering around this afternoon anyway. Where should I pick you up?"

"Well—that's the next part of the story. We have *Little Imp*."

She couldn't call the boat *Lost Change*. Mr. Grisham would have no idea what she was talking about.

"*Little Imp?*" he questioned. His curiosity was peaked. "How on earth did you manage that?"

"It's a long story. Can we tell you after you get here?

It'll be easier to explain in person."

"*Okay*—I'll hook the trailer up and meet you at the boat launch."

"Thanks—a lot!" she replied.

The Island Gang headed back to the boat, and began rowing *Lost Change* across the harbor to the launch.

"We need to tell Mr. Grisham about *The Sedgwick*, and what's going on at the mine," Travis said.

"No way! He's an old man! That would just freak him out," Curtis replied.

"Have you forgotten about the game animals in his shed?" stated Gary. "I think it would take a lot more than what's going on at *The Sedgwick* to freak him out."

Gary had a point. They'd heard some of his hunting stories. Grisham had been face to face with danger more than once. Maybe he was the right person to tell. And maybe he'd know how to break the story to their parents.

Grisham pulled up just as The Island Gang was tying *Lost Change* to the dock adjacent to the ramp. He was tuned to KMPS country radio, listening to George Strait sing, "Love Without End, Amen." He listened to the song right to the end as he waited for an opening on the ramp. He let the words of the tune run through his head while he considered how he should handle the situation he was in. He decided he needed to hear them out before jumping to any conclusions.

The Island Gang spotted Grisham as he backed the trailer down the ramp and quickly got *Lost Change* into position. They loaded the boat without much discussion, since there was a line to use the ramp. As they pulled away, the pace slowed a little. There was total silence. The air was so thick you could cut it with a knife. Someone was going to have to break the silence and end the misery.

"So who's going to start?" asked Grisham.

Gary and Travis were riding shotgun. Gary was first

to speak up, "During our maiden voyage to Dead Man's, we sort of spotted this secluded cove across Henderson Bay that we wanted to explore. We paddled over there to take a look at it. We knew our parents would never go for the idea—so we didn't tell them."

Grisham looked into the rearview mirror at Wendy, wondering exactly what she was thinking to do such a thing.

"*We decided to ask forgiveness instead of permission,*" added Tyler.

This habit of Tyler's—repeating things he heard the others say—was going to get them into trouble yet.

"Ah—forgiveness instead of permission," repeated Grisham. "Not always a good plan. "What's this about *Lost Change?*"

"After today's experience, we have a new name for *Little Imp,*" Justin replied, "The name *Lost Change* tells a story,"

"We needed some adventure—you know, you've had lots of them," Travis added, hoping to get Grisham's empathy for their situation.

Grisham listened quietly.

Gary continued, "We told our parents we were spending the night at Curtis' house, then after dinner we told Curtis' mom that we changed our minds and were going to spend the night at Travis' house. We spend so much time at each other's homes—we knew they'd never check on us. So, last night we headed out across Henderson Bay. We knew we'd be okay even if it rained—with the boat tent for shelter."

Grisham pulled the car over to the side of the road. There was no way he could give this the appropriate attention while driving. "You paddled across Henderson Bay last night?" he asked, shaking his head in disbelief.

Travis spoke up, "When we got there last night it was so dark we couldn't really see anything, so we decided to save our exploring for the morning. We were excited to use the boat tent—and knew we'd be safer out on the water than on land—so we pushed out past the rocky entrance and dropped the anchor. This morning Tyler woke up and stuck his head out of the tent, there was no cove."

"What do you mean there was no cove?" Grisham questioned.

"*No Cove!*" Tyler yelled, reliving the experience in his mind. "*So instead these guys tried to get us all killed!*"

Grisham raised his brow. It was obvious Tyler was wound up.

Curtis ignored Tyler's outburst and added his two cents, "'No cove' were my exact words. *It* hadn't moved—which meant—*we had!*"

"That's when we took the tent down, and I went for the anchor," added Travis. "When I realized that it wasn't hitting the bottom, I remembered that I had forgotten to allow for low tide when I set it last night. It was so calm as we crossed Henderson, I . . ."

"We," Wendy interjected. "None of us remembered to think about the tide. We were too focused on the cove!"

Travis appreciated not having to shoulder the blame alone.

Gary, anxious to get to the part about *The Sedgwick*, took the conversation, "The rising tide pulled the anchor free, and the tide carried us through the night to some point near the Narrows. We needed to get our bearings, so we found what we thought was a dock off the starboard side and decided to tie up."

"*That's when they almost got us killed!*" exclaimed Tyler. They were all reliving the experience, but it had taken a greater toll on Tyler. His communication was back to high volume.

"What's this about almost getting killed?" Grisham inquired.

"*You know—like dead,*" said Tyler.

"Tyler, why don't you let us tell the story?" said cousin Curtis.

"*Are you going to tell him the part about almost getting us killed?*" Tyler asked.

They were beginning to appreciate the impact the experience had on Tyler.

"Yeah, we'll get to that part," Justin said, "but let Gary finish."

"Anyway," Gary continued, "The dock turned out to be a pier, and after the experience we'd just had with the tide, we pulled *Lost Change* up out of the water onto the pier. Right when we were figuring out our location, this area that looked like a boarded up opening to an old abandoned mine—just opened up—and two men driving one of those trucks that can drive on railroad tracks pulled off the tracks and into the opening."

"Where about was this?" Grisham asked.

"We were sort of across from McNeil Island," Gary replied.

Grisham had spent plenty of time out in The Narrows and was trying to place the location of an old pier on the east shore. "Looked a little suspicious did it?"

"Exactly," said Gary.

"Did anyone see you?"

"Not at first," Travis said, "but we had a close call in the mine."

"*In* the mine?" Grisham asked, raising his eyebrows and tilting his head in disbelief.

"Yeah, it's called *The Sedgwick*. There's a sign hanging just inside the entrance," Travis said, "and it's not exactly abandoned."

Grisham had heard of *The Sedgwick*.

"A little while after they drove in, we decided we should check it out," Travis continued, "Something wasn't quite right, and we didn't want to leave without finding out what was going on."

"I can't believe you guys actually went inside?" questioned Grisham, not knowing whether to laugh or cry. "*What* were you thinking?" Their parents were going to hang him out to dry for getting their kids involved with the boat.

"Wendy, Gary and I were the only ones that went in," replied Travis. "We decided it was safer to leave a couple on the outside. Back inside, there was this large open area where these guys were growing all these plants. We're pretty sure it's drugs!"

Grisham was literally on the edge of his seat!

Gary spoke up, "We heard a voice over a radio relaying train schedules. We figured out they're using the track when they know they won't be spotted. We'd seen enough and wanted out, but the next thing we knew they were closing the barricade because a train would soon be coming—we were stuck!"

"They had enough lights to light up the ball field, and a ton of planters," Wendy added.

Marijuana, thought Grisham. "Sounds like a pretty intricate operation."

"They didn't know we were there, so we took off down different shafts, trying to find another way out," Wendy continued. "That's when we saw the pipes that supply water and power. We followed them thinking they would lead to an opening, but no luck. There was this big lab in there too—it had a terrible odor. We thought we'd never get out, but Shadow saved the day!"

"Shadow, huh?" replied Grisham, pleasantly surprised that they had the good sense to take the dog in with them. He'd had plenty of experience with dogs in the outdoors and knew they had a way of coming through in a pinch.

"Shadow found the other way out of the mine, which is where we had our narrow escape! We climbed these metal stairs that led out, and ended up at the top of this rock wall wondering how we were going to get down to where the others were."

"That's when they saw us," Travis added, "and we had to scale down the wall as fast as we could and then jump to the ground. A train was coming just as we jumped from the wall. We crossed the tracks ahead of the train and headed for the boat!"

"That train came at exactly the right time," stated Gary. "We ran back to the pier to discover that the tide was down—way down—and still on its way out. We had to push the boat from the pier, jump in, and climb aboard as we floated in the current. That's what got Tyler a little upset.

"*That's* the part where they almost got us killed," confirmed Tyler.

Grisham could only imagine the six of them floating in the current of The Narrows. He knew those currents had claimed several lives. He was grateful they were alive and anxious to get them home. At the same time, now that he was aware of a covert drug operation, he was obliged to act. "Could you show me the place?"

"We could show it to you from the water," replied Justin. "It's not too far from these nice buildings out on a point surrounded by a high fence."

Grisham put the descriptions of the location together in his head. Buildings out on a point sounded a lot like *Le Perle*, the nicest accommodations in the *Le Chateau* retirement community. "Would you boys recognize the men if you saw them again?" he asked.

"We talked about that once we finally got to the lighthouse," Travis said. "We never got a good look at them while inside the mine. Then we were in too big a hurry to get a good look while running for our lives. We heard several of them talking while we were in the mine, but they were never in view. We might be able recognize their voices."

"Do you guys know what I did before I retired?" inquired Grisham.

"No—what?" asked Wendy.

"I put in more than 30 years with the FBI."

"*The F-B-I!*" Tyler screamed out. "*Wow!*" he said, making the WOW sign with three fingers on either side of his wide-open mouth.

"I know who to call to have this checked out."

The fear of their parents finding out had just been replaced by another adrenaline rush. Grisham had worked for the FBI. The problem of getting their story to the police was solved.

"Have you called your parents?" Grisham asked.

"Yeah," replied Curtis. "Believe it or not, they haven't even missed us!"

"If I can get us a boat ride, would you be up for coming along to show us the spot?"

"Now?" asked Gary.

"The sooner the better," replied Grisham, "*if*—I can get us a ride."

Gary was first to answer, "Count me in! Does anyone *not* want to go?"

"I told mom I'd be home by dinner," replied Wendy.

Grisham reached for his cell phone, "Let me call some friends and see if I can get a boat to pick us up here in the harbor. If things work out, we can phone your parents."

"Are your friends in the FBI?" Travis asked.

"Sure are," he said. "And, they'll be very interested in what you've stumbled on to."

Grisham dialed Agent McGovney. "Bill, Reg Grisham here, how in the world are you?"

Agent McGovney tilted the mouthpiece upward and shouted to the rest of the office, "Hey guys, its Reg!" Returning to his conversation with Reg, McGovney replied, "I'm doing great Reg, how about you?"

"Just great! Say listen, I got hooked up with this group of kids from Raft Island over the past several weeks, and to make a long story short, they had a little boating adventure that ended them up just south of the Narrows Bridge this afternoon, where they came across something very interesting."

"Tell me about it," McGovney replied.

"Well, let me give you the short version now, and later I'll help file a report so you'll have the whole scoop."

He proceeded to tell Agent McGovney that his young friends had stumbled onto what sounded like a marijuana growing operation and a possible meth lab. Grisham explained that if McGovney could get them a boat ride they'd be able to pinpoint the spot.

"A boat ride—huh," McGovney, said with a sigh. "Let me make a quick phone call. There might be someone that can accommodate us. I'll call you right back."

It wasn't five minutes and Grisham's phone was ringing.

"Reg, I've got you a ride. Can you meet at the public dock?"

"Absolutely," Grisham replied.

"I'll have a boat pick you up in about 20 minutes. Agent Larsen isn't too far from there now."

"Agent Larsen?" he asked.

"Yeah. I don't think you know Agent Larsen. Just look for a boat named *Chance*. You won't be able to miss it—it's quite the boat!"

After hanging the phone up, Grisham said, "Well guys, we've got our ride. It'll be here in 20 minutes. McGovney says to watch for a boat named *Chance*. We're being picked up at the public dock at Jerisich Park. You should all call your folks and make sure it's okay to come along."

Grisham found a parking spot long enough to accommodate the car and trailer. The kids were taking turns calling their parents from Grisham's cell phone. "We've got a little time. What do you say we head over to Kelly's for ice cream?"

Grisham spoke with several of their parents explaining that the kids were with him down in the harbor and that he wanted to take them out for a boat ride. He assured them he would deliver the kids home once they returned. Wendy's mother was disappointed she'd be late for dinner, but she was happy that Wendy was having such a great time with The Island Gang and Mr. Grisham. The boys' parents were accustomed to hardly ever seeing them and were comfortable with the fact that they were in Grisham's care. They got their ice cream and headed back to the dock.

"Look over there!" Travis said in disbelief. "It's *Chance*!"

They couldn't believe their eyes. It was like one of those cigarette-racing boats they'd seen on TV! It was huge—and a *beauty*! They never imagined getting a ride on a boat like this! The boys ran the length of the dock to meet the boat. Wendy lagged behind with Grisham. As the boys approached the boat, they saw a lady on board.

"Are you Agent Larsen?" inquired Travis, given that she was the only one in sight.

"Yep, that's me," she replied.

As they were finishing their introductions, Grisham and Wendy walked up.

"Agent Larsen?" questioned Grisham.

"Most people aren't expecting a woman," she replied.

"You're right about that," he said, "but we're not complaining, are we guys?"

"This must be the team that agent McGovney was telling me about—the one that came across a questionable operation."

"Yep, that's us," Gary replied. "We think some guys

are growing drugs out there."

"Climb aboard, let's go for a ride," she said. As they boarded, Agent Larsen commented, "Five boys and one girl, huh? You boys need to even the odds out a little," she said, looking to Wendy with a wink.

Wendy just smiled

"Five boys, a girl, and a dog," added Gary, who was last to board. "Can Shadow come along?"

Shadow's tail had a case of "mad wag" as he waited patiently for an invitation.

"So this is Shadow," she replied.

"Sure is."

"He looks like a good dog," she said.

"He's a great dog. If it weren't for him, we might not have made it out of *The Sedgwick* alive!"

Shadow let out a single bark, confirming his involvement in the day's adventure.

"Well, we'd better take him along," she replied.

That was all Shadow needed; he was on the boat in a flash!

"Is this a cigarette racer?" asked Justin.

"Actually it isn't. It has the long sleek hull and overhead spoiler like cigarette racers do, but this boat sits a little higher on the water and has a fully self-contained cabin down below. The hulls on Cigarette racers are empty to keep them light and aerodynamic—making them real fast on the water. Unless you are into competing, that big empty hull is a lot of wasted space. *Chance* is a 32' triple engine Suncruiser. My husband and I go places for days at a time. We like having the comforts of home on board."

"This boat is *cool*!" said Curtis. "Can we check the cabin out?"

"Sure—wipe your feet on that mat on your way down. Mr. Grisham, do you know where we're headed?"

"From what they've told me, I have an idea of the

general location, but the kids are the only ones who have been there. From the sound of it, they had a close call. I told them we'd have them show us the location, and that the bureau would investigate later."

They pulled away from the dock. Agent Larsen turned to Grisham and said, "That's exactly how we'll handle it! McGovney tells me you retired some time ago. How long has it been?"

"I retired a little early due to my wife's ailing health—about eight years ago," he replied. "I stay in touch with some of the guys. A couple of us take a hunting trip now and then."

"Oh yeah? What for?"

"Usually we're after big game."

The kids were returning from below deck just in time to hear the hunting dialogue, and Tyler chimed in, "You should see his shed—*lots* of big game in there!"

"So you've had some success?" she asked.

"Are you kidding?" Travis chimed in. "He has at least one of all of the most dangerous animals in the world!"

"Not quite," Grisham replied with a chuckle. "The kids are easy to impress."

As they approached the mouth of the harbor, Agent Larsen asked, "So which way are we headed?"

"To the right," Gary responded. "It's back under the bridge, across the Narrows—past Hale's Passage."

"Oh, yeah. McGovney said something about McNeil Island," Larsen replied.

Reg added, "From the way they described it, sounds like we're headed out near *Le Chateau*. Are you familiar with the retirement community?"

"Is that the new one near Eagle Island?"

"It is," replied Grisham. "That's where my wife and I spent the last few years of her life. The luxury condos called *Le Perle* overlook the water right out on the point. We didn't have the view—a little out of our reach financially—but we were in a nice apartment. The important thing for us was to be close to medical attention and to avoid having to deal with the bridge."

"Sounds like a nice place," Larsen replied. "What were these kids doing out here in the Narrows?"

"Let's just say they went adrift and ended up out this way. They have big plans to explore the Puget Sound by water," added Grisham, "Their running across this drug operation was a real fluke."

"Their parents have a lot of trust in their ability," replied Larsen.

"Actually their parents have no idea," replied Grisham, as he took off his hat and wiped his brow.

"You're kidding?"

"I wish I were. They finagled a plan about spending the night at each other's homes, then snuck down to the boat last night and paddled out across Henderson Bay intent on exploring a cove. During the night, they drifted. The anchor was set, but they forgot to leave enough rope to accommodate the tide. At some point I have to figure out how to break all this to their parents.

"You?" questioned Larsen

"The boat they have was my dinghy."

Grisham told Larsen all about *Sea Imp*, helping the kids get *Little Imp* fixed up, and that the kids had just changed the boat's name to *Lost Change* after this overnight excursion.

"I can't believe they spent the night out here!" stated Larsen.

"That's makes two of us! I don't know all of the details, but I have heard enough of the story that I dread having to relate it to their folks."

"Maybe you've got an out," continued Larsen, "I'm sure McGovney will want to keep this under pretty tight wraps until they've had the chance to investigate. You may have to stall off telling their folks for a while."

"Good point. I hadn't considered that angle."

"By the way, sorry to hear of your wife's passing. How long has it been?"

"Close to a year now. I was really down in the doldrums for a while there, but I'll tell you what—these young rascals came around looking for a boat, and they've given me a new lease on life."

"Well, it's a good thing that they're keeping you busy," she replied, "We all need a reason to keep going, and what better than a good group of kids."

Grisham continued, "I've found myself doing things that I haven't done for years. Working out in the shed, getting this boat ready for the kids—I've really enjoyed it. Speaking of boats, how long have you had *Chance*?"

"My husband came into a fair sum of money. A wealthy aunt passed away leaving a nice inheritance. We always dreamed of having a cruiser, so we got it while we had the chance. That's where she gets her name."

"Hey," Gary piped up, "that sounds kind of like how we named our boat!

"There's Day Island," said Travis.

"You are familiar with these waters aren't you?" Agent Larsen said.

"Pretty much," replied Travis. "My family has owned boats since I was born. I've been through here quite a few times."

"Once we can see McNeil Island, we'll be close," added Gary, not wanting to be left out of the conversation, "There will be a pier portside."

"*It's across from Eagle Island*!" Tyler yelled.

They made good time in the cruiser. It was sure a different experience from paddling!

"There it is!" said Curtis.

They all agreed it was the right pier. As they approached, they looked for the barricade in the wall of rock, but the tide was out and *Chance* was sitting too low on the water.

"It's right up there," insisted Gary. "Once you're at the end of the pier, you'll see the barricade just off to the left. At the top of the rock, and a little further left of the barricade, is the top entrance. That's how we got away. They're delivering their next shipment tonight. We heard them talking about it."

That barricade looks permanent," said Justin, "but it's mounted to some kind of automatic opener."

"We saw one of the guys push a button," Wendy confirmed, "and the barricade just moved into place."

Agent Larsen took the readings from her GPS and wrote down the coordinates. She recorded some landmarks and listed the comments The Island Gang had made. "They do have a quiet location," Agent Larsen said, referring to operation inside *The Sedgwick*. "Hidden from the water, sealed up behind a barricade—they're conveniently invisible. I wonder where they are getting their power and water?"

"They've got it piped in!" Gary stated. "There are enough lights in there to light up a ball field! We followed water pipes down a long shaft hoping it would lead to a way out. But at the end, the pipes took a turn straight up through the top of the mine. We had to turn around and look for another way out."

"Well, thanks guys," Larsen said. "Let's get you guys back to the harbor before it gets dark. I'll get this information to McGovney. Hopefully, we'll be able to let you know how it all plays out in the near future. In the meantime, we can't let this get out. Depending on how things go, it may take a while before we get these guys. Sometimes there's more to an operation than what you see on the surface. We need you to keep this quiet until Mr. Grisham says it's okay to talk about it. You can't tell anyone!"

"Not even our parents?" asked Gary.

"Not even your parents. This needs to be hush-hush! It only takes one comment to the wrong person to ruin an investigation. If you remember something that you want us to know—or just need to talk—get to Mr. Grisham. He'll relay messages to the bureau. This is a lot of responsibility."

The Island Gang huddled up. It seemed odd to *not* tell their parents. But if being quiet about *The Sedgwick* meant they didn't have to tell their folks about the events of the day, they were all for it. They'd been hoping for a believable alibi that would allow them to keep their trip through *The Narrows* from their parents, yet permit them to turn the bad guys in—now the answer had been conveniently laid in their lap! And it was iron clad!

"Can you do it?" asked Agent Larsen, waiting for a response.

"You bet," came the reply, almost in unison.

While they were still huddled, Gary took the lead in their ritualistic pact-making ceremony. He was first to put his hand into the circle and was immediately followed by Wendy, who was positioned directly across from him. Gary glanced up, making momentary eye contact. He suddenly got the feeling that she intended for her hand to be second. Though he was certain their hands had touched before, somehow this time was different. The feeling caught him off guard as the hands quickly piled up.

Suddenly realizing that all eyes were on him awaiting his lead, he looked around the circle, making eye contact with each of them, and in chant cadence said, "Mums the word—until we've heard." His expression was their cue to follow. In unison they repeated the phrase three times, making eye contact with one another. Individual eye contact affirmed their vow to keep to the pact—no matter what. "Mums the word—until we've heard! Mums the word—until we've heard! Mums the word—until we've heard!" The message was clear. No one was to mention this to anyone outside the circle until they had word from Grisham.

It may have been Gary's imagination, but it seemed as though Wendy's hand lingered just a little at the end of their pact. The thought rushing through his head was, *I think she likes me!* He thought she was cute from the moment she'd caught them in Grisham's shed. For a split second he locked eyes with her once again, and then dropped his hand, hoping he hadn't blushed.

"A secret pact, huh?" said Agent Larsen, "Now I'm really impressed!"

Travis spoke up, "Whenever something's important, we make a pact. We know we can trust each other to be true to it."

The ride on *Chance* had given Curtis an attitude adjustment. This was the kind of boat he'd dreamed of. His outlook on their future plans could easily be influenced by an upgrade in transportation. It was all the rowing that bothered him. "I think another ride on *Chance* would be the appropriate place to fill us in on the details," stated Curtis, "once the case is solved, of course."

The motion was unanimously seconded.

"How about it?" Grisham asked.

"*Yeah, this is a cool boat!*" Tyler added in his loud, baritone voice, still not registering the fact that he was unnecessarily yelling all of his communications.

Agent Larsen's head was nodding in the affirmative, "Okay, I'll contact Mr. Grisham once the case is closed, and we'll arrange to take The Island Gang out for another ride. Maybe we'll even talk Mr. Grisham into a barb-b-que afterward. My husband and I would love to see his collection of trophies."

"That could probably be arranged," Grisham conceded.

12

In Search Of Crystal Cove

Time passed—it was the last day of school—and luckily, only a half-day. They were excited that the school year had finally come to a close. They talked as they left the bus stop and walked across the Raft Island Bridge, finalizing plans for the afternoon. "Everyone drop your stuff at home, grab some food, and meet at Grisham's," Gary said. "We'll finish this discussion then."

At the shed, they talked about everything that had transpired—then focused their attention on getting back to the cove.

"What do you say we bring Mr. Grisham in—make him part of The Island Gang?" suggested Justin. "He offered us sailing lessons. The cove could be our first destination!"

"Maybe we should," agreed Gary, "After all, it was Grisham's map that led us to the dream catcher. He must believe *Crystal Cove* exists! He may know more about it than we think!"

That had Tyler's attention, "*Get her rigged to sail!*"

"*Oh yeah*—we'll leave first thing in the morning," added Travis.

"*Exactly*," said Curtis sarcastically. "Mr. Grisham is just sitting around waiting for a chance to take us sailing."

"Curtis is right," replied Gary, "He may already have plans."

"*Stop the presses!*" shouted Curtis. "Gary just said I was right about something!"

"Don't let it go to your head," Gary added. "One

thing is certain, we'll never know if he's busy until we ask." Jumping to his feet, Gary issued the challenge, "Last one to the door is a rotten egg!"

Lately Grisham had been spending more time away. Gary figured he was planning a trip with some of his hunting buddies. He'd overheard a phone conversation one afternoon where he was talking about trapping himself a *vixen*. Gary seemed to recall that a vixen was some sort of fox, but wasn't exactly sure. Fox didn't seem like Mr. Grisham's style, but maybe he had all of the big game he wanted. Anyway, they'd seen his caddy in the driveway, so they knew he was home.

"Curtis is the rotten egg," shouted Gary as they arrived at the front door out of breath.

"No I'm not, Tyler is still coming," Curtis retaliated

"Like Tyler all of a sudden counts," added Travis, "Face it—you lost!"

With a tone of defeat, Curtis replied. "Whatever!"

"We've got to convince Mr. Grisham to take us to the cove," said Justin still panting, ignoring the competitive jabs between Gary, Travis, and Curtis.

Just as Gary began knocking on the door, Wendy reached out and rang the doorbell—*three* times in a row.

"Why'd you do that?" asked Gary. "You're going to make him crazy!"

"He won't mind," replied Wendy with a wink. "He'll just know we're excited about something." Really, it was just another one of Wendy's ploys to get Gary's attention.

Grisham answered the door, "Is everything okay out here?" he asked.

Gary reassured him, "Everything is fine. Wendy just got a little *anxious* with the doorbell."

"What can I do for you?"

Gary continued, "Well—a month or so ago my uncle told me about this Native American legend—the *Legend of Crystal Cove*."

Grisham's expression turned from concern to interest.

"At the time, I didn't know if he was making it up as he went along, or if there was really something to it. Since then, we've learned more about it. We believe it really exists."

"I've heard a little about *Crystal Cove* myself over the years," replied Grisham.

Gary had to ask, "Have you ever gone looking for it?"

"Is *that* what you were doing out in Henderson Bay—looking for *Crystal Cove*?"

Curtis was curious about this adult tactic of answering a question with a question, but he thought it best to keep his puzzlement to himself.

"We think we found it!" said Travis, "We were there, ready to search for the crystals—until the whole tide thing."

"We really *might* know where it is!" Wendy affirmed.

"You wouldn't be the first to think you were getting close," said Grisham. "I poked around out in Henderson Bay once upon a time—trying to confirm some information that I came across—but no luck. Of course, I can't say as I've heard of anyone finding the crystals," he said, looking out toward the bay, "I guess they could still be out there—*if* the legend has any substance."

Curtis was thinking quietly to himself, *Unless he's a really good bluffer—sounds like he hasn't already found the crystals.*

"That's the next thing we need to talk to you about," said Gary. "One time when we were out in the shed, Shadow ran up the stairs to the loft room, and pushed the door open with his nose. We knew the door was always locked, but when Shadow opened it, we couldn't resist the urge to have a look . . ."

"We know it's your private stuff," Wendy said, cutting into the conversation. "We're sorry."

"Over the years I've just sort of put things up there

that I didn't want to lose track of," replied Grisham. "The shed gets so busy, if I'm not careful things get misplaced. Whatever makes it upstairs is safe."

"There's more," said Gary. They all dropped their shoulders—a little ashamed of their actions. "While we were in there, this metal box sort of jumped out at us."

"My *treasure box*!" Grisham replied gleefully, as if they'd found something he had misplaced years ago. "Whenever I've come across unusual documents through the years, I tucked them away in that box. The plan was that after I retired, Lucille and I would spend our time sailing and exploring for hidden treasure."

"Did you ever do it?" asked Curtis.

"We certainly did," replied Grisham.

"Did you find anything?" asked Justin.

"We took the box every time we went sailing—we turned up a few trinkets here and there, made friends in some tucked away villages, and even came across some fairly old artifacts, but I can't say we ever uncovered a treasure, and we certainly didn't find any crystals."

"Why'd you quit?" asked Wendy.

"There came a time when Lucille couldn't go any more. Boat trips were just too hard on her."

"Did you ever make it to the cove?" Wendy asked.

"I don't think that we ever found *the cove*," Grisham replied. "Part of the reason I was anxious to help you with the boat has to do with your dreams to explore the region. Reminds me of myself not too many years ago—only you're young enough to do something about it. As determined as you are, you just might get lucky."

They were so relieved he wasn't angry that they began stumbling over their words as they vied for position as to who would talk next. Gary spoke the loudest and fastest, "We found a clue to the cove! We need you to come to Dead Man's with us so we can show you. The sooner, the better—like how about tomorrow?"

"*Get her rigged to sail,*" said Tyler, repeating his comment from earlier.

"Let's start by telling me what you've found at Dead Man's," replied Grisham.

"Well, when we found your box it was open, and in it we found the maps of Dead Man's," continued Gary.

"We think we figured out what the numbers in the legend mean," said Travis.

"We found the *dream catcher*!" Justin asserted with confidence.

Grisham's head was spinning as he tried to connect all of the dots to their comments, "You found a *dream catcher*?" asked Grisham. "So *that's* what the web was all about! *A dream catcher!* I spent the better part of two days carefully searching every corner of that cemetery trying to find some sign of a web!"

"We searched every nook and cranny too," replied Gary, "then we discovered it's the layout of the cemetery!"

"*The layout of the cemetery*?" Grisham echoed.

"Yeah," Gary answered. "I went out to edge of the plateau and climbed the old maple. There I was overlooking Henderson Bay, when I heard a voice in the wind saying, '*Dream catcher.*' I turned back to the rest of the guys to ask if they heard anything, and there it was! The cemetery—laid out in the pattern of a dream catcher!"

Grisham was thinking back to when he was there, "Huh, I never even considered that!"

"I don't think we would have either," conceded Gary, "If I hadn't gotten bored and climbed the tree. You've got to come with us to Dead Man's! We think we're close!"

Grisham was hooked, "When do we go?"

"How about tomorrow?" queried Gary.

"I can't go tomorrow," Travis chimed in, "family plans."

"I have to work all day Thursday, and Friday till noon," Justin offered.

"Let's leave Friday afternoon," suggested Curtis, "We can hit Dead Man's, get over to the cove in time to make camp. That'll give us all day Saturday to search for the crystals."

Throwing his hands up in the air, Tyler exclaimed, "Oh no, not this again! *Mate overboard! Bring her around!*"

"Whoa there, Tyler," said Curtis, "We're not going in the drink again, we're going to find treasure."

Using his pirate voice, Tyler made the forefinger of his right hand into a hook, closed one eye, and continued, "*Treasure you say? Now you're talking. When do we go—when do we go?*"

"You think your parents will go for an overnighter?" asked Grisham, looking Wendy's direction.

"With you as a chaperone, there's a pretty good chance," she replied.

"By the way, we haven't said a word about any of this to our parents," Gary added. "We want to wait until we know there's something to talk about."

"I understand," replied Grisham, "We'll just tell them we're having a sailing lesson."

Just the response they'd hoped for.

As far as parents were aware, the only time The Island Gang had been out in the boat was their maiden voyage. They knew how anxious the kids were to use the boat. With summer finally here, they were certain to go along with the kids' plan.

Their parents decided that if Grisham wanted to take the kids on an overnighter with the boat, it was okay with them.

There were a couple of near sleepless nights as The Island Gang waited for Friday to roll around. But it finally came.

They entered the shed Friday afternoon just in time to see Grisham making some final adjustments.

"Look guys," exclaimed Justin, "the *outboard*!"

"No more rowing," Curtis cried out with both thumbs up, "Now we're talking!"

Then they noticed "*TIG's LOST CHANGE*" had been stenciled on either side of the bow and along the back, in a font resembling twigs.

"We got our own logo!" said Travis.

"Look at that," added Gary. "Mr. Grisham's been at it again."

"I've been working on the logo for awhile," said Grisham. "After the name *Lost Change* came along, I finally landed on something I thought you'd like. The sign guy was here two days ago. Should be good and dry."

"This is *way* cool," added Wendy

Grisham had a way of adding excitement to their dreams. They didn't understand yet, but they had made quite an impact on his life, too.

"What do you think? Does she look ready?" asked Grisham.

"Boy does she!" replied Justin.

"With the outboard as back up, we're ready for anything!" added Gary.

"I figured it was about time to get it mounted," replied Grisham. "That motor's been taking up space in the back of the shed long enough. The cold storage bin had to go, but . . ."

" . . . What?" Travis interrupted, "What about the food?"

"Hold your horses there," replied Grisham, "*Lost Change* now has an outrigger," he said, pointing to the back of the garage. "One section is for food, and there's plenty of room for cargo."

"An outrigger!" shouted Justin, "No way!"

"*Way!*" replied Travis, as he spotted Grisham's handy work at the back of the shed. They all went over to get a look. Grisham had turned an old sea kayak into the outrigger.

"I doubt we'll need the keel with this setup," continued Grisham, "The outrigger should give us all the stability we need. We'll be a little crowded on board, but there should be enough room for the short trip—especially if we can fit all of the bedding and gear in the outrigger. I packed all my gear in the front section. The center section is for food, but the back is the largest, and it's empty."

Justin was curious, "Gear, what kind of gear?"

"Camp gear—and some other things that might come in handy," replied Grisham. "I have accumulated a collection of things that I always take when I go treasure hunting. You never know when you might . . ."

" . . . *run into a situation*," said Travis, completing Grisham's sentence and patting the sheath of the machete that was once again draped over his shoulder.

"Exactly," said Grisham with a wink. "Get your bedding, let's finish packing."

Lost Change was outfitted—it was time to get underway. They hitched the trailer to the back of the Cadillac and headed for the boat launch.

Once the boat was on the water, Grisham fired up the outboard. She let out a big puff of blue smoke, idled a little rough for a minute, and then smoothed right out. While the motor warmed up, Grisham dropped the trailer at his dinghy slot and parked the car up top in the approved parking area. Gary motored *Lost Change* over to the dock where Grisham and the others would board.

Justin, Travis, and Gary carefully untied the outrigger that had been lashed to the side of *Lost Change*, pushed it out from the boat, and fastened it in place. With Grisham at the tiller, they motored toward the bridge. As soon as they crossed under the bridge, Grisham killed the motor and called on the boys for some help, "Let's raise the mast!"

Their first sailing lesson was under way. Grisham had gone through the finer points of sailing back at the shed; now it was time to put what they'd learned into action. The mast was raised into position and cables were anchored to the appropriate cleats.

Grisham rigged the main sail, while Justin hooked up the jib. Then Grisham gave the command, "*Sheets to the wind!*" Grisham offered the crank to Tyler. "Time to crank her up! Want to give it try?"

Tyler took the crank in hand and put his all into it. Three quarters of the way up, the sails caught wind, startling him. "*Whoa there!*" he cried out. "*Not yet!*"

"Too late," replied Grisham. "Curtis, help Tyler finish the job."

Pressure of the wind in the sails made cranking more difficult. Though Tyler was the biggest of the boys, he had no concept of his size and strength. What was a struggle for Tyler was a challenge for Curtis and another chance to show that his size didn't mean he was a wimp. "I got it," he replied. Curtis took hold of the crank, intent on making an impression.

"We're underway," shouted Grisham. He was at least as excited as The Island Gang. He had a passion for sailing, and it had been several years since he'd had the opportunity.

The Island Gang nestled in opposite the sail and watched closely as Grisham maneuvered *Lost Change*. "Once you've got the wind, you've got to make sure you don't turn the boat out of it," he explained. "You can't always head directly for your destination. We got lucky this time. The wind is pulling us right toward Dead Man's. We won't be so lucky crossing Henderson," he said, as he pointed to the other side of the bay, about 90 degrees from their present heading.

A strong wind carried them to Dead Man's in short order. Gary and Justin helped Grisham lower the sails, while Curtis started the outboard, took the tiller in hand, and drove the hull up onto the beach. It was a different feeling with the outrigger, but one that he'd get used to.

Gary was first ashore. He steadied the boat while the others made their way to the front and across the bow.

Once everyone was off, Gary tied her to a large rock. Curtis raised the motor to avoid damaging the prop. Travis set the anchor off the stern. They wouldn't be there long enough to worry about the changing tide. They were on a mission to show Grisham the dream catcher—then they were headed across the bay.

"Over there," said Curtis, "That tree marks the trailhead."

Shadow led the way. He'd been through this drill once before.

As they walked the trail, Travis explained, "It was so overgrown through this area we had to use my machete to clear a path."

Grisham saw the results of their work and recognized the trail from his own experience several years earlier. Shadow was first to the top. He headed straight for the tall stone on the far side of the formation, where he stopped to point across the bay.

"Just a minute, boy," Gary said with a chuckle, "we're gonna show Mr. Grisham the rest of the puzzle first."

"Are you up for climbing a tree?" asked Gary, pointing to the old maple. "From about half way up you can see the dream catcher."

"I think my tree climbing days are over," replied Grisham.

"Well, you can sort of get the idea from that boulder,"

Travis said, pointing to a large rock formation off to the side of the maple. "From the backside it's an easy climb to the top."

Once atop the boulder, Grisham could see what they were talking about. There was definite symmetry to the layout of the burial ground.

Unfolding the map, Justin pointed out, "These numbers are sort of a combination. See—it says the center is the key," Justin continued, "Once we figured it out, we spotted that cove across the water," he said, handing Grisham the binoculars.

Grisham took a look, easily picking out the cove they were referring to.

"Come! We'll show you how the map's legend works!" volunteered Gary. "We tried lots of different ideas, but the only thing that finally made sense was to locate the proper point on the perimeter of the dream catcher!"

Gary and Grisham stood in the center of the formation while the others took their places at the far north end. Grisham watched curiously as Gary explained how he had figured out to subtract 3-West, from 7-East, finding the point exactly at 4-East. Wendy stood at 4 degrees East, which she had marked with a rock during their previous visit.

Gary continued, "Drawing an imaginary line from Wendy's position across the top of that tall stone and all the way to the other side of Henderson Bay puts us right in line with that cove. You can't see the water from here, so we got up on that rock and used the binoculars."

Forcefully, Travis added, "It has to be over there! There's no way the cove is here on Dead Man's!"

"I would have to agree with you on that," added Grisham, "Once I came into the map, I waited for low tide and walked every square inch of shoreline on this island—turned up nothing."

Seeing their excitement, Grisham went back over to

the tall rock and took another look through the binoculars. *What if the kids had figured it out?* He had seen enough to peak his curiosity. They headed for the boat.

Gary and Travis pushed off and climbed aboard. Travis quickly climbed across people and gear to get to the back of the boat, anxious to get his hands on the tiller under sail. Gary, looking for a place to sit, realized that the only seat left was next to Wendy, which he didn't mind at all. At this point, he was kind of intrigued with the prospect.

Gauging the direction the boat would need to head in order to get the most from the wind, Grisham maneuvered *Lost Change* into position and again gave the command, "*Sheets to the wind!*"

The kids were once again amazed by the surge of power as the sails caught wind, lunging *Lost Change* forward. They were headed to the mystery cove—only this time they had Grisham along—they felt assured of success.

Grisham got Travis focused on a point across the water and handed over the tiller, "Keep the tip of the bow centered on your target." Then he called for everyone's attention, "This is what I was explaining in the shed. We're aimed at that light colored area of beach, yet our destination is the cove," he said, as he simultaneously indicated the boat's heading and rocky entrance to the cove. "To get the most out of the wind, we'll hold our direction until we've gone a distance beyond the line between us and the cove. Then we'll bring the main sail about, changing our heading to a point back across to the other side of the cove. We'll repeat the sequence several times until we get within striking distance. Then we'll lower the sails and motor in. This zigzagging action is referred to as tacking." Grisham drew imaginary lines on the floor of the boat as he explained the process. He had them imagine that he was using tacks and string on a map—they got the idea. With the wind blowing like it was, he didn't dare get the map out. While in the shed, he had shown them how to stay clear of the boom as it traversed the deck, but the real world has a way of providing experience that cannot be had in a shed.

"Okay," shouted Mr. Grisham, "time to come about!" Grisham pointed out a new focal point to Travis, "On my command, change our heading to that point!" Grisham coached the others on remaining clear of the boom. Several of them would have to hit the deck, but they were smaller and younger. "Gary, man the starboard line. Curtis, you get the line portside! Gary and Curtis each took a crank in hand. Looking to Curtis, Grisham continued, "As soon as Gary begins loosening his line, crank hard and fast. The faster the boom moves securely into position, the less momentum we lose. Keep your eye on the boom or it'll knock you right out of the boat! Ready? Okay Travis, *new heading!*"

As Travis changed their heading, Gary quickly let his line out, and Curtis cranked hard, taking up the slack. All who were in the path of the boom ducked as it swung over their heads into its new position. Tyler was amused as he watched the process from his comfortable position in the bow. Once again they caught the wind, which lifted the outrigger out of the water. Quickly, Grisham lay back across the rear beam connecting the outrigger, placing as much of his weight as possible outside the boat. "Gary, go put your weight on the forward beam, keeping your legs in the boat—like this!"

Gary got into position, mimicking Grisham's pose. The outrigger made *Lost Change* maneuver almost like a catamaran.

"Adding our weight to the outrigger allows for greater resistance, causing the sails to catch more wind and carry us faster."

"We're doing it—we're sailing!" shouted Curtis, "*That's* what I'm talking about!"

With the help of a good coach, they managed all of the necessary maneuvers. They took turns manning the different positions as they crossed the bay, learning the importance of being precise and working as a team. After tacking several times, they were in close range of the cove.

"Let's lower the sails," suggested Grisham, "It's too risky to get any closer to those rocks under sail. It's going to be tricky enough motoring in."

"Last time we beached her right over there," offered Wendy, pointing to the sandy beach area.

The boys used the oars to keep *Lost Change* off of the rocks as Grisham got her carefully to the beach. It wasn't as dark as it had been the last time they were there. Extra daylight, combined with Grisham's presence, gave everyone extra confidence. They began where they had left off several weeks earlier, scouring the shoreline for an opening that might reveal hidden crystals.

Grisham had other priorities. He was anxious to find a smooth, flat piece of ground. The only things on his mind after a full afternoon of hiking and sailing were a meal and a good night's rest. Wendy figured the best way to show gratitude for accompanying them was to give Grisham a hand. They found a place not too far from the boat. He and Wendy visited as they gathered wood and got a fire going.

"Looks like you're fitting in pretty good with the boys," Grisham remarked. "Aren't there any girls your age on the island?"

"Not that I am aware of. I was the only one at the bus stop. But that's okay. These guys are a lot of fun and they're good boys," she replied. "Sometimes a little crazy—I seem to fit right in."

Grisham sensed she was referring to the day out at *The Sedgwick*. "It's just a good thing no one got hurt on that little excursion. That could have been disastrous!"

"We were lucky," she replied, "but the guys are pretty smart. Whenever we get in a tight spot, they seem to know what to do."

"Which one is the smartest?" he asked. Grisham had seen the glances between Wendy and Gary and was curious what her response would be.

"I don't know," she replied, "maybe Gary. He's generally the one leading the way. The others really look up to him."

It was as Grisham figured. "Well, time to rally the troops." Grisham called out to the boys, "I could use some help down at the boat!"

Travis, Justin and Curtis were close by and responded quickly.

"We need to get the outrigger right up along the shore so we can unload all of the camp gear. If you'll help me get to the food, I'll get supper started while you guys shuttle the rest of the supplies up the hill."

The mention of food had their attention. "No sweat, we can do it," replied Travis.

Travis was in shorts, so he waded into the shallow water, pushing *Lost Change* off shore and bringing the outrigger parallel to the shoreline. They quickly located the camp stove and lantern.

"I'll take those," Wendy offered, carrying the stove and lantern up the hill.

Mr. Grisham got into the cooler. He had a surprise—foil dinners. Steak and vegetables—seasoned with onion, garlic salt, cracked pepper and slice of butter. He pulled his shoulder bag from the cooler and headed up the hill.

Gary had been the farthest away when Grisham called the boys to help and straggled in a little late. "What's going on?"

"We're getting the gear up to the camp area while Mr. Grisham gets dinner ready," replied Curtis.

They'd been so excited from the day's activities they'd almost forgotten about food. "Food! A most excellent idea! How can I help?" asked Gary.

"We're going to set up camp while Mr. Grisham cooks," replied Curtis.

The boys had set up plenty of tents. In no time they had raised the large tent and staked it over a ground tarp. They also set up the small dome tent. Grisham was impressed at how quickly they worked and how well they worked together. "Nice work, guys! Now go make sure *Lost Change* is tied off and anchored, and check to be sure you have all of the bedding. I should have dinner ready by the time you get back."

"What's for dinner?" asked Travis.

"It's a surprise," came the reply. "Hurry back!"

The boys straightened *Lost Change* out, got her anchored, and secured everything that wasn't going up to the campsite. They talked of what they would do with their riches once they discovered the crystals. Curtis thought it a bit odd that the last time they were at the cove they had pushed out and slept on the boat, yet this time they were gregariously walking up and down trails. He watched Shadow, who was still cautious. Shadow paused now and then to listen and smell the air, but overall seemed at ease.

As they walked up the trail, they could see Grisham poking around in the coals.

"We're ready," offered Curtis from a distance. "What ya got?"

Enthusiastically, Gary added, "Ready? I'm *way* past ready!"

Justin saw Grisham pull a large clump of foil from the fire pit, "*Foil dinners*? Right on! What's in them?"

"You're just in time," Grisham said with a smile, "come have a seat." He handed each of them an old paper sack, upon which he placed a large wad of sizzling foil. Grisham watched as they opened the foil to find a large juicy steak with a mix of carrots, string beans, and potatoes.

"Just what the doctor ordered," Travis replied as he

dug into the meal.

After dinner, Gary offered to take the silverware down to the water to wash up. Grisham collected the paper sacks that hadn't been soiled so they could be used again. The foil was wadded up, put into a zip lock bag, and stored away so the scent of food wouldn't attract unwanted visitors.

Though they'd had a little cloud cover through the day, it was a clear night. Gary finished washing up, wrapped the knives and forks in a dishcloth, and laid them on a rock near the water. He was looking at the stars, when he suddenly had the impression that he wasn't alone. He turned to look, but could see no one. It was then he wished he'd brought a flashlight along.

A twig snapped, and he quickly turned to look again. He knew someone was there. "Is that you Travis?" he called out.

"No. It's me," Wendy replied.

"Oh, Wendy," you startled me.

"Sorry about that. I just came to see if you'd finished the washing." Really she'd been watching him for some time—wondering what he was thinking as he looked skyward. Something was obviously on his mind. "What ya thinking about?" she asked.

He'd found an old button down near the water as he was washing the silverware, which got him thinking about his great-grandmother, who died a few years back from cancer. She had a collection of buttons, at least three large coffee cans filled to the top. His brothers and sisters and he used to spend hours stringing buttons, matching styles and colors. Memories of great-grandmother brought the taste of home bottled peaches from the trees in her yard to mind, as well as the sweet smell of lotion on her hands as she held his face, kissed his forehead, and then pulled him close for an embrace. He'd been taught about God and Heaven, and that life continues after death. Deep inside, he hoped it was all true—he believed it was. He didn't share any of this with Wendy, he was afraid she wouldn't understand.

"Oh nothing," Gary replied, "just enjoying the peace and quiet.

"You want to be alone?" she asked, thinking that maybe her presence was unwanted.

"No, not at all," Gary replied.

She was relieved and stayed to visit. They sat on a log near the shore and visited until Grisham decided it was time to gather the troops for bed.

Once they were all inside the cabin tent, Grisham suggested bedtime prayer. After prayer, he announced that the small dome tent would be Wendy's quarters. He reached through the opening and pulled the dome tent right in under the awning of the cabin tent so that the two openings were facing each other, just inches apart. "There you go, Wendy," he said. "You'll have some privacy—without being completely alone.

Wendy would have been fine to sleep in with the boys, like she had during their previous trip to the cove, but she understood that adults had a way of wanting things to look right, even when there was nothing to worry about. "Thanks, Mr. Grisham. See you all in the morning."

They were up early. This was the first time they had seen the cove in full sun. Wendy and Shadow followed a trail that circled up and around, looking down over the cove and campsite. Tyler had walked up the trail behind Wendy, then turned and headed the opposite direction following a path that led out toward the point at the entrance to the cove.

Shadow had a strange curiosity with a large piece of rock that jutted out of the ground right up top. Wendy assumed it was the scent of another animal that had his interest.

After awhile, Gary and Travis joined Wendy up top. Maybe that vantage point would reveal something they couldn't see from the water. After all, they had been right on top of the dream catcher, but hadn't figured it out until Gary climbed the old maple.

Grisham was over at *Lost Change* getting into one of his duffel bags. Before they knew it, he was climbing into a dive suit.

"Hey, what's Mr. Grisham doing?" asked Gary.

"Hey, Mr. Grisham, what's up? Did you find something?" Travis called out.

They headed back down to the beach.

"I didn't bring any air, but the water is so cold I thought I would put my dry suit on to keep a little warmer. There are some shadows down in the end of the cove that I want to get a look at from underwater."

So that's what Mr. Grisham meant by being prepared, thought Gary, wondering what else was in those bags.

"I have my wife's gear if any of you want to join me," he offered. "I'm sure it would fit. Any takers?"

"If you find anything interesting, I'll join you," offered Gary. "In the meantime, I'll hang here with the others."

The Island Gang searched every inch of shoreline multiple times, but kept turning up a big fat zero.

"Whatever Curtis thought he saw last time we were here must have been a shadow," muttered Gary. "Speaking of Shadow. *Shadow!*" he called out, "Where are you boy?"

Shadow came running. Gary gave him a scratch under his collar and looked him straight in the eyes, "We need to find some Crystals. Can you help us? I wish I had one to show you—that would help, wouldn't it boy?" Shadow ran back to where he had been when Gary called him, which was up above. "I wonder what he finds so interesting up there?" asked Gary.

Grisham went snorkeling—The Island Gang went back to walking the shore.

Suddenly Travis had an idea. "We should get the binoculars and line up our position with Dead Man's."

"It's worth checking out," agreed Gary. "Maybe we're off by a few degrees."

He said the words, but in his heart he knew that the rocky entrance was the same one they'd seen from Dead Man's.

Gary and Travis got the binoculars and headed up top. They wanted to get as high as they could, hoping to get a view of the tall rock at the burial ground.

"We should check from up there," suggested Travis. "We ought to be able to see to the big rock at Dead Man's from up on top of this boulder."

What they could see of the boulder they were climbing onto was at least twice the size as the largest rock over at Dead Man's, and it appeared that it went deep into the ground. Gary climbed to a ledge in the rock about halfway up. Travis followed. Within a few minutes they were atop the boulder.

"I've got the rock at Dead Man's," Gary said as he focused the binoculars on the burial ground, "but, it's impossible to know where the point at four degrees east is—we'll never be able to tell if we're lined up. Here, you take a look"

"What's Shadow all worked up about?" Travis asked, pointing down at the base of the boulder. "He's trying to dig into the side of the rock!"

"What is it boy? What did you find?" Gary asked.

Shadow let out an anxious whine as if he were trying to tell them something.

"Let's check it out," said Gary.

"Shadow seems to want to get under it," Travis said.

"Like that'll ever happen," exclaimed Gary. "This boulder's going nowhere! It's huge, and firmly planted in the earth!"

There was no way of knowing how far below the surface it went, but every indication was that there could be as much of it below ground as there was above.

Shadow continued scratching at the side of the boulder, which is when they realized he wasn't getting anywhere. Gary climbed down to get a closer look. "It's all rock," said Gary, referring to the entire area upon which they were standing. They hadn't realized it due to the sparse brush growing here and there, but they were indeed standing on a huge rock formation. Somehow the sparse vegetation had been able to take root and survive.

Gary took a closer look at the area where Shadow was digging. There was a crack between the base of the boulder and the rest of the formation—a deep crack. He couldn't see into it, but as he put his ear to it he could hear the sound of water.

Travis got down on his knees next to Gary. "Where's your flashlight, Travis?" Gary asked. "I wonder if we can see anything in there."

"Do you think this crack goes all the way down to sea level?" questioned Travis.

Gary used Travis' flashlight, but the beam wasn't bright enough to see through to the other side of the crack.

Travis ran to the head of the trail and called down to Wendy, "Hey, get Mr. Grisham and come here! Bring a big flashlight! *Hurry!*"

Wendy waited for Grisham to surface. "Mr. Grisham," she called out, "come here! The boys found something up top!"

While Grisham was getting out of his mask and fins, Wendy got a large flashlight from the boat, and the two of them headed up to the boulder. Curtis and Justin heard the commotion and were making their way across the rocks from the other side of the cove.

Travis met Wendy and Grisham at the top of the trail, "There's a crack at the base of that large boulder. We think we can hear water down inside there." Shadow let out a whine as if to say, "It's about time you paid attention."

"Actually, Shadow was the first to find it," Travis added. "He's been frantically digging at the side of the boulder. When we realized he wasn't getting anywhere, we took a closer look."

Shadow let out a bark as his name was mentioned. He knew he was being acknowledged.

"Let's take a look," said Grisham as he got down on his knees, putting his ear to the crack. "It does sound like water. There must be open area down inside there. This could be our cove!"

They tried the flashlight, but even the larger one wasn't bright enough to do any good.

"I need you guys to stand at the head of the rock formation in line with this crack and be my guide. I'm going back in the water."

Grisham retrieved his underwater flashlight from the boat and put his mask and fins back on. Once he was positioned directly in front of Gary, he dove. A minute later he surfaced, took another bearing, and dove again. One more time, to the surface, and under again. This time two minutes went by—then 3, then 4.

"He either found something or he's dead!" said Gary, unsure whether to be excited or concerned. "No one can hold their breath this long!"

Curtis was getting a little anxious, "He can't be dead?"

"You can all relax," replied Travis with his ear to the crack, "I hear something. Mr. Grisham, is that you?"

"It's me alright," came the reply. "I'll be right out. I'm going to need some help."

"What is it? Did you find the crystals?" asked Travis.

But it was too late. Grisham had already gone back underwater. They all hustled down by the boat to see what

Grisham had found. Within a minute, Grisham appeared. He had something in his hand.

Are you ready, Gary?" Grisham asked. "I could use a hand in there, and I think you're the one for the job. You'll have to hold your breath for about a minute to make it into the cove. Are you up to it?"

"I can try," Gary responded, having never really counted out the seconds before. "Let's see what you found!"

"It's a crystal all right, a *large* crystal!" In the light of the sun, the crystal took on new beauty. "I'm not sure what we have here, but there are plenty just like this in there," Grisham said, holding it up for everyone to see.

Justin was first to handle the crystal. It was amazing! He couldn't help but wonder the value of the treasure that lie in the cove. He wondered how long the crystals had been kept there in the dark and what they would look like as they were brought into the light.

Gary determined he was up for the task. "I'm coming," he answered excitedly.

"Get the other dry suit on, and bring a couple of those catch-bags from the duffle."

While Gary suited up, Travis located the mesh bags. Shadow was all over Gary as he attempted to dress. People always say dogs are just animals. Gary knew there was more to it, at least in Shadow's case. Shadow just made a significant contribution. He wanted some attention, and he wanted it now!

Using his best sweeter than sugar voice, Gary grabbed Shadow's face looking him straight in the eyes and said, "What's the matter boy—are you being ignored? You did real good—yeah, you're the hero of the day—yes you are." As Gary praised him, he gave him a good rub down, which was Shadow's favorite form of praise. Then Shadow took a few steps back for a full body shake while Gary finished suiting up. Travis handed over the bags he'd retrieved from the duffle bag, and Gary prepared to join Grisham in the water.

All at once, Shadow heard Tyler off on the far side of the cove, and took off to go check on him. Shadow had a sense for Tyler's condition and was quick to respond when he sensed anything might be wrong. Curtis realized what was going on and followed Shadow.

"Have you ever been in a dry suit before?" Grisham asked of Gary.

"First time," came the reply.

"Well, I think you are going to like it. It's called a dry suit for a reason. The only part of you that's going to get wet is your head. You'll actually stay fairly warm."

Gary had never let the temperature of the water bother him, but the idea of not getting wet while submerged in water was intriguing. "This is great!" he said as he waded into the water, stopping to slip the fins over his booties. Before donning the mask, Gary gave it a quick rinse—spitting into the lens, swishing it around so that the saliva would coat the inner surface, and then giving it a final rinse with the salt water. He'd been taught that this ritual helped prevent the mask from fogging up. He slipped the mask on and was ready to go.

"Holding your breath in cold water like this can be a different experience," warned Grisham. "I want you to practice a couple of times right here in the open to make sure you're up to it. We'll get into a tight area down there on the way to the cave. Let's see how long you can hold your breath."

Gary gave an affirmative nod, took a breath and went under. The group counted out loud. Upon surfacing he cleared his snorkel, showing Grisham that he was no stranger to a mask and snorkel.

"That'll do it," said Grisham. "You want to try one more time?"

Gary gave a negative nod of the head as he pulled the

snorkel from his mouth, "No, I think I'm ready."

"Do you get claustrophobic?" asked Grisham

"Sometimes," came the response.

"Alright. We'll move as quickly as we can through the tight area. Take a couple of deep cleansing breaths," said Grisham, demonstrating the procedure. "Then hold your breath and follow me. Stay real close. It's a bit of a maze down there. When we get to a tunnel area, hold on to my fins. It gets dark and a little tight," Grisham warned again. "I'll pull us through the narrow opening. If you run into any problems, tug on my fins real hard. Any questions?"

By then, Gary once again had a mouth full of snorkel, so a nod was all he could manage. Grisham started the three count. "Ready? We go on three. One—two—three!"

Grisham and Gary submerged simultaneously and they were off.

Gary made it to the area where Grisham veered off to the right, when all of a sudden he slapped real hard at one of Grisham's fins, and headed back to the surface!

Grisham felt the slap and turned to see Gary heading the other direction. Grisham followed.

"What's up?" Grisham asked as they surfaced.

"Didn't you see that? There's—something in there!" gasped Gary. "Something with little beady eyes, in the rock, right where you made the turn!"

"I'll be right back," said Grisham, as he dove down to have a look.

Soon he was back. "That is one big wolf eel! He won't bother you, if you don't bother him. Wolf eels look a lot more dangerous than they really are. If you qualified to be his dinner you'd have reason for concern, but you're much too big for that. He is a lot more afraid of you than you are of him," Grisham said, trying to reassure Gary, who hadn't yet put his mask back on. "I was on a dive once further north where we actually got a pair of wolf eels to come out of their holes and feed and play right around us."

Gary wanted to believe. "Okay," replied Gary reluctantly, "I'll follow you, but don't take your time getting past that eel." Gary was generally pretty brave, but there was something about being under water with an unfamiliar creature that was a little different.

Gary and Grisham went under for a second time. Gary could see what Grisham meant by a maze. No wonder it took him several dives to find the way in. Gary was curious as to where the other underwater passageways led, but knowing that Grisham had already reached the crystals, he determined to keep hold of Grisham's fin as he had been instructed. After waiting a couple of minutes, the rest of the gang ran back up top to the crack.

"Are you guys in there?" Travis hollered into the crack.

"We're here," came the reply.

"What can you see?" Travis asked, hardly able to contain his excitement.

"Not much yet," Gary answered, "but there's a big open area inside here! You can walk around completely out of the water."

"You guys need to back away from the crack for just a minute," said Grisham to the guys up top.

"Okay," responded Travis.

"Take a look over there," Grisham said to Gary, pointing upward.

As the guys up top moved, sunlight came through the crack, and one straight shaft of light was shining directly on a large stack of crystals that lay on a natural rock shelf, up away from any threat of the rising tide.

"How'd they ever find this place?" asked Gary.

"My guess is the cove was good fishing," replied Grisham. "If you spend enough time in a small cove like this, sooner or later you learn everything about it."

They climbed up to where they could reach the crystals and began loading them into the catch-bags. As the first bag filled up, Gary looked at the pile, which didn't seem to be getting much smaller. "*Holy Smoke!*" he cried out, catching the attention of those assembled up at the crack. "You won't even believe how many crystals are in here!"

"Be careful not to drop them," warned Grisham. "They'd be lost for good down there," shining the light on layers of rock below them.

"How many are there?" asked Wendy.

"A lot!" replied Gary as he filled the second bag. "We're going to have to make a couple of trips!"

As the second bag filled up, they realized that what they thought was a rock shelf turned out to be a bowl-shaped area in the ledge of rock.

"Can you even believe this?" exclaimed Gary to Grisham. "Look at all of them!"

Both bags were filled to the top, and there were plenty of crystals remaining.

"We're going to need more bags," replied Grisham. "I think I only have four total. We'll have to empty these, and bring all four bags back in order to get them all! You want to come with me, or wait here?"

"I'll wait here if you don't mind."

"That's fine," replied Grisham. "I'll be back as quick as I can."

Overhearing their conversation, Travis headed for the boat to locate the other bags. He knew Grisham would be there soon, and he was anxious to see what two bags of crystals looked like. The others followed. They were stunned at what was happening. They'd actually discovered *Crystal Cove!* It *was* real!

Travis located the additional catch bags and combined the remaining contents of the two duffels into one, leaving one duffel bag empty for the crystals.

Grisham's hands were full with the two bags of crystals, so he left the light behind. Gary climbed down from where the crystals were and took a seat on a ledge of rock below. He thought back to discovering the dream catcher and solving the combination. Though he had just helped fill two bags with crystals, it seamed unreal that they had actually found an ancient treasure. As he sat, he swept the light across the various formations of rock—still amazed that anyone had found the underwater cave. Suddenly, something caught Gary's eye. Slowly retracing the path the light had taken, he searched to see what it was. There on a rock toward the top of the cave, almost directly across from the crystals, was a shiny object.

"There's something else in here," Gary said, thinking there was still someone listening up above. "Is anybody there?"

Then he realized that they'd probably all gone to see Grisham and the crystals.

Gary decided to get a closer look. He climbed to where he could reach it. It was a metal box-shaped object—gold in color. As he removed it from the rock, he was surprised how heavy it was. It looked very old. "I wonder if it's gold," he said aloud. He tipped it sideways for a look at the engravings on the outside. As he did he felt something move on the inside. "There's something in it!" he said, once again talking to himself.

"In what?" asked Wendy, having returned to the crack in time to hear the comment.

"There's something else down here," Gary replied. "It's a box! I think it's made of gold!"

Wendy relayed the message to the guys down on the beach, "Hey guys! Gary found a gold box!"

Grisham was underwater on his way back to the cave and missed the excitement. Everyone gathered near the crack.

"What does it look like?" asked Wendy.

"It's tall, and square. There's something inside—but, I can't get it open."

It was rectangular in shape, about three times as tall as it was wide. Gary fiddled with it until Grisham returned. Although Gary anticipated Grisham's return, he was startled as Grisham immerged from the black hole of water.

"Look Mr. Grisham! Look what I found!" Gary said, handing him the item. "I think it's made of gold, and there's something inside!"

Grisham removed his mask, shook the water from his hair to keep it from dripping into his eyes, and took the object from Gary. "Where did you find this?"

"Right up there," Gary replied, shining the light on the piece of rock.

"It is a curious piece," agreed Grisham. "By its weight, it could be gold."

Everyone up at the crack was going crazy. They wanted to be down in the underwater cave.

"Should we take it with us?" asked Gary.

"Absolutely," replied Grisham, giving it a shake, "We need to find out what's inside. I'm sure it was placed in here with the crystals. Whatever's inside probably tells a story."

Grisham took the flashlight, taking a look around the cave. He couldn't believe he had missed the gold box. He made an attempt at opening it, but it wasn't immediately clear how it opened. "Boy, it is really sealed off!"

Gary was anxious to see it in the light of day. "Do you think it's waterproof?" he asked.

"I don't see any other way out, so it must have come in the same way we did, which tells me there's a pretty good chance that whatever is inside is safe."

They finished packing the crystals. Four full bags.

"Hey guys," Gary shouted to the rest of The Island Gang, "four more bags of crystals!"

Four bags plus the box was a big haul. Grisham tried tucking the box under his arm. It wasn't going to work. It would be too cumbersome passing through the tunnel. It was going to take two more trips to get it all. Gary was anxious to take the box out to show the others. "I'll leave one of the bags of crystals so I can bring the box."

"Why don't you leave both bags behind," replied Grisham. "It's pretty difficult to maneuver through that opening with both hands full. We'll need to make another trip either way. With your other hand free, you can carry the light."

"Are you sure?" asked Gary.

"Absolutely! I made the last trip in the dark, and it was more difficult. Take the light and lead the way."

"Uh—okay. I guess I can do that."

Grisham sensed a little reluctance in Gary's voice. "You'll do fine," he stated, reassuring Gary, "After all, there's only one way out. And, unlike the trip in, once you turn the corner, you'll see daylight. Just follow the light.

Gary was glad it was dark. He didn't want Grisham to see the concern in his expression. The dark didn't bother him all that much—it was being underwater in the dark that brought uncertainty!

With the light in one hand and box in the other, Gary took a deep breath and led the way. His fears were quenched as he uneventfully made his way through the underwater maze and emerged into the cove. Grisham was right. Light from the destination made *all* the difference!

The others had waded out to their knees to greet them.

"Let's see the box!" shouted Travis.

"Yeah," Wendy added. "What is it anyway?"

Grisham surfaced right behind Gary with two extremely full bags of crystals.

"Holy Smoke," sighed Justin, pointing in the direction of Grisham. "Are you looking at that?"

With huge eyes Travis asked, "What's all this worth?"

Grisham shrugged his shoulders, handing the bags to Wendy and Justin, "A lot!" he replied. "Careful with the bags, they're pretty full. Put them with the others. C'mon Gary, we've got one more load."

Hearing all of the commotion, Curtis, Tyler and Shadow immediately headed from the point back toward the boat.

"Where's Gary?" asked Curtis.

"Back in the underwater cave with Mr. Grisham for the last of the crystals," replied Travis. "Get a load of this!" He held the two sides of the unzipped duffel open for Curtis and Tyler to see.

"*Holy Smoke!*" shouted Tyler, "*We found the crystals!*"

Shadow let out a single bark followed by a long whine.

Travis took his turn examining the box. "It has to open—there's stuff inside!" he said, as he tried to get his fingernails under the edge of what appeared to be the top portion of the box. "It's stuck!" He headed for the boat, intent on getting a screwdriver to pry it open, but he caught himself before completing the task, realizing that was probably not the best idea he'd ever had.

Soon Gary and Grisham returned. As they added the final bags of crystals to the duffle, everyone's heads were spinning. *Crystal Cove was real!*

"I can't believe it," stated Gary, "The dream catcher was the key! We found a treasure!"

"And," exclaimed Justin, sizing up the quantity of crystals, "we're on our way to a bigger boat!"

As inconspicuously as she could, Wendy cleared her throat and sent a piercing glance his way, as if to say, "Are you trying to hurt Mr. Grisham's feelings. He's put his heart and soul into *Lost Change*." No words were exchanged, but her meaning was clear.

Justin back-peddled the best he could, "Anyway, it doesn't hurt to dream. Either way, we'll never retire *Lost Change*. She's earned her place in history!" Justin looked to Wendy for approval.

Out of the corner of her eye she caught his stare and put a content expression on her face, keeping her gaze fixed straight ahead in an effort to draw less attention.

Lost Change had exceeded their wildest expectations—until, of course, you introduce a fortune into the equation. One thing is sure, they were all one hundred percent converted to the whole legend thing, even Curtis—who suddenly couldn't keep his mind off Grisham's treasure box. *With Crystal Cove proving out—maybe there was something to those other legends.*

"What do you say we take all of this back to my place," suggested Grisham. "We won't be able to catch anyone in town until Monday. I'll keep everything safe and secure until then."

The Island Gang agreed. Grisham's would be the safest place.

Curtis liked the idea and was busy working on a plan to get to the treasure box.

"Once word gets out that we found *Crystal Cove*, we'll have more attention than we know what to do with. I know you're all anxious to tell your folks about the crystals, but I think we should keep quiet until we can get them into the right hands. I hate keeping secrets from your folks, but like *The Sedgwick*, the smaller the circle the better."

They understood. The Island Gang threw their hands into a circle, entering into a pact of silence.

Given the circumstances, no one was in the mood for a sailing lesson on the return trip. They had been in the cove longer than planned, and they just wanted to get back. They started the outboard and headed for home.

On the way back, Gary had an idea, "I've got it!"

"You've got what?" asked Wendy.

"I know who we can show the box to!"

"Who's that?" questioned Justin.

"Wes! He knows lots about Indian stuff . . ."

" . . . You mean Native American stuff," Wendy interjected.

"Yeah, anyway, he might even recognize the origin of some of the engraving. If not, he'll know who to ask!"

Wes was an older gentleman the boys knew from church. He had lived in Gig Harbor most of his life, and had taken particular interest in northwestern Native Americans. Though The Island Gang had never discussed *Crystal Cove* with him, they were positive he'd heard of the legend.

"Can he be trusted to keep quiet?" inquired Grisham.

"Absolutely! Wes is as trustworthy as they come," Gary answered.

The rest of the boys agreed.

"I'm sure you know of him," Gary continued. "He has the totem pole in his front yard over on Pioneer."

"Why certainly," answered Grisham, "I know the totem pole. I can't say I've ever met the man, but everyone knows the totem pole in front of that bright orange and yellow house!"

"That's Wes," confirmed Gary, "'Righteous orange' he calls it. It's his favorite color. As for the totem pole, he made it himself—from scratch! He did a lot of research so it would tell a story, just like authentic totem poles do, and then he put it right on his property. He did all the carving, painting—everything."

"Sounds like quite a guy."

"He's something else," confirmed Travis, "and he knows Indians—Native Americans, that is. He's actually quite the history buff."

"Maybe we should go by and see him together," suggested Grisham. "I wouldn't mind sizing him up a little before we let him in on our find."

13

The Crystals

When they arrived at Grisham's, he invited them in.

"Let's count the crystals," Travis said. "I've got to know how many there are!"

"That's not a bad idea," Grisham added, knowing how much kids like to count. "Why don't you take them out on the deck where you can spread out? I'll dish up some ice cream."

"Ice cream?" replied Tyler as he raised his eyebrows and licked his lips. "I better help Mr. Grisham."

Grisham welcomed the help—he and Tyler headed for the kitchen.

Wendy, Travis, Justin, and Curtis went to the deck and emptied the duffel bag into one pile in the middle of the large round table. Gary went to call Wes to see if it would be okay for them to stop by later. There was no answer, so he joined the others out on the deck, resolving to try Wes again later. They each had a paper sack from Grisham's kitchen and began filling the sacks as they counted.

"They're amazing—aren't they?" commented Gary. "The crystals of *Crystal Cove*. I can't wait to find out if they're really diamonds!" He took a seat at the table and began to count. It would have gone a lot faster if they'd been counting marbles, but they handled the crystals with far greater care than they would a marble, examining each one as they went.

Grisham and Tyler had been visiting in the kitchen as they served the ice cream. They arrived on the deck as the group was reporting their results.

"I have 152," reported Curtis.

"153 over here," Justin added

"170," Wendy reported.

"147," said Travis.

Gary, who was last to join the counting, was also last to report, "I have 115."

"Seven hundred thirty-seven," reported Tyler, having totaled the figures in his head as they were verbalized.

"Seven hundred thirty-seven!" repeated Grisham.

"That's right," confirmed Tyler. "Seven hundred thirty-seven."

"Remember when we first found the box in Mr. Grisham's attic?" asked Justin.

Travis let out a chuckle, "Yeah, I remember. Curtis dropped it on his toe, and started doing the hop dance." Travis mimicked the scene as he grabbed hold of his right foot and began hopping around the deck, and then fell to the floor rolling onto his back—hanging onto his foot through the entire routine.

Everyone laughed. Even Curtis got a smile on his face. "It's a lot funnier now than it was at the moment—that's for sure," Curtis said.

They were all in great spirits. They'd fantasized about moments like this ever since then—questioning in the back of their minds the validity of *legends*.

It was time to give Wes another call. This time he was home. "Hey, Wes, it's Gary Nielson."

"Gary Nielson," Wes repeated, struggling to put a face with the name, "and what are you up to this fine evening?"

"Well, we came across this Native American artifact that we'd like you to take a look at."

"You did, did you—who's we?"

"My buddies from Raft Island and I—and Mr.

Grisham."

The mention of Raft Island was all Wes needed to help him match a face with the voice on the other end of the phone. "I don't think I know a Mr. Grisham."

"He's our neighbor."

"Okay. So what did you find, and where'd you find it?"

"That's a long story, but we'd like to come by and show it to you, we can tell you then."

"Well, bring it on over, let's have a look."

"Now?"

"I don't see why not, I'm not going anywhere. Does tonight work for you?"

"I think so—just a minute," Gary said, holding his hand over the mouthpiece, "Mr. Grisham, I got Wes on the phone. He wants to know if we can go by right now."

"Sounds good to me. Tell him we'll be there shortly."

Grisham put the sacks of crystals into his pantry. Gary got the gold box, and they headed for the car.

There were three short flights of concrete stairs leading to Wes's front door. At the head of each flight was a landing, at which point the stairs made a 90° turn. Wes had seen them pull up and was on his way to the door as they were climbing the last flight of stairs. Gary led the pack, prize in hand.

"Greetings and salutations," Wes said as he opened the door. Then he saw Gary's entourage. "Holy smokes! You brought the whole neighborhood!"

"We were all there when I found it," Gary replied, "so I decided we should come together."

"C'mon in," said Wes, holding the door as they entered. "Let's see what you have there." Wes took the gold box, intently studying the engravings. "*Where'd you find this?*"

"Over the last few weeks we've been doing a little exploring out in Henderson Bay, said Gary, "It came from a secluded cove out across the bay."

"This is quite something," Wes responded, turning the box on every angle, examining the artistry and craftsmanship. "So, tell me the story."

"Before we get into it, let me introduce Wendy and Mr. Grisham. They're neighbors from Raft Island."

"I was wondering when you'd get around to introductions." Wes turned to Wendy, "Tell me how a beautiful girl like you got saddled with the likes of these rascals?" he asked, bantering with the guys he knew to be rabble-rousers down at the church building during scout night. Wes could tell that Grisham was pretty close to his same age, and was a bit curious as to how he managed to keep company with the youngsters. As he extended his hand he offered his standard welcome, "Greetings, Mr. Grisham. This is quite a brood you're hanging with."

"You can call me Reg—and it sure is. They've been keeping me busy the past month or so, which is just what the doctor ordered." Grisham would have been more frank with Wes as to how the kids company had helped him get through the loneliness of losing his spouse, but it didn't seem the time or place.

Wes figured there was more to his comment than the words spoken and was interested in exploring it further, but before he had the chance Gary piped up, "He helped us fix up his old boat so we could get out on the water, and it was his treasure box that led us to discover *Crystal Cove*."

Whatever had been occupying Wes's mind, instantly fled. The mention of *Crystal Cove* had his full attention! "What's this about a treasure box—and—did you say, *Crystal Cove?*" asked Wes, switching his glance from Gary to Grisham.

"It was all these guys," said Grisham, "they took me

along, but it was their genius that led to the discovery. You've heard of the legend I take it?"

"Surely! Who hasn't heard stories of the '*Legend of Crystal Cove*'? But, you say you've discovered its location?"

"We sure have," Gary answered, "and right there in the underwater cave with the crystals was this box. What do you think?"

Wes didn't know where to start. He knew the *Legend of Crystal Cove* was as old as time. He was more of a believer in ancient legends than most—it just seemed unreal that this group of youngsters would chance upon it. "The box is wonderful! Tell me about *Crystal Cove*—where are the crystals?"

"There at my place now," replied Grisham. "Monday I intend to get them into town. I have a connection from my years with the bureau. I think he'll be able to give me an appraisal."

"The bureau—you mean the *FBI?*" Wes asked.

"Thirty plus years," replied Grisham.

Anxious to see the crystals, Wes inquired, "I don't suppose I could get a peek at them?"

"Tonight?" asked Grisham.

"I'd be delighted, if you'd oblige," came the reply.

"I don't mind telling you that we're keeping this as quiet as we can." Throwing a head gesture in the direction of the kids, Grisham said, "We aren't even telling their parents yet, not until we can get the crystals into a more secure location."

"I understand," Wes replied.

"You've made quite an impression on the boys. They've all vouched for your trustworthiness. Gary couldn't wait to get you involved. He says you have quite an interest in Native American things. We're hoping your knowledge of northwest tribes and culture might prove useful in determining the origin and authenticity of the gold box and crystals."

"The box looks pretty authentic to me," replied Wes, continuing to examine the item. "It's obviously very old. I know exactly where to take it to learn more. The gentleman most schooled in these kinds of things has been away, but he may have returned. I'll check tomorrow. If he is back, I'd like to show this to him. Can I hang onto it?"

Grisham looked to Gary, "What do you think?"

"I don't see why not."

"I guess that settles it," said Grisham. "Shall we take that ride out to my place?"

Wes decided to follow them so they wouldn't be inconvenienced by having to bring him home. Gary climbed in with Wes. He'd be able to point Grisham's house out if the cars got separated.

As they drove, Gary continued his questions about the box. "What do you think is inside?"

"Hard to say," Wes replied, "but if I went to all of the trouble of leaving something behind, it would be something of worth—you know, like some folks bury time capsules, recording memories they don't want to be forgotten. My bet is that it contains something like that—events that some-body wants to be remembered."

"I guess that makes sense—whatever it is can't be worth *anything* compared to the crystals!"

"So, the box was right with the crystals?"

"Yep. It was sitting on a ledge of rock just across from them. It's really cool in there. You have to swim underwater for almost a minute to get into it, but then it opens right up into this big cave. We'd have never found it if it weren't for Shadow."

"*Shadow*?" questioned Wes.

"Yeah, he sniffed out a deep crack up on top of this rock formation overlooking the water, right in the end of the cove. When we listened real quietly at the crack, we could hear water. That's how we found the cave the crystals were in."

"Dogs are something else," replied Wes.

"Shadow was brilliant," continued Gary, "Once we knew where the cave was, we walked out to the edge of the rock and guided Mr. Grisham. He had to dive a couple of times, but he found it. He needed some help to get all of the crystals, so I went into the cave with him. It was so cool! There was a shaft of light coming through the crack, shining directly on crystals. We figured there's only a span of about an hour that that phenomenon occurs. I imagine we would have found them with or without the ray of sunlight, but it was awesome to see them lit up by the sun. I'd have never found the box without a flashlight. It was nowhere near the crystals."

"Could be some meaning there," said Wes, squinting his eyes deep in thought. "I wonder if that ray of sun would have reached the box at a different time of day?"

"I don't think so," replied Gary, "the way the boulder sits, I don't think the sun's rays ever got to it."

Wes and Gary were just crossing the Raft Island Bridge. The intensity of their conversation caused them to lag behind, "Take the middle road," directed Gary, "When it ends, take a left, then another left. Grisham's place will be on the right."

Gary and Wes pulled in as the others were entering the house. Clouds gathered through the late afternoon—it was beginning to drizzle. They wasted no time getting into the house. Grisham directed them into the dining room and went for a bag of crystals. "Here you go," he said, holding the bag open to Wes' view.

Wes was in awe. "They're wonderful," he stated, taking one into his hand, "and so many of them!"

"Shall we tell him?" asked Grisham, looking to The Island Gang for approval.

Wes looked from face to face, he could see the pure delight in their eyes, "What—tell me *what*?"

Slowly nods of approval came. They looked to Gary to break the silence. "This is just one of the bags. There are four more just like it."

"Holy Smokes!" stated Wes, "You're kidding, *right*?"

Having heard Wes use that expression several times now, Wendy wondered if he was responsible for teaching Gary the phrase.

Travis, Curtis, Justin, and Wendy each went into Grisham's kitchen to retrieve the other bags.

"Here they are," Wendy announced as they returned.

Wes was overwhelmed. They stayed at Grisham's into the night, sharing the stories of how they had come across the treasure box, their first trip to Dead Man's, discovering the dream catcher, and their first attempt at exploring the cove that nearly ended in disaster. They carefully avoided any mention of *The Sedgwick*. The time to bring that up had not yet arrived.

As they prepared to go their ways, Grisham reminded all to keep quiet until he had a chance to get the crystals someplace safe.

"So you don't mind if I show this to a few folks tomorrow?" Wes asked, with the gold box in hand.

"I don't see any problem with you showing it around— if you can show it without telling where it came from," stated Grisham.

A bit puzzled at the prospect, Wes hesitated, and then replied, "I can do that. It'll drive Skip crazy," he chuckled to himself, "but eventually I'll be able to tell him the whole story—he'll be fine with that."

Grisham, continuing the conversation, offered, "Monday, I'll take some crystals into town. I don't imagine it will be too long before we have some sort of determination, then I'll get them to a secure location. We'll be able to share our adventure at that point."

Curtis' mind was once again on Grisham's treasure

box. Unable to contain his thoughts any longer, he leaned over to Justin who was seated next to him and whispered, "I wonder if there's anything to the rest of those legends?"

"What legends?" Justin replied.

"The ones in the *box*!" he whispered adamantly. "The papers in the treasure box had a whole list of legends! There could be something to them—just like *Crystal Cove*."

"I didn't see any other legends," answered Justin.

"That's because you guys were too busy gawking at the *Crystal Cove* stuff," said Curtis. One of the papers referred to "*Legend of Walking Sick, Legend of the Masks, Legend of the Orcas,* and a couple of others that I can't remember. Who knows what all is in there? There could be a *lifetime* of adventure, right in that box!"

The hour was late—it had been a long day. It was definitely time for sleep! There are a few necessities for kids the age of The Island Gang, and high on the list is sleep.

Monday, Grisham took 10 of the crystals to a jeweler the bureau had used to appraise items they recovered on the job. "I'd like to get a rough appraisal on these," he said, handing them to the man.

The jeweler took the crystals from Grisham and started for a back room.

Stopping the man, Grisham asked, "Would you mind examining them right out here? I'm really not comfortable letting them out of my sight, not even for a moment."

The jeweler had only taken a quick peek at the crystals, which were neatly wrapped in a table linen. His curiosity was heightened.

At Grisham's request, he laid the linen on the glass counter, and spread it open. Putting a jeweler's glass to his right eye, he took a closer look at one of them. "Where'd you come across these?" he asked, as he made his way around the counter toward the front door of his store. "They've been exposed to the elements—it appears for some time."

Grisham watched as he locked the door and flipped the sign over that read, *Closed Temporarily.*

Grisham wasn't sure what to make of it and stammered the response, "I—actually—some friends of mine just sort of came across them."

The jeweler could tell Grisham was a bit on edge, "Don't be alarmed by my having locked the door," the jeweler said, "whenever I feel the need for added privacy or security, I lock up for a few minutes—it's common practice among merchants in this part of the city."

"Oh—well, anyway, I told my friends that I knew where to have them looked at, and voila! While I was with the bureau we used to send you items. I was certain you could be of assistance."

"You were with the bureau, huh? I thought you looked familiar. Haven't seen you in some time."

"I retired about eight years ago," came the response.

After some examination, the jeweler reported, "They're authentic alright! Diamonds! Six of the ten average 3 to 4 carats each. These four here are closer to 6 carats— they'll be smaller once they're cut, but you have a decent find here. I haven't had the privilege of dealing with many raw diamonds." The jeweler took one of them to the buffing wheel. "Fact is, I have never seen uncut diamonds this size with such color and clarity. Mind telling me where you found them?"

"Well, not just yet. But one day I'm sure you'll get the whole story," Grisham replied with a nod.

Curious, the jeweler asked, "Are there more where these came from?"

"No," replied Grisham. "I'm confident that we got them all."

The jeweler had learned to listen to words and watch faces. *First Grisham had said some friends came across them, yet his last statement indicated that he was there when they were found. Hmmm . . .* thought the jeweler.

"Can you give me a rough value?" asked Grisham.

"These smaller crystals could bring $300 per carat on the wholesale market. I'll give you $500 a carat for the larger ones if they're for sale?"

"They're not for sale at the moment, but I'm sure they will be. Here's a little for your time," Grisham said, offering a $100 bill.

"Oh no, not necessary," replied the jeweler, "but I would like to be at the top of your list when you decide to sell them."

"I'll keep that in mind."

"You aren't interested in sharing the location of your discovery are you?" asked the jeweler.

"Not really," was Grisham's response.

"Didn't think you would be, but I'd be a fool not to ask. When you're ready to sell one or all, my offer stands."

If he only knew, thought Grisham. "Thanks again," he replied on his way out.

After pulling away from the jeweler, Grisham pulled into a parking lot and got a calculator from his glove box to do a little math. Knowing the crystals he had taken weren't among the largest of the collection, he figured the average size of the crystals to be around 6 carats. "Let's see," he said, "Seven hundred and thirty-seven, times an average of 6 carats, times $500—$2,211,000. *Wow!*"

It was time to find a safe home for the diamonds. Grisham didn't want to risk having something happen to them. He headed straight home.

There was a car in his driveway as he pulled in. He could tell from the plate it was a government vehicle. He pulled alongside the car where he read, *Department of Fish and Wildlife. What could the DFW want?* he wondered.

There were two men at the front door where they waited as he got out of his car. "Hello gentlemen," "What can I do for you?"

"Are you the man of the house?"

"I sure am."

"Do you own the boat registered as *Little Imp*?"

As they asked the question, Grisham realized that *Lost Change* was indeed still registered as *Little Imp*.

"Yes."

"Did you have the boat out last weekend?"

"As a matter of fact I did. I was out with some friends. What's this all about?"

"We're following up on a report that you were out clamming over the weekend."

"Clamming?" questioned Grisham. "We didn't do any . . ."

"Where were you boating?" they cut in before he could finish his sentence.

"Out in Henderson Bay, just south of here," Grisham responded. "And if we were clamming, what of it?"

"Well, only that clams are out of season, and the report states that you were seen taking several large bags of clams out of a cove across the bay."

Grisham hoped he wasn't telling a story through his expression. This was a very suspicious visit. He wondered who knew they had been in the cove! It was time to get rid of these guys and take action.

"Well gentlemen, I'm not sure what else to say, but I can promise you that we didn't take a single clam. May I ask where the report came from?"

"Actually, that's generally confidential information—people fear retaliation for making a report. But, this was anonymous."

"Well, I was giving a sailing lessons, and we spent

some time in a cove out across Henderson, but we didn't take any marine life, so I'm not sure what your anonymous report is all about."

"Okay," they replied, handing Grisham a pamphlet, "We'll take your word for it. For future reference, this outlines seasons and regulations for taking shellfish in the Puget Sound. It is our mission to maintain a healthy level of marine life for future generations. Please share this information with your friends."

"I'll do just that," Grisham assured them. "Thanks for your concern. You should know that we have every intention of following regulations. The kids I was out there with are the most honest kids I have ever had the pleasure of associating with."

"Thank you for your time," they replied. They got in their car and drove away.

"That was truly strange," Grisham said, as he watched them pull away. "Someone suspects that we've found something. There's no way *anyone* really believes that we were clamming! I've got to get McGovney on the phone. Maybe he'll let me store the crystals down at the bureau."

Grisham went to his car, hit the remote to his garage, and backed his car in. Next he called FBI headquarters. "Agent McGovney, Reg Grisham calling."

"Hey Reg, we were just talking about you. The case on your entrepreneurs out at *The Sedgwick* is really heating up. As of now we'll bust at least 16. I'm sure Agent Larsen will be getting a hold of you in the next month or so to share the news."

"That's great," Grisham replied. "I need another favor."

"What's up?"

"I have something I need to store in your safe for a short time."

"Are you bringing us more trouble?" asked McGovney.

"I don't think so, but I can explain more when I see you. I know it's close to going home time, but I *have* to get this into the safe today. Would you mind hanging out until I arrive?"

"Sounds serious."

"I'll fill you in when I get there. I should be able to make it in about 45 minutes."

"I'll be waiting with bated breath," replied McGovney, "You've *really* got my curiosity now!"

Keeping in the shadows, Grisham walked from room to room looking out each window as he locked up. He didn't spot anything suspicious, but he knew that didn't necessarily mean a thing. He was sure his place was being watched. Whoever had called Fish & Wildlife had probably followed the car to his home—*if* the men that just left were even with the DFW at all! The whole thing was way too fishy.

Grisham quickly loaded the crystals into his trunk—and left for downtown. Once he was safely on the freeway, he figured he'd made a clean get away. Habit had him checking his mirrors. As far as he could tell he wasn't being followed. He made it to the bureau in record time, where he pulled into the roundabout, parking under the flags right in front of the main doors.

After opening the trunk to retrieve the crystals still wrapped in the linen, he headed for the lobby. "I'm here to see Agent McGovney," Grisham reported to the receptionist.

"You must be Agent Grisham," she replied, "He told me to expect you. I'll ring McGovney right away."

"Thanks."

"He'll be right down," she reported.

"I figured since its closing time my car would be okay in front there for a few minutes."

"You figured right," she replied, "I'll keep an eye on

it for you."

"Reg, good to see you again so soon," McGovney said as he entered the lobby. "I'd of never guessed we'd be seeing this much of you after retirement."

"Is there someplace we can talk for a minute?" Grisham asked.

Having overheard them, the receptionist responded, "Conference room B is open just around the corner. It's nice and private."

"That works," McGovney replied, "Is it locked?"

"Not sure—here's a key—just in case," she replied, handing over a large key ring with a single key on it.

Once they were secluded in the room, McGovney inquired, "What's up, Reg?"

"These youngsters are keeping me busy."

"Is this the same group that stumbled onto the drug operation?"

"One and the same," Grisham replied, reaching into his pocket. "Take a look at these!"

"Those aren't diamonds are they?" inquired McGovney.

"Sure are! About forty carats worth!"

"Where'd you get them?"

"You're not going to believe it," Grisham continued, "This is what the kids were after when they happened upon the drugs."

"Don't tell me you've been anywhere near that mine?" pleaded McGovney.

"No, no," Grisham replied. "The boys had been anchored outside of a cove along way from *The Sedgwick* the night before they stumbled onto the drugs."

"Oh yeah, Larsen told me about the anchor and the rising tide."

"The cove where they attempted to anchor is where the diamonds were. It's the *Legend of Crystal Cove—cove*!

These are the crystals of *Crystal Cove*!"

"Be serious! You found *Crystal Cove*?" asked McGovney in disbelief.

"I kid you not. It is a long, involved story, which I am more than happy to share with you, but I may have a bit of a situation."

"What's that?" asked McGovney.

"I was with the boys when we found the crystals. We stored them at my house over the weekend, and then today I took this linen of crystals to one of the jewelers the bureau uses downtown. We wanted to know for sure what we had. When I returned from the jeweler, two men from the DFW were on my doorstep—following an anonymous tip that I had been seen taking several bags of clams from Henderson Bay over the weekend. Apparently clams are out of season, but we weren't clamming. We were harvesting diamonds! As far as we knew, we were all alone. Whoever saw us made darn sure we didn't see them!"

"How many of these crystals do you have?" asked McGovney.

"There are five bags in my trunk—seven hundred thirty-seven in all!"

McGovney gave a nod, "*Now* I understand why you need access to the safe!"

"Whoever made the report must have taken the registration numbers from the boat. My guess is they used DFW to locate me."

"I see you haven't lost your instinct," said McGovney. "Let's take your car up to level four of the parking garage."

McGovney climbed in with Grisham. Security at the fourth level waved them through. They proceeded to the far end of the garage, parked the car, and carried the bags in through a doorway that led to where the bureau logged suspect evidence. Behind the counter was a large safe. McGovney tagged the bags, "McGovney—Private," wired them shut, entered them into the log, and handed them over to be placed in the safe.

Maybe I should accompany you back to your house just in case any of your suspicions prove out."

"Well, I hate to inconvenience you, but in light of the circumstances I would appreciate the company. If it's a false alarm, we can always get dinner and watch some football."

"Now you're talking! I'll follow you so you don't have to run me back to my car," said McGovney.

"Sounds good. I really appreciate this."

14

Illegal Entry

On the way back to Grisham's, McGovney phoned Grisham on his cell to tell him that he was famished and asked if he knew a good Chinese food place where they could stop for some take out. Grisham knew just the place. They made a quick stop and were on their way.

It was the 2nd of July. The Island Gang had gathered at Grisham's to plan their activities for the 4th.

Gary turned to Travis, "Hey, has your dad gone to the reservation yet?"

"Nope! But we're going—he promised he'd take us tomorrow."

Justin jumped in, "Count me in! I definitely want to go!"

"I'm going too," said Gary.

"And me," Curtis added.

Wendy couldn't figure out what the excitement was all about, "What's this about the reservation?"

"The Indian reservation. It's the best place to go for fireworks," replied Justin.

"Where is this reservation?"

"They're everywhere! But the one we go to is about 30 minutes away, out near Puyallup."

Wendy knew Puyallup. Her parents had taken her out by the state fairgrounds once. "Why would you go all the way out to Puyallup, there's a firework stand right in Gig Harbor?"

"Because the reservation is where you get the *good stuff*!" replied Travis.

Wendy thought her family usually had some pretty good fireworks, and they'd never been to a reservation. "So what's the good stuff?"

Justin started in, "Bottle rockets, firecrackers . . .

" . . . And if you want to blow anything up, they've got the goods out at the reservation," interjected Curtis.

"We've all got a little pyrotechnic in us," said Gary.

"Pyrotechnic?" questioned Wendy, "Sounds more like *pyromaniac* to me! You can count me *out* of blowing stuff up. The last thing I need is to be grounded for the rest of my childhood!"

Justin spoke up, "Good point. We don't want to get on the Major's black list. I guess we can resist blowing things up this year—at least while you're around."

"Hey, does anyone know what's up with Grisham and his special announcement?" Gary asked.

Grisham had told them that he had some news he'd be announcing at the 4th of July celebration. He wanted to make sure that all of The Island Gang would be in attendance.

"Maybe he's going to give us an award for helping the FBI bust those guys out at *The Sedgwick*," offered Wendy. "McGovney told Grisham they might not have discovered them without us."

"Boy, that would blow our folks away," replied Justin. "I wonder how they'll respond to our helping break a drug ring."

"I'd like to think they would praise our bravery," said Travis, "but something tells me they'll be madder than heck!"

"Particularly when they learn where *The Sedgwick*

is," added Curtis, "Maybe we can ask him to leave that part out!"

"It may have nothing to do with the mine," said Gary, "I overheard a phone conversation a couple of weeks ago where he was talking about trapping a vixen. Maybe he's got another one of his hunting trips planned."

"Isn't that a fox?" Wendy asked.

"I think so," replied Gary, "and there's no fox in his collection, so that would make sense."

"Maybe," Travis replied, adding his two cents, "but what would be the point in announcing a hunting trip to the islanders—*unless* he's decided to take us with him as a reward."

"That would be *great*!" Gary said, excited at the prospect. "I've dreamed of doing something like that ever since we first saw his trophies." Gary's mind drifted to a safari, chasing elephants, lions, and giraffes. He'd watched the scenes on TV and had no problem picturing himself right there on the African range.

Wendy brought him back to reality, "You do have an imagination! We'll just have to wait until the 4th to find out what his surprise really is. But if we end up on an exotic hunting trip—*I'll* be shocked."

Just then, Grisham and McGovney turned onto the driveway. Seeing the shed open, Grisham said, "Good timing! Looks like the guys are here now. I'm anxious to introduce you to them."

Grisham got out of the car and called everyone over. "I've got someone here I'd like you to meet. This is agent McGovney, the man that lined agent Larsen and *Chance* up for us. And this is Wendy, Gary, Travis, Justin, Curtis, and Tyler." Shadow let out a whimper. "I guess I better not leave Shadow out. He's as much a part of The Island Gang as any of them."

They each responded with, "Hey," as they were introduced.

"Well," McGovney responded, "I've sure heard a lot about you guys lately. Sounds like you're keeping busy."

"Dad always says 'the busier you are, the less trouble you'll get into,'" Gary replied.

"Sounds good in theory, but I'm beginning to question," McGovney said.

"What brings you to Raft Island?" Gary asked.

McGovney knew that Grisham hadn't had the chance to tell them about the DFW folks, and it wasn't his place to break that news. "Well, I hadn't visited out here for some time, and . . ."

Grisham interrupted, "I appreciate your thoughtfulness McGovney, but we can tell these guys what's going on. They might even prove helpful."

They all gathered around.

"Tell us what?" Travis asked.

"Did any of you see anything suspicious out at the cove?" Grisham asked.

Curtis got that puzzled look on his face and muttered, "How is a question an answer to a question? I don't get it!"

"Let me back up a little," said Grisham. They could tell by his posture and tone that he was concerned about something. "I told you I was going to take some of the crystals to the jeweler today. When I got back, there were a couple of men here at the house. They said they were from the Department of Fish and Wildlife, and their car confirmed that, but I'm still suspicious."

"What did they want?" asked Travis.

"They were here because someone filed a complaint against us for clamming out of season—said they spotted us taking several large bags of clams out of a cove on the other side of the bay."

"What did you tell them?" asked Gary.

"I told them that we hadn't taken any clams."

Wendy put the pieces together, "Someone was watching us?"

"Sounds like it. And whoever made the report must have been close enough to see the bags and get the registration numbers off of the boat. That's the only way DFW could have located me. The question is, do they really believe we were poaching clams, or do they know something about that cove and the diamonds?"

"So they *are* real diamonds?" Justin asked.

"They sure are," replied Grisham. "*Authentic raw diamonds!*"

"We're rich!" hollered Curtis.

Gary and Travis ran toward each other and jumped as they gave each other high ten and chest bump.

"It appears they're pretty valuable," confirmed Grisham.

"Someone's after the crystals?" asked Curtis.

"We better get them moved," exclaimed Gary, realizing the danger of having them at Grisham's.

"I already did," Grisham replied. "They're secure in a safe downtown at FBI headquarters. I didn't have time to discuss it with you. I had to act quickly."

"What if they saw you move them, and followed you downtown," asked Curtis.

"I'm sure I wasn't tailed, besides, they're in a safe at headquarters."

"You think someone actually knows we found them?" asked Justin

"It's possible that others figured out the location of the cove, but were unsuccessful finding the underwater cave. Maybe they were watching the location to see if someone else would have better luck. I need to know if you guys saw anyone while we were out there."

The Island Gang talked amongst themselves for the

next several minutes. They had no recollection of seeing any other people, or boats for that matter. But they were so caught up in the adventure of it all—they agreed it was possible they could have missed something.

Tyler had started to wander deeper into the shed while Grisham was talking. He caught their attention when he began to chuckle, talking to himself as he went.

"What's up Tyler?" Gary asked.

"Nothing," Tyler replied.

"C'mon," Curtis scolded, "whenever you start this—talking to yourself, it's always something. What's up?"

"The guy by the rocks," replied Tyler. "He was so funny."

"What guy—by what rocks?" demanded Curtis! "This is important! Tell us!"

"This guy—was climbing out of the water, and then he looked up, saw me, and went right back in. I think he slipped."

"Then what happened?" Grisham asked.

"That's all. He just went back underwater."

"He never came back up?" asked Curtis.

"Nope!"

"You never saw him come back up for air?" asked Grisham.

"Nope!"

"Tyler, I need you to think real hard about this," said Grisham. "Did the man have an air tank on his back?"

"He had—like what you had on—a suit and stuff."

"This must have happened out at the point, before I got there," said Curtis. Maybe that's what got Shadow's attention!"

"He must have had air," said Grisham. "This must be the guy that called DFW. I wonder what he's up to. Agent McGovney and I will make sure the house is secure. We'll have to keep a close eye on things for the next couple of days. If someone is after the crystals, they won't wait long to surface."

Agent McGovney interrupted, and with a wink of his eye said, "In the meantime, our Chinese is getting cold."

The Island Gang took the hint—it was dinnertime. They headed home. McGovney hadn't been to Grisham's in years, and as they walked from the shed to the house he remembered what he liked most about Grisham's location. "You do have the view out here, Reg. You sure you don't want a permanent houseguest? I could get used to this!"

Grisham had a response, but not one that he was ready to make public just yet. He'd promised to make his announcement during the festivities of the 4th. He held his tongue and joined McGovney as he walked up onto the deck and looked out across the bay. From the deck, they entered through the side door, which took them directly into the kitchen. Grisham got a couple of plates from the cupboard, and they ate their dinner.

Conversation over dinner focused on memories of their time together in the bureau. They reminisced about the good times, laughed over the blunders, and remembered those who had lost their lives on assignment.

Having finished dinner, they decided to retire to the family room.

"See if you can find the game on TV while I put a few things away," Grisham ordered.

McGovney had no sooner left the kitchen than he noticed things out of place in the entryway. "Reg you'd better come have a look!"

Someone had clearly gone through things in Grisham's house, leaving the kitchen untouched.

"Oh my gosh!" exclaimed Grisham, "I had a feeling something was up!"

It was clear from the condition of the molding on the inside of the front door that it had been forced open. The closet in the entry had been ransacked, along with book-cases, the hutch in the family room, and closets and drawers in one of the bedrooms.

"Makes you wonder why they stopped here," Grisham said, questioning the logic. "Why would they go to the effort of breaking in, and not search the entire house?"

"They obviously didn't find what they were look-ing for," replied McGovney. "Good thing you followed your impression to move the crystals!"

It was tempting to pick up the mess, but they decided to leave it until they could get someone on the scene to dust for prints. By the looks of things, forensics wouldn't find much. Every indication was that the perpetrators knew what they were doing, which means they would have taken proper precautions. It was as if they were making a statement by leaving the mess.

After a rough search, Grisham could find nothing missing. He was convinced that whoever had been there was after the crystals. "Now you see why I was uneasy."

"I'll file a report tomorrow," offered McGovney, "and I'll get someone from forensics down here early in the morn-ing. Do you want to get out of here for the night?"

"No," Grisham replied, "I think I'll stay put. I'll make sure it's locked up and set the alarm. But in any case, they won't come back while I'm home. They don't want a con-frontation, they're just looking for the loot."

McGovney walked the house with Grisham as he completed the rounds. They got to the back bedroom to find the window open and screen pushed out. "So, this is why they didn't search the entire house," exclaimed Grisham, "Take a look!"

There was obviously a hurried exit through the bed-room window. The screen was torn and sitting out on the deck. Marks on the wall indicated they hadn't taken their time getting out.

"That's puzzling," replied Grisham, "how could they have made that mess without making noise. We'd have heard this racket—even from the kitchen!"

"The kids either scared him off, or perhaps the intruder was prompted to leave when we pulled up," concluded McGovney. "Noise from this room wouldn't have been heard out in the shed."

Grisham and McGovney took the back door out to the porch. In the planter just below the raised deck, Grisham's flashlight revealed a couple of branches that had been broken off of one of the rhododendrons.

"There's the escape path," McGovney pointed out. They headed right down to the beach! Do you suppose they had a boat?"

"That would explain how they got away without being spotted," answered Grisham. "The shoreline is private property in both directions. Maybe one of my neighbors saw something."

"I'll have an agent knock on a few doors," McGovney replied, "People should be alerted to the fact that there's been a break-in. I know it's remote, but there's always the chance that this had nothing to do with *Crystal Cove*. Either way, a heightened sense of awareness can't hurt."

"Good point," agreed Grisham.

15

4ᵀᴴ Of July

The next day passed quickly. The boys went with Travis' father to the reservation to get the *good stuff*. Wendy stayed home to help her family with preparations for the following day. Her mom had volunteered the family to be on the food committee in hopes of becoming better acquainted with neighbors.

Grisham's immediate neighbors were alerted as to the trouble at Grisham's. Nobody had seen a thing, so they weren't any help with the break-in, but at least they now knew to take appropriate precaution to keep their homes safe. At daybreak, Grisham had taken a walk down to the water while forensics scoured his house for clues. There were no obvious signs of a boat having been there. He worried that the intruders might return since they hadn't found what they were after. On the other hand, they couldn't possibly believe the crystals would still be in the house, even if they had been the first time. In that sense, he felt fairly safe. Nonetheless, he kept his field glasses nearby, keeping frequent watch over the shoreline and perimeter of his yard.

That evening, the boys, with the exception of Tyler, got together for their weekly scout meeting. Sometimes Tyler joined them and other times he didn't, it just depended on his mood. While the troop was making final plans for the next hike, The Island Gang boys were at the back of the room busily making plans for the 4th.

"What time are you guys going to the All Saints Center tomorrow?" Travis asked.

The All Saints Center was a common area of Raft Island that could be scheduled for use by any of the residents, and was the gathering place for most island events. It had a lodge, a couple of outbuildings used as dorms for youth camps, several acres of grounds, and some waterfront with a dock and a couple of rope swings that swung out over the water. When the tide was out there was room to walk the shore, but there wasn't an actual beach like down at the boat ramp. There was a large, sloped grassy area between the shore and the lodge that had several groupings of apple trees, as well as setups for a variety of outdoor activities—among which were badminton, croquet, and volleyball. At the top of the hill alongside the lodge was an outdoor basketball court, which doubled as the launch pad for fireworks. Off to one side of the lodge was a swing set and big toy for the little guys. Up on the deck that extended around two sides of the lodge were a couple of ping-pong tables. The All Saints Center was outfitted to accommodate most everyone's interests, and residents looked forward to their gatherings at the facility.

Begrudgingly, Curtis replied, "I'll probably be down there all day. Mom thinks she's in charge, which means we've been drafted to be her slaves for the day."

"I'll head down early and give you a hand," volunteered Travis.

"We have guests coming tomorrow," Justin replied, "so I'm not sure what time I'll get there, but we're coming—guests and all."

Gary was thinking that it would be nice to arrange a sleepover with one of the guys so that he could get out of his chores and get there early himself. Listening to the guys talk, the only appealing option was Travis' house, but he was doubtful his folks would go along with it. They already told him to plan on going as a family. "Mom said we're going as a family, which means you'll see us when we get there."

Travis added, "I hear Tyler's dad is going to play pyrotechnic again. That means my dad will join him, and the good stuff will be cleverly mixed in with the junk from town."

Gary spoke up, "We need to get together sometime during the festivities to make plans for the crystals . . ."

"You mean plans for the *money* we're going to get," Justin interjected.

"Good point," Gary continued, "and we need more sailing lessons. We need to log plenty of hours so that we are ready for the San Juan's next year."

"Like our parents are really going to let us go to the San Juan's," exclaimed Curtis.

"If we have Grisham with us, they'll let us," replied Gary. "And so far, having him along has been good luck."

Justin asserted, "We'll need his treasure box for sure! Curtis says there are all sorts of legends in there."

"What do you mean 'all sorts of legends'?" asked Travis.

"Tell them, Curtis!"

"Well, you guys remember all of the folders, right?"

"Sure," Gary answered. "They had maps of all the different island chains of the Pacific Northwest."

"Yeah, all the way up to Alaska," added Travis, "What of it?"

"While you guys were busily engrossed in the DMI folder, I found papers that listed a bunch of legends," replied Curtis. "I didn't think much of it. At the time, I figured it was all—just stories—the same way I felt about *Crystal Cove*. Needless to say, my opinion has changed!"

"Did you recognize any of them?" asked Travis.

"Nope," Curtis replied. "They weren't familiar to

me."

"Do you remember the names? Maybe one of us will recognize them!" asked Gary.

"I don't remember all of them—one had something to do with Walking Stick, others were *Legend of the Orcas*, and *Legend of the Masks*—there was a drawing of one of those ancient face masks carved in wood. That's all I remember for sure."

"We need to get to the treasure box!" Gary stated emphatically.

Talk about another overdose of adrenaline—and here it was, bedtime. Chances of getting much sleep weren't very good.

It was finally the 4th, and anticipation of the evening's events was high.

Gary was up early. He snuck out of the house and headed for Grisham's. He had phoned Travis—they were going after the treasure box. Gary made sure he had his school ID card, just in case they needed some plastic to jimmy the upstairs door. He met Travis at the head of Grisham's driveway.

"What are the chances it will be unlocked?" asked Travis.

"Doesn't matter. I have a key," replied Gary, holding up his ID card.

"Gotcha!"

The door was locked as anticipated, but the ID card did the trick.

"We're in! Now where's that box?" asked Gary.

They looked high and low, but no box.

"Grisham must have it in the house," stated Travis.

Suddenly, a ringing phone startled them! They

hadn't even noticed a phone the last time they were there. Across the room, surrounded by clutter on the third shelf of a bookcase was a phone. One of the lines lit up as the ring continued. Gary walked toward the phone. He got to it just as the ringing stopped, and quickly picked up the handset. He looked back across the room at Travis and gave the *quiet* signal, placing his finger to his lips. Travis remained silent, but his eyes were about to bug out of his head! He couldn't believe Gary was going to eavesdrop!

"Good morning Reg! Just thought I'd wake you up and wish you a happy 4th of July."

Grisham knew the voice. It was McGovney. "You'll have to try a little earlier if you want to wake me," replied Grisham. "I've been up for hours."

"A bit nervous about tonight are you?" asked McGovney.

"Not really. But I do have plenty to take care of beforehand. Are you and Jean coming?"

"Are you kidding? We wouldn't miss this for the world!"

"Say, is there any news I can give The Island Gang tonight? I'll be recognizing them this evening, and it would be wonderful if I could mention some specifics."

"Not yet," asserted McGovney. "We have a loose end, and we believe this guy is a major player. That rail truck disappears into a tunnel up north. We haven't been able to figure out where the tunnel goes. The truck eventually comes back out the same end of the tunnel it went in—they either meet someone inside, or the tunnel leads to a drop location. The tunnel isn't on any maps. We're trying to plant a man on the inside—we need a little more time."

"I understand. See you this evening."

Gary waited for two clicks before hanging up the phone, and then related the conversation to Travis. They were disappointed at not finding the treasure box, but excited that Grisham planned to recognize The Island Gang. They agreed to keep Grisham's conversation to themselves, and just act surprised later that evening.

Down at the All Saints Center, Curtis was trying to stay motivated. Chairs and tables had to be arranged both inside and out, as the evening's festivities would be carried out in both places. With the warm weather, they preferred to be outdoors as much as possible, but as often as not, the 4th was plagued with at least intermittent rain—so they had to be prepared. They brought out the large barbeque that was custom built to accommodate a crowd, and set it up away from the serving tables. Fourth of July decorations were everywhere.

Curtis' mom would've been happy if they could have gathered the apples that littered the lawn in various parts of the property, but it was no use—there were literally hundreds of them. She knew that meant there would be an apple fight. But there was at least one apple fight every year, and other than the year Tyler's younger brother had to get five stitches in his head, apple fights had been fairly uneventful.

By 4:30 in the afternoon, people began showing up. There was no paved parking, just a field that had been lightly covered with gravel adjacent to the front lawn that had been designated as such. Some of the older boys were given the assignment to act as lot attendants. Tall stakes strung with yellow tape marked off the parking area. As folks got out of their cars, they were given a rundown on the evening's events. "Enjoy food and fun until 7:30. At 7:30, we'll gather in the lodge for announcements and entertainment."

Everyone knew the center of entertainment would be the Island Band that consisted largely of the Livingston family, local islanders. They were actually pretty good.

The dad and older brother played electric guitar, a younger brother was on drums, and their mom switched between bass guitar and bongos. There were a couple of guys from off the island—one was amazing on keyboards, and the other played acoustic guitar and was lead singer for most pieces. Several others took turns singing and shaking tambourines or huaraches. They had quite the sound system and were always fun to listen to.

Gary finished his chores and arrived at the All Saints Center early, but not before getting into an argument with his mom. He needed a little time alone to blow off steam before interacting with others, so he headed straight down to the water for a walk. He rehearsed the argument over and over in his mind, trying to figure out how he could have handled it differently. He didn't like fighting with his mother, but sometimes these lectures and accusations seemed to come out of nowhere—he just couldn't figure it out.

Wendy had been helping her mother set the food out when Gary arrived. She'd seen Gary head for the water and decided to follow him. She lagged behind, curious what he was up to. As she watched from behind an old cedar, she could see that something was troubling him. He paced the shore, stopping now and then to skip a rock across the water. He was talking to himself, but she was too far away to catch the conversation.

Then while his back was to her, she quickly scurried down to the water sneaking right up behind him, "Boo!"

Gary tried not to let on that she had startled him, "Oh—it's you. What's up?"

"I saw you down here, and thought I'd come say hello. Is everything all right?"

"Yeah—I guess. I had a little tiff with my mom. Sometimes I'm just going along doing my thing, when all of a sudden something sets her off! I can't figure it out."

Wendy could relate. She had experienced similar

confrontations at her house. But regardless, it seemed only right to defend her gender. Chuckling, she said, "Women are supposed to be complicated, that's part of the intrigue."

Not sure whether to be amused or consoled, Gary replied, "*Is that right?*"

"Yep! Dad told me all about it. He says the day he figured it out marked one of the best days of his life! Now he can usually tell when mom just needs to rave for a while. He calmly hears her out, agrees with her, and then goes on about his business."

It was Gary's turn to chuckle, "So your dad has it all figured out, huh?"

"I don't think he has it all figured out, but he seems to know when it's time to lose his opinion and just listen. It made things better at our house."

"I don't know if I can do that. When you feel like you're being attacked, it's awful hard not to defend yourself!"

"Yeah, but if you learn to listen quietly, then say what you know she wants to hear, the lecture will pass quicker. It takes my mom awhile, but she often figures out when she has blown things out of proportion and comes back with an apology."

"Sounds like it's worth a try," conceded Gary. "Thanks for the advice—I guess."

Just then they saw Tyler climbing down the ladder on the far side of the pier. They knew he'd walk the shore gathering seashells, stones, and small pieces of driftwood—like he always did. The pier sat at the far end of the property. It was familiar territory to Tyler, and he had plenty of room to wander without getting into trouble.

Wendy and Gary were further down the shore near the rope swings. So as not to be seen, Gary grabbed Wendy's hand and pulled her along as he ran up toward a tree to which one of the rope swings were tied. He had grabbed her hand without giving it any thought. As they got to the tree, he noticed it again—that feeling he'd had when their hands had touched on Agent Larsen's boat. A rush of emotion passed through his body. His heart was racing, but it was different from being out of breath. This sensation was new—just since Wendy had come into the picture. It was a good feeling, yet at the same time—a little uncomfortable. He wondered if Wendy was experiencing the same thing, but was too embarrassed to ask. He let go of her hand and they continued walking side-by-side up toward the food.

As they were getting something to eat, Justin and Travis came over, "Hey, where have you guys been?"

"Down by the water," Gary replied. "Did you guys just get here?"

"No," Justin answered, "we've been up on the deck playing ping-pong. My sister wants us to join the older guys for volleyball after we eat."

"Sounds like fun," said Wendy. "Count me in."

That was all the encouragement Gary needed, "Me too."

"Anyone seen Curtis?" asked Travis.

"Not yet," Gary replied, "but he was here early to set up. I'm sure he's around somewhere."

Grisham had been to the All Saints Center earlier in the day, and told Curtis all about the break-in. Curtis found the others while they were eating, and brought them up to speed.

After listening to Curtis relate the entire story, Travis exclaimed, "Can you believe it? Someone *is* actually trying to steal the crystals!"

"Good thing they'll never find them," replied Justin.

"If we didn't have Mr. Grisham, we'd be in a world of hurt!" added Travis, thinking back to the times Grisham had bailed them out.

Wendy was thinking back to when the guys were

first trying to make him an offer on his boat. They thought he was going to be an old, gruff, insensitive ogre. Now they knew him to be a caring, sensitive man that enjoyed helping them. She hoped they had learned not to judge a book by its cover. It brought her a sense of satisfaction to know that she had played a part in bringing them together.

They finished eating, played several games of volleyball, a round of croquet, threw Frisbee, and had a brief apple fight. Time passed quickly, and at 7:15 the announcement came reminding everyone that it was time to gather in the lodge.

The band was warming up with a couple of Beatles tunes as people entered. After their warm up, Mr. Livingston approached the microphone. "We'd like to welcome you all out to Raft Island's annual 4th of July celebration. It's always nice to take a break from our hectic lives and enjoy some down time. We'd like to introduce the newest addition to the island." Wendy's family stood as they were recognized. "We also have a very special guest here this evening."

"Oh no, not this again," Curtis whispered to The Island Gang. "Every time he announces a special guest, someone walks in dressed like Elvis and tries to dazzle us with their impersonation. I wonder who the unlucky sucker is this year."

"Before the introduction, we'd like to dedicate this next song to our guest."

It was Bette Midler's "The Rose."

Throughout the song, eyes searched the audience trying to determine to whom the dedication belonged.

At the conclusion of the song Mr. Livingston said, "Rose, would you please stand. Ladies and gentlemen, I would like to present, Rose."

Rose was an elderly lady in a beautiful dress that perfectly identified the patriotic occasion for which they were gathered.

"Who's she?" Travis asked.

"She's seated at Mr. Grisham's table," replied Wendy. "Must be a friend of his."

No one seemed to know for sure.

"Mr. Grisham, would you please come forward and properly introduce Rose?"

"What's going on here?" Gary asked in a puzzled tone, "Is this Grisham's surprise?"

Grisham stood and made his way to the front of the room.

"I am indebted to the island community for making me feel welcome here for so many years," he started off. "Most of you know of my terrible loss this past year. I was married to Lucille for forty-three years before multiple sclerosis claimed her life. I will always love her. If I were to have gone before her, I would have wanted her to seek companionship, and I'm sure that she understands my need to do the same. I have asked Rose to be my wife. She has accepted, and the wedding will take place August 1st, right here in the lodge. You are all invited!"

There was a standing ovation. After it quieted down, Grisham invited Rose to join him up front as he continued, "I didn't expect that this day would come so soon, if at all. I was in quite a state of turmoil and depression at the passing of Lucille. There for awhile, my life was totally out of control, and while I didn't think so then, I know now that I was at a loss as to where to begin to put things back together."

You could have heard a pin drop. Silence reflected the respect of those in attendance.

"Since this community has everything to do with the turn around that has taken place in my life, I've asked if I might say a few words," Grisham continued, "First, most of you know that I spent my career in the employ of the FBI. During my thirty years with the bureau, though the majority of my assignments were domestic, I was constantly aware of events taking place around the world. I learned to have a great appreciation for the United States of America. You can search the nations of the earth, but you'll not find one with a greater sense of community than the USA."

Another round of applause followed.

Having appropriately acknowledged the purpose of their gathering, Grisham now continued with the introduction of his fiancé. "Rose suffered the loss of her faithful husband this past year. Knowing that everyone will want to hear our story, we've decided to eliminate the possibility of repeating ourselves 20 or 30 times by sharing it with you now."

Rose leaned toward the microphone and took the lead, "We actually met while we were nursing our spouses through the terrible final months of their lives at *Le Chateau*. My husband and Lucille had favorite places in the lovely indoor gardens where Reg and I would take them on walks. We occasionally passed each other in the halls or the gardens. Other than exchanging pleasantries, we were both too busy caring for our spouses to really notice one another."

Grisham picked up the story, "*Le Chateau* called a month or so ago upon discovering that I had left a few things behind. When I went to pick the items up, Rose was there delivering a bouquet to the staff. We remembered meeting in the garden and a conversation ensued. That led to lunch— and here we are!"

There was another standing ovation. When the crowd finished, Grisham asked The Island Gang to stand and come to the front. They were making their way up when Curtis realized that Tyler wasn't with them. "Has anyone seen Tyler?" he asked.

"I wonder if he's still down by the water," replied Wendy. "Gary and I saw him down there earlier."

"I'll go get him," replied Curtis.

The rest of The Island Gang worked their way around

the crowd and up to the front.

The applause quieted, and Rose continued, "I'm meeting these youngsters for the first time, but I've sure heard a lot about them." She turned to The Island Gang, "Please introduce yourselves."

Grisham saw that two of them were missing and asked, "Curtis and Tyler, are you out there?"

Justin was standing closest to Grisham, and leaned over to whisper in Grisham's ear, "Curtis went for Tyler, he was last seen down by the pier."

"It seems the two of them are occupied at the moment," Grisham announced, "but I've just been assured that they'll be along shortly.

Tyler's parents keyed in to the announcement," but knowing Tyler, they decided to wait patiently for Curtis to return before becoming too alarmed.

As they introduced themselves, Rose took each one by the shoulders and studied them as if she were memorizing their every feature. After they stated their name, she gave each of them a big hug and thanked them for being a friend to Grisham.

Grisham leaned toward the microphone, "Rose and I have decided that we'd like the boys to be in tuxes at the wedding. They'll all be best men. We'd like Wendy to be our maid of honor and ring bearer. Will you do it?" he asked, sending a wink Wendy's way.

They agreed, and then Gary reached for the microphone and asked, "I have one question. What is a vixen?"

Grisham got a puzzled look on his face, and then realized that the boys must have overheard one of his conversations. "So you've been doing a little eavesdropping, have you?" he replied, blushing at the thought of Rose figuring out that he had referred to her in such terms.

The exchange evoked a round of laughter. People were still laughing as Curtis burst back into the room, "*I can't find Tyler anywhere!"*

This wasn't the first time this had happened. Islanders had known Tyler to wander off on occasion and had formed search parties more than once. They knew that Tyler's parents were instantly nervous.

Mr. Livingston reached for a microphone, "Ladies and gentlemen, this will go much quicker if we take just a minute to get organized. Would those with cell phones please come forward and give your numbers. We'll stay in touch as we search the island. I'm sure we'll find him in no time."

Quickly, groups were formed and people were headed in various directions. Tyler had never wandered off of the island. He understood that was not permissible. With this number of people looking, he was sure to be found soon.

Fearing the worst, Grisham got McGovney and headed for his place. Rose and some of the other elderly remained at the lodge, in case Tyler should happen to show up. Tyler's parents dialed 911. An island neighbor who was on the Gig Harbor police force was on duty and was sent to the island.

Gary, aware of the break-in, used the excuse that crazy things sometimes happen on the 4th, and talked his dad into heading for the bridge where they could check cars leaving the island to make sure Tyler hadn't been abducted.

The message light was flashing on Grisham's phone as he and McGovney entered the house. Pushing the play button they heard, "We have the boy—he's safe. He will not be harmed. We'll contact you at midnight to make arrangements to exchange him for the crystals."

"Oh my word!" exclaimed Grisham, "They have Tyler!"

Grisham and McGovney listened to the message several times, hoping for clues. There was something—an odd noise in the background.

"Sounds like they could be on a boat," said McGovney.

"Is there any chance of getting a chopper out here?" Grisham asked.

"Let me see what I can do."

Grisham didn't know what to do next. Should he call off the search? He knew that Tyler probably wasn't on the island, but he didn't want to explain the whole story to the islanders right at the moment. He had to get to Tyler's parents. He couldn't leave them in the dark!

Grisham called Mr. Livingston's cell, "Rich, its Reg. I need you to get in touch with Tyler's folks and have them meet at my place as soon as possible."

Anxious for the news Livingston asked, "Have you found Tyler?"

Not wanting to alarm the entire island and ruin plans for the evening, Grisham measured his words, "We've located him."

Livingston wasn't exactly sure what to make of Grisham's response, but replied, "I'll give them a call and have them head your way. We'll call off the search."

"Thanks," replied Grisham.

McGovney came in from the other room, "I have a chopper on standby, but I haven't ordered them out here yet. We should wait for a solid clue before putting it in the air. We need to think this through—we don't want to aggravate the kidnappers. Do we have any idea where they might be headed?"

"None. Must be the same guys that ransacked the house the other night," stated Grisham, remembering that as best as they could figure, the intruders left by boat.

"The diver Tyler spotted must be in on this, he's the only one that could have taken the registration numbers off of the boat," lamented Grisham, "If only we had spotted another boat, or anything out of the ordinary out at the cove.

We have nothing to go on!"

"We'll have to wait for the phone call," replied McGovney. "In the meantime, we should get the city cops over here and fill them in on the information we have.

There was a knock at the door. "That's probably Tyler's folks," Grisham said, "I'll get it."

"Mr. and Mrs. Webb, c'mon in. I'd like to introduce you to agent McGovney of the FBI. Agent McGovney, meet Tyler's parents."

"It's bad news, isn't it?" Mrs. Webb blurted out.

"I am sorry to say that Tyler has been abducted and is being held ransom," replied Grisham.

Mrs. Webb began sobbing immediately, "I knew it was bad! *Ransom*! We don't have any money! What is going on?"

Grisham shared the events surrounding the crystals. "The abductors left a message on my answering machine. They said that they would call back at midnight to make arrangement to trade Tyler for the crystals."

"We have to wait until midnight?" Mrs. Webb questioned. Then in a pleading yet confident tone, she stated, "You will make the trade?"

"Of course we will," assured Agent McGovney.

It was 9:25 p.m. With the sun finally sinking behind the Olympics—it was time for the fireworks to begin. Shadow saw the fireworks being laid out and immediately split. Something about dogs and fireworks—it's not a good combination.

By about 10:00 p.m., the fireworks were over. The Island Gang headed over to Tyler's to check on him. They got to Tyler's, but nobody was home.

"Where do you suppose they are?" asked Wendy.

"Mr. Livingston said they'd gone home for the evening," replied Justin.

"Maybe Tyler got to feeling better and they've gone

down to the beach for the good stuff!" said Curtis. "Tyler can be relentless if he doesn't get his way."

"No way!" Travis exclaimed, "They know we all want to be there for the reservation stuff. Something is up. Their cars aren't even here!"

"We should check down at the beach anyway," added Justin.

They were within eyeshot of Grisham's just in time to see a police car pull into his driveway. "Did you guys see that?" Travis asked.

They broke into a sprint for Grisham's.

As they rounded the bend in Grisham's drive, they saw all of the cars.

"Something's up!" Travis exclaimed.

Shadow had joined them and led the way down the drive. The men who had just pulled up were on the doorstep. The Island Gang ran down the drive so they would be there when the door opened.

"*Hold it right there!*" shouted one of the policemen, as both officers quickly turned, drawing their guns.

The Island Gang froze in their steps—wondering why these guys were so jumpy. One of policemen shone a bright light in their direction.

Shadow was freaking out. "It's okay, boy. Come! Sit!" Gary commanded.

Grisham answered the door to see the police with weapons drawn, shining flashlights on the boys.

"We're just here to see Mr. Grisham," Gary stated.

"What's going on?" asked Grisham.

"We were waiting for you to answer the door, when we heard voices and footsteps running down the drive," answered one of the officers.

"These are The Island Gang boys," said Grisham, introducing the boys, "they're no threat."

"What's up?" asked Gary.

"Come on in—we'll fill you in," offered Grisham.

Inside they found Rose, Agent McGovney, and Mr. and Mrs. Webb.

"Where's Tyler?" asked Wendy

"Tyler's missing," answered McGovney.

"Again?" replied Curtis.

"Not again," Mr. Webb cut in, "still!"

Grisham spoke up, "Did Curtis tell you about the break-in?"

"Yeah," Travis answered, "do *they* have Tyler?"

Grisham nodded, "McGovney and I came here when the search for Tyler began. I just had a feeling there might be trouble. There was a message on my machine. They're going to call at midnight to arrange an exchange—Tyler for the crystals."

"So Tyler has been missing this whole time?" asked Justin.

"He's being held ransom?" asked Curtis.

"That's right," replied McGovney.

Mrs. Webb's eyes were still moist. Curtis went over and gave his aunt a hug. "Don't worry—they'll get him. Everything will be okay."

It was 11:15. Forty-five minutes before the call would come. The phone was wired. They were hoping for a trace.

"Where are the crystals?" asked Gary.

McGovney responded, "I had some of them delivered here to the house. Whoever we are dealing with evidently saw you guys out in the cove. We'll get these guys, and you'll have all of the crystals back."

"That's not important," replied Travis, "I mean, I hope you catch the guys and all—but Tyler comes first!"

16

Rescue At Dead Man's

It was precisely midnight when the call came. Grisham answered, "Hello?"

"Do you have the crystals?"

"I do."

"We'll be on the south shore of Dead Man's at 1:00 a.m. Come alone or you'll never see the kid alive again!"

"How am I supposed to . . . ?"

"Look, we don't care how you get there! Just be there—alone—with the crystals at 1:00 a.m. sharp!" click.

"No luck with the trace," said McGovney, "they weren't on the phone anywhere near long enough. But—these guys are either new at this game, or they are cleverer than we think. How do they plan on evading us at Dead Man's?"

"It's too dangerous to send a bunch of guys out there," Grisham spoke up. We have no idea who we're dealing with. We need to comply with their request. I go alone."

"I agree. We'll make absolutely sure Tyler is in no danger. Is there a boat we can use?" asked McGovney

"Our boat is in the marina," replied Mr. Webb. "You can use it."

"Reg, let's step outside for minute," said McGovney motioning toward the door, "we need to cover a few things."

McGovney and Grisham stepped out to where agents Strong and Fisher were waiting with officers Iselin and Dexter of the local police force. "Strong, I want you and Fish on that island ASAP!" exclaimed McGovney. "Grisham says you'll just about be able to walk your way to Dead

Man's. There's a spit extending from Dead Man's that nearly reaches the southwest corner of Raft Island during extreme low tides. Lucky for us, a −3.1 tide peaked a couple of hours ago—the spit is still exposed. I need you in full black—I want you invisible!" McGovney stated emphatically. "They'll have a lookout—you mustn't be spotted! Watch for Grisham coming around the far end of Raft Island. He'll be alone in the boat, but I'll be in tow—don't worry Reg, I'll be in dive gear, well below the surface. They'll never suspect a thing." Turning to Strong and Fisher he continued, "I'll let loose as he rounds the south end of Dead Man's, making my way to the island unnoticed. Reg, as soon as you make the exchange, I want you and Tyler to get out of there. If need be, we'll call in the helicopter, but not until after you and Tyler are well out of the way."

McGovney continued as he handed wireless ear buds and transmitters to Fish and Strong, "These are all set on the appropriate frequency. There will be a transmitter on the boat with Grisham. We'll be able to hear everything that goes on. Iselin and Dexter, ever used infrared scopes?"

"You bet!"

"Who's our marksman?" McGovney asked.

"That'd be me," answered Dexter.

"Hey—wait just a minute," Iselin protested, "I know how to handle a rifle!"

"Do you have weapons with you?"

The response was affirmative on both counts.

"Good," McGovney replied, handing each of them a large, hard-sided case, a set of ear buds and receivers, "Take these. Get in position to where you can see the spit and maintain watch of Dead Man's plateau. Like I said, they'll have a lookout—he'll be up top. We need to know his position right away. Stay alert—if the boys need backup, they'll let you know. "Lots of communication guys—no action until you know Tyler and Reg are clear of the island. Let's go!

We're going to take these guys down!"

Fish and Strong donned their ear buds and quickly got dressed in black. Dexter and Iselin headed out through the thick stand of trees off the back of Grisham's property, crossing the yards of several neighbors in the process in search of the ideal location to accomplish their task. They all listened in as McGovney completed his instructions. "The tide is going to require us to circle the island as we leave the marina. Reg, how long will it take to circle all the way around the island?"

"About 20 minutes."

They are undoubtedly aware of the low tide and will be watching for us to come around the island. I want to take them on the beach at Dead Man's. Any questions guys?"

"We'll have the position of their lookout shortly," assured Dexter. He and Iselin had just a short hike from Grisham's to where they had a view of Dead Man's and the spit. "Strong, let us know when you and Fish get close to the spit. We'll have things scoped out."

"10–4," replied agent Strong.

The final radio was given to Police Chief Knight. "Monitor the line," directed McGovney. "Let the folks inside know when Tyler is safe. It could get a little dicey out there—and I . . ."

" . . . Got it!" Knight said, interrupting McGovney mid-sentence, "I'll only share the good news."

McGovney couldn't tell if it was just Knight's personality to be gruff or if he begrudged the fact that the bureau had taken control of the operation that was geographically in his jurisdiction.

"If we need the helicopter, I'll ask you to contact Agent Willard. He's standing by at this number," said McGovney, handing Knight a slip of paper. Knight gave a nod.

Iselin and Dexter were set up in short order. The vegetation they were in was so thick they'd never be spotted.

They had clear view of Dead Man's. Just their luck, there were a couple of kids hanging out on the spit. "What do you suppose these guys are doing out here at this hour?" asked Dexter.

"Who knows, but they might actually make a good decoy," commented Iselin.

"Good point," replied Dexter, as he got on the radio, warning Strong and Fisher of the kids' presence.

"Yeah, we see them," Fisher answered, "We'll try to get past them without drawing attention."

McGovney and Grisham were at the boat. It took just minutes for McGovney to get into his dry suit and get a rope tethered to the boat below the waterline.

Moments later, Dexter was on the radio, "We've got the lookout. He's in the large tree at the far end of the plateau."

The lookout was sporadically moving his field glasses from one view to another. "Looks like he's watching the marina and the far end of Raft Island's north shore," stated Dexter.

"Doesn't make any sense," commented Iselin, "he has to know there's no access from the marina!"

"Maybe he's too deep into the island to see the effects of the tide."

"You've got a point," replied Iselin, "The good news is, from his vantage point there's no way he'll be able to see McGovney go ashore."

McGovney was riding in the boat with Grisham until they got to the north end of Raft Island, where he would get into the water before they were in view of the lookout. He would then be towed the rest of the way to Dead Man's. "Good work guys," replied McGovney, "and thanks for the heads up! Reg, once I'm in the water you'll have to slow her down a little, but we've got plenty of time."

Dexter continued to watch Strong and Fisher, while

Iselin kept an eye on the kids hanging out on the spit. They began wandering from the spit—it looked as though they were preparing to go for a swim. The first kid dove.

"Did you see that?" asked Iselin. "Watch the water as that second kid goes in!"

"What in the world?" replied Dexter, "The water—it lights up in some kind of—neon green color as the kids swim."

Iselin continued, "I've heard something about bioluminescent plankton, but this is the first time I've ever witnessed it firsthand."

Strong and Fish made it to Dead Man's quickly and without being spotted. Hearing Iselin's commentary, they turned in time to witness the phenomenon.

"Are you guys watching the lookout and the agents or being entertained by some kids?" barked McGovney.

"Sorry, I've got the agents," replied Dexter.

It was time for McGovney to get in the water. Just before going under, McGovney gave Grisham some final instruction, "The towline is secured to the left side. You may have to compensate with your steering to maintain a straight course."

"Thanks for the warning, I'll pay close attention," replied Grisham.

"Strong and Fisher—you guys in position?" asked McGovney.

"We're getting there. We'll be in place by the time you drop."

Soon after McGovney went under, Dexter knew the boat had been spotted. He saw the lookout fix his view on the northwest corner of Raft Island. Then he signaled down to the beach and began climbing out of the tree.

Dexter let the team know, "The lookout is on the move. Do you copy? The lookout is on the move!"

"We copy," acknowledged Strong.

"Copy," replied Grisham.

It was two minutes to 1:00 when Grisham hit the southwest corner of Dead Man's. Well concealed below the water's surface, McGovney dropped and headed for shore. Grisham rounded the end of the island, coming into view of the beach in time to see the lookout repelling down the face of the cliff. "I've got our lookout," he reported, "He's repelling the cliff. There's only one other man—he's got Tyler!"

The man holding Tyler pointed a bright light toward Grisham, completely negating the benefit the moonlight had provided in navigating the boat.

"*Stop right there! Stand up and show me the crystals!*" the man called out, holding Tyler close with a gun to his head.

Grisham took the boat out of gear and stood, holding up the crystals.

"*If there's anyone else in that boat I'll shoot the kid! Come ashore right here!*" he called out, as he indicated a path with the beam of light.

Grisham lightly beached the boat and cut the motor. The guy that had repelled the cliff was readying their boat for departure.

"Are the bags tied off?" came the question from shore.

"Yes," Grisham answered.

"Toss them up here to the beach."

Grisham tossed one of the bags onto the beach. He hoped the others could hear the conversation and were watching what was going down. He didn't want these guys to get away, and he knew McGovney wouldn't make a move while there was any chance of Tyler getting hurt.

The guy on the shore untied the bag to check its contents, "You did real good," came the reply from shore. "You have a real nice find here. Unfortunately for you, we found the spot first—we just had a little trouble locating the crystals. Throw me the rest of the bags!"

Grisham tossed two more bags onto the beach as carefully as he could.

"Kid, get in with the old man," he barked. "Old man, I want you to take a look at our boat," he said as he swept the light across to the other boat. "My help has a gun on the kid's head. You keep your hands in the air while we split, and no one gets hurt—it's that simple."

McGovney was waiting in the shadows at the far west end of the beach, but unable to contribute to the situation. It was too risky.

The guy shuttled the bags to their boat and climbed aboard. They put it in reverse, pulling away from the shore, and then threw the throttle forward. They were off!

"He's making a clean getaway!" Grisham shouted into the radio once the boat was out of hearing range.

"Just get out of there," ordered McGovney, "Get Tyler to Raft Island, we'll handle this. Knowing that he had two sharp shooters on Dead Man's, McGovney barked, "Strong! Fish! Get a bead on these guys!"

"Roger that!"

Suddenly a familiar voice came over the radio, "Want some help with these guys?"

"Is that you Larsen?" asked McGovney.

"Right you are," came the reply. "I was monitoring radio frequencies on our way back from fireworks, when I heard all the excitement. I talked my husband into coming out here just in case you needed a hand. We're riding in stealth mode at the moment. Check us out at about eight o'clock—I'll flash the lead running light."

"Got ya!" replied McGovney.

Want us to intercept them and head them back to shore?"

"Strong, you guys catching all this?"

"Roger! We'll hold fire."

"Head them to shore, Larsen," said McGovney.

Larsen circled, got up alongside them, threw two spots their way, and hollered across the bullhorn," Back to shore boys—fun's over!"

They'd been so busy watching behind—they were taken completely by surprise! With the light in their face, they couldn't even find their guns. The driver of the abductors' boat veered off 90 degrees, putting them on a course that would take them between Dead Man's and Kopachuck State Park, which was on the mainland.

Grisham heard the update on the kidnappers' route. He had just passed by the piece of water where the spit was located. "The tide has come in a little; the spit is just below the waterline. Chase them this way and they'll hit it for sure!"

"We've got'em!" shouted McGovney. "Strong and Fish, get back to the north end! Quick! Dexter, you and Iselin get your sights on these guys!"

"Got it!" replied Dexter.

Agent Larsen headed north along with the kidnappers, allowing a little room in case they had located their guns. *Chance* had the power to outrun them, but at this point they didn't need to use it.

"As we get to the north end of Dead Man's, they'll have no choice but to turn," Agent Larsen said. "Low tide won't allow them to cut through Raft Island Marina."

"Exactly," confirmed McGovney. "We'll nail them on the spit!"

At the north end of Dead Man's, Larsen nudged the throttle forward, forcing the abductors a little closer to shore, and then quickly veered off to the right, circling around.

Before the abductors could figure out what Larsen was up to—it happened! They hit the spit, bringing their boat to an abrupt stop, throwing the passenger straight out over the bow and slamming the driver into the steering wheel and up across the windshield.

Chance sat deeper in the water than the other boat, so Larsen was being cautious due to shallow conditions. Larsen and her husband approached the wreck slowly, throwing all the light they had toward the abductors. One of the men lay still, draped across the windshield—he looked to be in bad shape. The other guy appeared injured as well and was limping back toward the boat.

Agent Larsen took aim in his direction and shouted through the bullhorn, "*Freeze right there!*"

He ignored her command, keeping his focus on getting to his boat. Agent Larsen fired a shot! The man dropped to the water—then realizing from the sound that it was a handgun, he continued in a crouched position toward the boat, hoping he was out of range. His partner had rolled off of the windshield into the boat and tossed him a gun.

That was all the invitation that Dexter needed. He fired a shot at the guy outside the boat, hitting him in the arm—the gun dropped into the water. The man cradled his arm as he yelled out in pain, "Where did that come from?"

Iselin fired near the man in the boat, letting him know that he, too, was being watched. The man rolled over the edge of the boat into the shallow water, "They're all over us!"

Now both abductors were in the water on the far side of the wreck—momentarily out of Dexter and Iselin's view. Dexter gave an update, "I hit one of them in the arm—he dropped his gun in the water. We can't see them at the moment—they're behind the boat—they can't get far. Once they're in view, we'll hit'em again."

"We're almost there," came the call from Strong and Fisher, who were still making their way to the north end of Dead Man's.

McGovney was also enroute to the north end, but he had greater challenges due to his position and the terrain. It was killing him to be missing the action.

"They have no chance," Larsen chipped in, amused by their plight, "They're injured, unarmed, and surrounded!"

Fisher and Strong had split up as they came to the descending ridge that nearly divided the island. Strong took off on a run as soon as he hit level ground. It was only a minute until he could see the two crawling up toward the beach. "I've got them!" Strong took aim, hitting the one that was moving the best in his right leg.

"Got one in the leg—he's down!" Strong reported.

"That one came from the island!" said the man, grabbing his leg. "How'd they get on the island? I thought you were watching from the tree?"

"I was! The old man was alone! The moon lit the boat up clear as day—he was alone!"

Still in shallow water, the abductors were on their knees with their hands in the air, "Okay, we give up!"

"*Keep your hands where we can see them*!" came the call from the bullhorn.

Agent Strong was first to get to there and quickly put the men in cuffs. Larsen had gradually motored *Chance* as close as she could to the scene. Larsen's husband radioed for an ambulance to meet them at Raft Island's dock, while Agent Larsen waded out to the wounded with a couple of old t-shirts to apply tourniquets.

Grisham arrived on the scene as Strong and Fisher were loading the abductors onto *Chance*. He had dropped Tyler on the shore down the hill from his home where friends and family were waiting, and headed back to see if he could be of assistance.

McGovney finally made it to the wreck, where he gathered the crystals and searched for guns and other items to hold as evidence. There wasn't much, only a boat log and a couple of maps that appeared to be of any importance. McGovney took the line that was still dragging in the water behind the boat Grisham was driving and tied it to a cleat up near the bow of the wreck. The wrecked boat was in bad shape and barely stayed afloat as it was towed to the Raft Island's boat ramp, where it was hauled away to be held in impound.

A significant crowd had gathered at the ramp. The dock area had been closed off with yellow caution tape, and additional law enforcement people were on the scene. Ambulances and paramedics were crossing Raft Island Bridge as they tied up. The two men were treated, loaded into the ambulance, and taken to the hospital.

Once all that were involved in the evening's events had given statements, it was time to head home. It was late. There would be another day to share war stories. Grisham invited The Island Gang and their families to his place for a bar-be-que the following day. It was time to tell the story of discovering *Crystal Cove*.

17

The Day After

McGovney phoned Grisham the following morning with an update. "The lead abductor is a guy named Arthur Bricketts—his accomplice was Montell Greene. They claimed to be just a couple of treasure diggers who freaked out when they got beat to the crystals. They assumed they would scare you and the boys into turning over the crystals, or at least a portion of them, and be on their way. They never suspected you'd be retired FBI."

"Do you believe them?" inquired Grisham.

"I'm not sure what to make of it. Initial ID checks show them to be who they say they are, but a thorough background investigation is underway. Neither has a record until now, unless of course these are aliases."

"I'll wager there's more to this than meets the eye," replied Grisham, who was very upset that The Island Gang had been put through this ordeal.

"They say they are part of a local club that dives wrecks and hunts for lost treasure. These two supposedly identified what they were certain was *Crystal Cove* but were never successful finding the crystals. Arthur was on his way to give it another try the day you were there. This time he had dive gear. When he saw you guys, he watched from a distance. Had he not been alone, or had he been armed, I'm sure he would have confronted you at the cove."

Grisham listened, but replaying in his mind the visit from DFW—he was suspicious.

McGovney continued, "He decided to watch you,

and when he saw you and the kids emerging with bags, he was certain you found the crystals—he retreated, called the DFW, and you know the rest of the story."

McGovney felt certain this wasn't the first bad choice these guys had made, but it was the last they'd make for awhile.

That afternoon, Grisham shared the story with The Island Gang and their families. Everyone was grateful Tyler hadn't been harmed. He was a little traumatized, but the experience he'd gone through the night before wasn't much different from some of the events that played out in his mind on a regular basis.

Gary's dad was first to speak up, "So how did you guys find these crystals? I can't believe the kids were even involved!"

"Involved is the wrong word," replied Grisham. "If it weren't for them, we wouldn't have the crystals at all! I tried to figure out the link between Dead Man's and the cove several years ago, but was completely stymied!"

"Dead Man's?" questioned Gary's father.

"Right, the clues to the cove's location are at Dead Man's!"

Each of The Island Gang contributed bits and pieces as they relived the experience of figuring out the dream catcher and how the legend on the map led them in the direction of the cove. They told about finding the map at Grisham's and confessed to having checked the graveyard out during their maiden voyage. They told of begging Grisham to accompany them for the final adventure, convincing him not to tell their folks about *Crystal Cove* until they actually had some crystals. They didn't want to suffer the accusations of being *dreamers* or told to stay away from Dead Man's before having the chance to follow every clue.

They intentionally left out their initial attempt to explore the cove. Investigation at *The Sedgwick* was still underway.

"We'd have never found the crystals without Shadow," said Gary, "He's the one that noticed the crack alongside of this huge boulder that overlooks the cove. His curiosity with that crack led us to figure out that the entire formation in the end of the cove is rock—and that deep inside the rock was a cave—only accessible by going underwater."

Shadow let out a bark and began making the rounds for attention.

Wendy sat quietly, watching the excitement on Gary's face as he wrapped up the final details. Suddenly she realized he'd forgotten something. "You didn't tell them about the gold box!"

It wasn't till that moment that they realized they hadn't seen Wes at the 4th of July celebration.

"Gold box?" questioned Gary's mother.

"Yeah, I stayed in the cave while Mr. Grisham took the first haul of crystals out. We needed more bags, but there was no need for both of us to make the trip. While I waited, I used his flashlight to look around the cave, and I found this really cool gold box!"

Grisham, concerned that Wes hadn't made it to the festivities the previous evening, went for the phone to give him a call.

Wes answered, "Greetings and salutations!"

"Wes, its Reg Grisham."

"Reg—sorry we missed the festivities! I understand congratulations are in order?"

"Congratulations?" asked Reg.

"Don't play sly with me, I heard all about your announcement—I think it's great that you're going to tie the knot again."

"Oh, thanks—we hope you can make it. I'm anxious for you to meet Rose."

"And we're anxious to meet her. Some friends came

to town unexpectedly, and we ended up meeting them in Seattle for the evening. Anyway, we had no idea you'd be breaking that kind of news!"

"It all happened rather quickly," Grisham replied. Without going into the happenings of the previous evening, he simply added, "You missed an eventful 4th! I'm sure the kids will want to fill you in. The purpose of my call was to ask if you learned anything about the gold box. We're finally sharing our adventure with everyone, and when the gold box came up, we realized we don't have it and hadn't spoken with you since leaving it in your care."

"Who's everyone?" asked Wes.

"The Island Gang and their parents are all here," confirmed Grisham.

"Alrighty then—I'll be right over. I have quite the story."

Wes arrived at Grisham's in no time. Grisham let him into the family room, made the obligatory introductions—though most knew Wes—and then gave him the floor.

Wes began, "So I took the box, which, by the way, *is* made of pure gold, to a Native American friend of mine. From the moment I pulled it out of the bag, he couldn't take his eyes off of it. First thing he did was interpret the engraving on the outside of the box. It reads, *'Here lies life's treasure.'*"

Everyone in the room presumed the engraving referred to the crystals.

Wes continued, "My friend Skip, now eighty-eight years old, has studied his people's culture and ancestors for years. The history of his people records that a single tribe migrated to this region years ago. They chose to leave their homeland, located in a group of islands to the far north, because of a division among their people. Island living suited them, and it is believed that they eventually settled in what we now call the San Juan Islands. Anyway, Skip has the knowledge, tools, and chemicals to work with ancient artifacts. He got the box open, and inside was a scroll. Here is the interpretation," Wes pulled a piece of paper from his pocket, and read:

"You have come upon the great treasure of the Skyanabo. The treasure of which I speak is not found in the crystals, although it is my hope that they will serve you as they served my people. The light reflected by the crystals is constant and unchanging, bringing hope, and reminding those who look upon them of the Great Spirit who is the giver of light. There have been seasons when these crystals have proven very valuable to my people, and seasons like now when my people allowed darkness to rule their lives and turned from the goodness that otherwise was in their nature. My great grandfather, Aboabo, hoped to leave the ways of the Skoterga in the islands to the north, but alas, they have surfaced again. It is with deep sadness that I lay the crystals of Aboabo away in this secret place. However, I take comfort in knowing that where I go from here, the Skoterga cannot follow. As I pass through the final dream catcher, I will enter the world of spirits, where evil cannot come. There I will find peace. In the words of Aboabo, 'may the Great Spirit rest upon you, may you never take from the world more than you need, may you share the bounties of the earth with all, may you see that justice comes to those who will not walk in peace . . . these things do, and happiness will be yours.' This knowledge is the great treasure of the Skyanabo. May Aboabo's words of wisdom be your guide. May you find the strength and determination to do much good among men. Look to the light of the crystal, remember the giver of light, and the greatest treasures in life will be yours."

A solemn feeling of obligation to accomplish good works came over Gary. He wondered if the others were feeling the same thing.

Wes continued, "I know you didn't want me to divulge the origin of the box—and I didn't. But the words on the scroll made it clear where the box had come from. The crystals tie right in to the stories Skip has been told all of his life. His people continue to worship light today. More than once, dissenters have ridiculed them for the practice, but his family is among those that have hung on to their beliefs. Your discovery has brought Skip great satisfaction."

"Does that mean we have to give him the crystals?" asked Curtis.

"Not at all," replied Wes. "Legend holds that Chief Aboabo hoped the treasure would bring wisdom and lasting happiness to those who find it. But Skip is so excited with your find; he would like permission to take the box with him to the Aleutian Islands. He has developed friendships with tribal leaders there, and this is the best evidence he has found of his family's migration from islands to the north. Skip asked if he might have the record from the box. He wants to see that it is preserved—possibly in a museum that his people are planning."

"I say we let him have the gold box and the record," replied Gary.

"And some crystals," asserted Wendy. "They're important to the story!"

Everyone agreed.

18

Back At The Sedgwick

Gary couldn't forget the conversation he overheard a couple of days earlier while he and Travis were in Grisham's attic looking for the treasure box. The FBI was close to nailing the underground—if it weren't for the roadblock out at "the tunnel." Getting a man on the inside could take a while. The writings of the Skyanabo made a lasting impression on him. He understood these guys were just like the Skoterga dissenters. They were disrupting peace and order by promoting an industry that takes away personal freedom, and they were undermining the law. They had to be stopped.

In all of the excitement at Grisham's the previous evening, one of McGovney's radios had accidentally been pushed behind a planter on the deck rail. Gary spotted it during the barbeque and found the right opportunity to slip it down under the edge of the deck behind a rhododendron. He had every intention of returning it, but first—he had a plan. He would have to get Travis on board. He knew it was too dangerous to go alone.

The next day, Gary took Shadow out for a walk. During the walk, he thought about what he would say to convince Travis to join him. He took a different route than usual—one that would take him to Grisham's and then by Travis' house. He didn't want to phone Travis with his idea—he had to see him in person. Travis was out front as Gary arrived.

"Travis," Gary called out, running toward him, "I have an idea! We need to talk!"

"What's up?" asked Travis. It was obvious Gary was

in one of those serious moods.

"Up there," motioned Gary, indicating that he didn't want to talk to him where others might hear. They climbed the ladder to Travis' tree house, where they would have privacy. Shadow followed the boys up the ladder.

"I'm going back to the mine—tonight!"

"You're what?"

"I'm going to *The Sedgwick!*" he repeated as he held up the radio. "Somehow I'm going to get this into that truck so that the FBI can track these guys. McGovney said they disappear in *the tunnel,* and that they don't know where the tunnel goes. If we can get the radio into the truck, they'll be able to trace them!"

"First of all—you're crazy! Second of all, what if they switch vehicles in the tunnel or leave the truck and go somewhere on foot—or any one of a hundred other things? Then what?"

"Good point. We'll have to get the radio into the shipment."

Travis looked at Gary in disbelief. "You've flipped! This time—you've really lost it! How do you plan to do all this?"

"We'll figure it out once we get there."

"*We?*" What do you mean *we?*"

"You're coming with me—aren't you?"

Travis was always up for adventure, but going back into *The Sedgwick*—without telling a soul—no backup—it was the stupidest thing he'd heard yet. "These guys are criminals! We were lucky the first time! We can't just go waltzing back in there. We need to tell Grisham your plan. He'll help. He always does!"

"Not this time. He'll never go along with this. He and McGovney will both think it's too dangerous."

"That should be your *first* clue," replied Travis.

"I feel it," Gary said. "This time I feel it. The other

night when Wes read the interpretation from the box—did you feel anything?"

"Yeah, it was cool! We found a piece of history—ancient history."

"It's more than that. We are the ones that found the treasure—the ones the writing referred to—the ones who will accomplish much good! We have to do this! I know we can!"

Travis just stared at Gary, wondering what he was thinking.

"We've been in *The Sedgwick*—all over it as a matter of fact. We have the advantage of knowing the layout. Plus, we have an FBI radio! We'll be able to call for help as soon as we need it."

"Provided anyone's listening," chided Travis.

Travis could see Gary was determined. He couldn't let him go alone. "*Okay*—so when do we go?" he asked, "And exactly *how* do we get there?"

"We leave ASAP! We go by foot. It's too risky for the two of us to try to maneuver the boat across The Narrows. Besides, the only *sure* entrance into *The Sedgwick* is up top."

"And what do we tell our folks? Don't worry mom, we're just going for a little jaunt over to Tacoma—on foot—nothing to worry about."

"We give our parents the same old routine. I'm spending the night at your place—you're spending the night at mine."

Travis knew Gary was right. That had always worked. For just an instant, he wished it hadn't.

They climbed out of the tree house. Gary phoned home to tell his mom, while Travis tracked his mom down to let her know their plans. Then they went to the garage for a few supplies. Travis had one of those garages that are a combination of your worst nightmare and a garage seller's dream. Stuff—was piled everywhere. The thought of heading to *The Sedgwick* on foot wasn't a pleasant one. "Let's take the bikes," suggested Travis.

"What would we do with the bikes when we get there?" asked Gary. "They'll just get in the way, or we'll lose them!"

They located a backpack containing a first aid kit, flashlight, matches, and four packages of ramen noodles. They shoved everything but the food items into Gary's waist pack. Travis went inside for a daypack. Gary followed, raiding the fridge and kitchen cupboards. Apples, pudding packs, sliced deli turkey, pretzels, a couple of bagels, and the last of the Oreo's. *That should hold us over.*

They made one last pass through the garage, which is when something caught Gary's eye. "Scooters! Grab one— let's get out of here!"

They each got a scooter—and they were off. Gary sent Shadow home. He didn't want him along this time. Too many roads—too much traffic—he worried Shadow might get hit. They had a long way to go, but with the long summer days, they wouldn't see dark until after 9:00 p.m.

After crossing the bridge, they followed surface streets where they could make better time. Each time they passed undeveloped land, they made their way through the trees and brush to a view of the water, where they would look down the coastline for signs of the mine.

After several hours, they came to a ridge that looked down on the tracks, just in time to see the dark green truck riding the track. "There it is," said Gary, taking Travis by the arm and pulling him to where he would be able to catch a glimpse before it disappeared from view, "See it?"

"That's the truck! We must be getting close!"

They collapsed their scooters, slung them over their shoulders, left the street, and followed the ridge.

"I can't believe they cruise up and down the track right in the middle of the day, and no one suspects a thing," said Travis.

"It is kind of secluded out here," replied Gary. "There's not much chance of them being seen—after all, they know the schedules and completely avoid trains. If the truck were seen, most people would think nothing of it. Those type of trucks ride the track all the time."

"True," replied Travis, "just the same, it's a little suspicious. It seems someone-somewhere would report an *unmarked* truck running up and down the tracks."

"You're assuming someone sees it on the tracks," said Gary, "Don't forget they can get on and off at will."

At the next clearing, they found themselves on the wrong side of a heavily wooded ravine, separating them from the next possible location of *The Sedgwick*.

"Holy smoke!" complained Travis, "This is ridiculous! How many more hills do we have to climb?"

"It sure doesn't look this rugged from the water," agreed Gary, "but we're almost there. I'm sure of it!" Once again, adrenaline kept Gary going. He would not be deterred.

Finally, at the top of the next hill, their surroundings began to look familiar. "Look, there! Isn't that where they park their cars?" asked Travis, pointing toward an opening in the vegetation ahead.

It was approaching dusk. The sun was soon to make its way behind the Olympics, causing shadows in the view ahead.

"You might be right," acknowledged Gary, "we'd better drop down the bank into the brush."

Well hidden in the heavy brush, they made their way slowly along the bank.

"There it is," whispered Gary, pointing to the hatch door that led into the mine.

They froze for a moment—watching and listening.

"Stay here and keep an eye on that door," said Gary,

laying his scooter at Travis' side, "I'm going up to check for cars."

Gary was back in minutes. "No cars," he reported, as he headed straight for the door. "Hurry, let's get inside while the coast is clear!"

Travis ditched the scooters in the thick brush and followed. Once inside, they were sure to close the hatch, which made climbing down the stairs a little precarious. At the base of the stairs, they paused to listen—*no* cars didn't necessarily mean *no* people. There was a faint glow of light ahead. It was coming from where they had previously been able to look down on the operation. Gary pulled a flashlight out, and they headed slowly toward the overlook.

"I think we're alone," offered Travis.

"Let's get down there and take a look!"

They made their way around to the main entrance and then slowly into the room where all of the planters were.

"Take a look at this!"

The area was monstrous, much larger than what they'd anticipated. They walked among the planters, looking in wonder at all of the tall plants.

"So this is all marijuana?" asked Travis.

"I guess," replied Gary.

A string of old beat up tables ran the length of one entire side of the area they were in. Just above the tables were a series of large heaters. Along the back edge of each table were zip lock style plastic bags of various sizes.

"This must be where they package it," stated Travis.

There was a peculiar odor.

"What is that smell?" asked Travis.

"Must be the marijuana," replied Gary.

They went out to see if there was a shipment in the truck. Gary lifted the corner of the tarp that was stretched across the bed. There were several boxes back against the cab.

"They're ready to make a delivery," offered Travis.

Gary dropped the tailgate for a better look and muttered, "And there's just enough room for us."

Travis had wandered from the truck, missing that comment. "Over here! There's another tunnel."

There on the opposite side of the truck was a tunnel they hadn't seen the first time they'd been in the mine. They followed it a short distance to where the incline became extremely steep. There were steps cut into the earth. Climbing the steps, they came to a familiar juncture.

"This is where we were when we couldn't decide which way to go," Travis chimed in. "That way led to the long shaft that was a dead end!"

"Right!" confirmed Gary. "Let's check out the lab again."

They turned the corner and were greeted by a familiar odor. "And I thought the marijuana had a bad odor!" exclaimed Travis. "This is putrid!"

They wandered around, picking up bottles and jugs that lay on a long counter, trying to read labels to figure out what was in them. Chemicals of some kind—was all they could make out. There were several sinks—looks like they were used for mixing stuff. They were certain that some sort of drug activity happened there. Everything looked about the same as it had before. It was time to get back to the truck.

As they were walking, they suddenly heard voices coming from the hatch door.

"Quick! To the truck!" whispered Gary in a panic.

They hustled, tracing their path back to the truck, trying not to break their necks on their way down the steep steps.

"In here!" whispered Gary, pointing to the open tailgate.

"What? I thought we were just going to plant the

radio," replied Travis.

"There's no time. Hurry! Get in!"

They climbed in and carefully backed their way under the tarp. Gary raised the tailgate as quietly as he could and closed the latch. They waited silently, breathing as shallow as they could. It was so dark under the tarp they couldn't even see each another. Travis was glad; he didn't want Gary to see the expression of pure fright that he was sure adorned his face. He felt as though his eyes were about to pop out of his head. This wasn't part of the plan—at least not part of Travis' plan!

Hearing the men come closer, they scooted a little deeper into the bed of the truck. There was a familiar voice. "How long till we head out?" the man asked, as he opened the truck door.

Gary was almost certain that it was Streets! They could hear him doing something inside the cab.

Suddenly Travis' nose began to itch—he was sure he was going to sneeze. He grabbed his nose, shut his eyes, and pinched for all he was worth. It was seconds before the urge passed, but pass it did. The truck door closed and they could hear the man walking away.

"That was close!" Travis whispered, "I might be allergic to this stuff. I just about sneezed!"

"Don't even!" Gary whispered back. "I sure hope this delivery is going north."

Gary knew from McGovney's description that the tunnel giving them trouble was up north.

"And what do you propose if we do get to the tunnel?"

"We'll figure that out when we get there."

"When we get there?" asked Travis. "We'd better figure it out long before that! I swear—you have a death wish!"

A muffled voice came from back inside the mine,

"Just got the report. All tracks clear till 9:05 p.m.—time to get on our way. Who's going with me?" the voice asked.

"I'm up," came the reply.

"That's Streets!" whispered Gary, "I know it!"

Fearing the men might check the merchandise before taking off, Gary and Travis decided to get even deeper into the bed of the truck. There were two rows of boxes with room on both sides and a gap down the center. Gary took the middle, and Travis was on the passenger's side. They avoided the driver's side all together. There were layers of gunnysack just inside the tailgate. They each grabbed a piece of gunnysack and pulled it up over them as they backed into the bed.

"Easy there," came a voice from behind Gary. He nearly left his skin!

"What! Is that you, Wendy?" whispered Gary, doing his best to slow his heart down before it pounded its way out of his chest.

"Wendy?" inquired Travis from the other side of a stack of boxes.

"Who else? You thought you were just going to sneak off and have all of the fun by yourselves?"

"How'd you get here?" Gary asked.

"I saw you guys leaving the island. I had a feeling you were up to something—so I followed you, and then when I figured out what you were up to, I climbed in and waited."

They could hear the electric motor opening the mine entrance. The doors to the truck opened and shut. As the truck started, an empty feeling came over them.

"Here goes nothing," remarked Travis.

Gary wanted to comment, but unsure of *what* to say, remained silent.

They could feel the action of the train wheels lowering, putting them squarely on the track. Though they had experienced passing trains many times, they had never actually ridden on a train. The feel of metal on metal was dif-

248

ferent. The tarp rose a little with the wind as they whirred along. They made their way forward to the tailgate where they could watch the scenery out the back.

"Water's on the right, we're headed north," confirmed Gary.

Sarcastically, Travis responded, "Great! That means we have one in a thousand chances of ending up in your *tunnel.*"

"Funny," replied Gary. "I doubt they have a thousand drop sites to the north. Looking at the size of the delivery, our chances might actually be pretty good."

The gunnysack added a little comfort to the ride. They talked for what seemed like hours as the truck swiftly made its way through the night. After a time, the water got further and further from view, indicating that they were headed inland. Suddenly they came to a halt. They could feel the train wheels raise beneath them, after which the truck left the track. They were on loose gravel for a short distance, then a paved road. There was a little traffic, so they knew they were near civilization. They crowded up against the tailgate, trying to identify a landmark—but it was no use. They were in a town, but there was no way in knowing *which* town. They decided to lay back and get comfortable. Then all at once, they left the highway without warning. The bumpy ride indicated a dirt road.

"What in the world?" stated Travis, confused at the change in terrain, "Feels like a logging road!"

"Just be thankful for the gunnysack," answered Wendy. "It could be a lot worse!"

The tarp was flopping up and down, giving them limited glimpses. They hit one big bump, and the tailgate dropped.

"Good job with the tailgate," commented Travis.

"Hey, I shut it as quietly as I could," Gary retorted.

Luckily the men up front hadn't noticed.

"Look out there, we're in the toolies!" said Wendy.

The bumpy road lasted quite awhile. Then they were once again on a semi-smooth surface.

"Asphalt," Gary said. "But, no lines," he commented, benefiting from clear view through the open tailgate.

Asphalt soon led to gravel. They had positioned themselves closer to the tailgate curious as to their surroundings, but the impression suddenly came to move deeper in the bed of the pickup. All at once, the truck came to a stop. They quietly covered themselves with gunnysack.

"Good evening, gentlemen," came the greeting from a man who was obviously standing alongside of the truck, "How was the drive up?"

"Uneventful," Streets replied, "and a beautiful night for a drive."

"Uneventful is the way we like it," came the reply, "I'll get the gate."

"Gate?" whispered Wendy in questioning tone.

The truck had barely started moving when the man guarding the gate hollered out, "Hold it!"

The driver stopped and stuck his head out the window to see what was up.

"Your tailgate's down—I'll get it for you."

The guard didn't bother to look under the tarp. He just lifted the tailgate and pushed it shut. "You're good to go," he said, waving them on.

Once the truck was moving, Gary quickly moved toward the tailgate where he could watch the night sky. It was gone!

"*We're here!*" gasped Gary, "This is it! We're in the tunnel!"

"Now's a good time for that brilliant plan you were going to come up with," said Travis.

Gary reached into his pocket, caressing his good luck piece. He'd taken one of the crystals the previous evening and was counting on it for luck. "As soon as the truck slows, we have to get out of here and keep out of sight!"

"What if there's nowhere to hide?" responded Travis, "We are in a tunnel."

"We'll find a place," assured Gary, "then we'll watch."

"No sign of slowing yet," said Travis, "makes you wonder how long this tunnel is."

"Sooner or later they'll slow down," said Gary. "Be ready! We'll have to act fast! I'm going to wrap myself in a piece of gunnysack, and roll out the back of the truck. Everybody get back alongside of the boxes. Once I'm as far as the tailgate, grab an end of gunnysack and roll—follow me."

"I'll go second," stated Wendy.

"I'll be right behind you," added Travis.

Gary crawled across the layers of gunnysack, reached up and carefully let the tailgate down. They waited patiently for the truck to slow, but it kept on going—deeper and deeper into the tunnel.

As Gary sat on the pile of gunnysack, he suddenly remembered the radio. Reaching into his waist pack he pulled it out and turned it on. He peeled a piece of duct tape from the pencil he'd stuck in his shirt pocket. He'd wrapped a little duct tape around the end of the pencil—just in case. With the button taped in the down position, the FBI would be able to hear everything. He messed around with the buttons, trying to see if a signal was getting through, when suddenly the truck hit a big bump, toppling him over. Just as he was recovering, the truck began to slow. Without thinking, Gary grabbed the edge of a layer of gunnysack and said, "Here goes!" He rolled himself into a cocoon, and just kept rolling right over the edge of the tailgate.

"*He's nuts!*" said Travis.

Wendy nodded in the affirmative, crawled into position, latched hold of a layer of gunnysack and rolled out behind him.

Travis hesitated for a split second as he watched the two of them bouncing along behind the truck, then he took a deep breath grabbed a couple pieces of gunnysack and rolled for all he was worth. After a few tumbles he untangled himself from the gunnysack, and got up against the wall of the tunnel. Wendy and Gary were making their way toward him dragging their gunnysacks behind them. The truck came to a stop.

There were headlights off in the distance. The drop was going to take place there in the tunnel. People were getting out of both vehicles. It was then they realized how narrow the tunnel was. There was barely enough room for the two cars to pass by each other.

"What sort of tunnel is this?" asked Wendy.

"C'mon. Let's get a little closer," said Gary, motioning for them to follow.

The oncoming vehicle had cut its headlights so they were protected in the shadows. Slowly they made their way along the wall, ducking into a recess just beyond the back of the truck.

"Got the goods?" came the question from the driver of the other vehicle.

"But of course!" came the reply

"Are the extra kilo's on board?"

"Was there any doubt?"

"It's a limo!" exclaimed Travis.

It was long and dark, probably black, but too dark to tell for sure. There were running lights stretching the length of the roofline.

The back door of the limo opened—a man got out, "Hey uh Joe, beautiful night, eh. Gotta love it when the stars are out."

"Yeah, summer brings the good weather," replied Joe.

"Mole doing okay, is he?"

"Yeah, all is well."

"The project—it's coming along okay, eh?"

"Slow but sure. He hopes to finish by fall."

"That's good. Tell him we're ready for him. Is that Streets with you?"

"I *told* you that was Streets!" Gary said excitedly.

"It's me," Streets replied. "I'll get the cargo."

Streets walked to the side of the truck for one of the boxes. As he unsnapped the tarp, he saw the tailgate was down again. Passing Joe to make the exchange, he noted, "We better get this tailgate looked at. The dang thing is down again."

Joe thought that was odd. He walked to the back and closed it, giving it an extra tug to make sure it was secure. Then he got the remaining boxes and met Streets up front.

"Here you go," said the driver, handing over a briefcase.

"Hey Harley," Joe said, talking past the driver to the guy standing at the rear of the limo, "Mole sure likes the briefcases! He gives them as gifts."

"Gifts, eh?" questioned Harley.

"Yeah, whatever occasion comes along—birthdays, anniversaries, Christmas. The execs all carry one—sooner or later everyone's gonna have one of your briefcases. Then he'll open up down at farmer's market—and sell them," Joe chuckled.

"I'm glad he likes them," came the reply. "See you next week."

Gary, Travis and Wendy listened to the conversation in awe! *How big was this organization anyway? Who were these execs he was talking about?*

Joe and Streets climbed into the truck. They watched for a minute as the limo backed down the tunnel.

"Is that limo going to back all the way out?" asked

Wendy

The truck started up, which was their cue to get clever—quick. They bunched up together in a big lump against the side of the tunnel, pulling the gunnysack up over them. Gary reached in his pocket for the crystal and said a silent prayer. Once they heard the truck pass by, there was a sigh of relief. Gary lifted the corner to take a peek. Grateful they had once again escaped harm—he came out from cover. Wendy and Travis waited a little longer. The headlights came on as the truck backed into an alcove.

"Did you see that?" asked Streets.

"See what?"

"That glimmer off to the side back there," Streets replied, pointing back to where they had come from.

Joe, answering a bit sarcastically said, "I have this little limitation. I only have eyes in the front of my head, and I was looking over my shoulder!"

"Funny," Streets replied. "As you backed, the lights swept across the tunnel. I thought I saw something—like a camera flash—back on the left side.

Gary stood there holding the crystal, waiting for the truck to pull from the alcove and head the other way, but he suddenly realized the headlights were turning back toward him. Instantly, he was back under the gunnysacks.

"Where'd you see it?" asked Joe.

"It was right back there," said Streets, pointing off to the left.

Holding their position and putting on the high beams, they took a long look down the tunnel. "Must have been nothing," Streets replied, "Let's get out of here."

There were piles of dirt and rock here and there throughout the tunnel. The layers of gunnysack fell across the kids, giving the appearance that they were just another pile of dirt—they blended right in.

With the truck gone, Travis got his flashlight out,

"Now what are we gonna do?"

Thinking back to the hatch door at *The Sedgwick*, they were hopeful of an inconspicuous exit out of the tunnel. They walked to the alcove the truck had used to turn around. It was a dead end. They tried several other alcoves—nothing.

Exasperated, Travis started in, "Great! We're stranded in a guarded tunnel miles from nowhere, it's the middle of the night, and there isn't a soul who knows we're here! Now what do you propose—genius?"

Gary wanted to knock him upside the head, but exercised great restraint and replied, "Gee, I don't know—*Curtis!*"

Travis got the picture. He was tired and scared, and the combination caused him to act out of character. Curtis was the eternal pessimist, and none of them cared for it.

Gary felt a curious attraction to the crystal in his pocket. As he pulled it out, there was a clear picture in his mind—similar to the experience he'd had discovering the dream catcher. He wasn't ready to disclose his secret to the others, so he tucked the crystal back into his pocket. "We go that way," he insisted, pointing the direction the limo had gone.

"What makes you so sure?" asked Wendy.

"Just a feeling," he replied.

It seemed unlikely that the end of the tunnel the limo had used would be unguarded, but in this case, the unknown seemed more attractive than the known, and in light of Gary's experience with the crystal, he was rather persuasive.

The tunnel got really tall just past where the limo had stopped, and there were a whole string of alcoves, or possibly shafts—they weren't sure which. Even with the flashlight, shadows obscured the view, making it uncertain.

"Looks like another mine," stated Wendy.

"What's with these guys and mines?" asked Travis.

Gary continued the inquisition, "I wonder what was mined here?" Using his flashlight, he looked down a timber-reinforced shaft. The thought of exploring it entered his mind, but reason prevailed, and they pressed forward. Exploring would have to wait. Further ahead they were finally able to discern night sky coming through the opening at the end of the tunnel.

Gary reached into his pocket and caressed the crystal. *Thanks*, he thought quietly to himself, wondering at the strange power that appeared to be couched in his good luck piece.

"C'mon," said Gary, breaking into a run, "this is our way out."

They exercised caution as they neared the opening. It didn't appear to be gated, but that didn't mean it wasn't guarded. Gary slowly stuck his head out of the opening looking in all directions. "*No one!* C'mon!"

"Hey McGovney, listen to this," said agent Strong, storming into McGovney's office with a radio in hand. McGovney's team was working late, making up for a loss of office time. They'd been pulled out for a special assignment, which in their minds should have meant time off for good behavior—but instead—it meant overtime to get caught up. "I was monitoring several channels, when all of a sudden I hear this conversation. Sounds an awful lot like our infamous Island Gang. I think we've located our missing radio. They're playing around in a tunnel somewhere."

"At this hour?" replied McGovney.

The two of them listened further.

"Where are we?" asked Travis.

"Good question," replied Gary, "The length of time we were in the bed of that truck, we could be almost anywhere."

"Bed of a truck!" exclaimed McGovney. "You don't suppose . . ."

McGovney stopped mid-sentence as he heard yelling in the background.

"Look—water!"

"Get a trace on this signal," shouted McGovney. "Sounds like The Island Gang may have found the other end of our tunnel!"

Wendy and Gary hurried to Travis, who had wandered up a short incline. There they found a boat landing, well hidden in the night shadows cast by a thick stand of dogwood, alder, and maple. Using their flashlights, they could see that there was an outcropping of land to either side. The whole area was heavily wooded. It was a small, protected cove. Maple branches at the opening to the cove reached from both sides, nearly touching in the center.

They walked parallel to the shore until they could get a clear view of the body of water in front of them. Across the water was a length of shoreline, uniformly lined with lights, "Probably streetlights," said Gary. "But is that an island, or is this a bay?"

A bright moon revealed several boats out on the water. There was a fresh wake. Due to its line of travel, it looked as though it could have recently left the landing. Gary grabbed Travis' shirt, pulling him close, "Come here! Quick!"

Gary dug into Travis' daypack locating the binoculars. The boat was a distance off, but a certain series of lights looked familiar. "Here—look!" shouted Gary, once again pulling Travis close, putting the binoculars to his eyes, "Doesn't that look like the lights from the limousine?"

Travis agreed. The boat they had spotted appeared to be a small ferry—possibly only capable of ferrying a single car—at least one as long as the limo.

McGovney slammed his fist on his desk, "How is it our illustrious Island Gang has such a propensity to be in the middle of all the action?"

The FBI had kept watch on the *known* opening to the

tunnel for some time while the DEA and ATF were doing their thing. But they'd kept their distance all the while—trying to locate the other end from the air. The tunnel wasn't charted on any map. Until they knew more, they resisted the urge to storm the gate. That would only signal the network to go deep. They were exercising patience. Like fishing—patience tends to bring a larger catch.

Remembering that he was still carrying the radio, Gary reached into the pocket of his cargo pants where he had shoved the radio after recovering from tumbling out of the back of the truck and said, "Hey, it's still on! The tape held!"

"I thought you were going to plant that on the shipment," stated Travis.

Gary ignored the comment. That had been the plan, but things happened so suddenly. Gary peeled the tape away, releasing the button. He listened for a second or two, and then pressed the button again, "Is anyone there?"

There was a brief cheer from McGovney's office, followed by the reply, "You've got McGovney and Strong. What are you kids up to?"

Excitedly, Gary replied, "We sort of took a ride in the back of a truck, which led to watching a deal go down in the tunnel, and now a limo is on a ferry headed across the water!"

McGovney shook his head thinking to himself, *Sort of took a ride, huh!* He was grateful the kids hadn't been harmed, but somehow these kids were going to have to learn the meaning of the word *danger*!

Putting the sequence of events together, McGovney asked, "What on earth possessed you to go back to that mine?"

They could hear the lectures starting.

"Do you have any idea where you are?" asked McGovney.

"We were in the truck a long time. Could be Boundary Bay," answered Gary, "I think that's Canada across the water.

"Canada?" questioned McGovney.

"Maybe," Gary replied. "This mine is on the water too—way north—several hours at least."

"*Mine*?" questioned McGovney, reaching for a stack of maps sitting in a box on the floor next to his credenza.

"Definitely," Gary continued, "and bigger than *The Sedgwick*.

It irked McGovney just a little that The Island Gang knew more about the inside of these operations than his men.

"Any landmarks?" asked McGovney.

"A string of lights along the opposite shore—looks like street lights, and we're near a point of land. There's a little landing here, but there's no way it's marked on a map. It'd be hard to see from the water—particularly at night."

"I take it they didn't see you?" asked Strong.

"Nope! We had a close call—but we're okay."

"We'll send a helicopter right away. We should be able to find the mine on one of these maps. Keep a look out for our helicopter, and try to find a way to send a signal. There's an awful lot of shoreline out there."

McGovney got dispatch on the phone, which in turn directed the call to agent Willard, the chopper pilot on duty. McGovney explained the situation, giving his best guess as to the approximate location. Willard retrieved a couple of maps and headed out.

"We need a flare gun," said Wendy.

"That would be nice, but it's highly unlikely we'll find anything like that out here," replied Travis.

"There's always one handy in the movies," replied Wendy. She and Travis headed back toward the landing, leaving Gary to watch the ferry. Wendy looked for an emergency kit around the landing area. Travis went back to the opening of the mine. He didn't know exactly what he was looking for. Something they could use to signal the helicopter.

"I can't believe we're supplying Canada," said McGovney. "B.C. is supposed to be one of the largest growers in North America. They must not be able to keep up with consumption," he said jokingly.

"Either that or it's easier to pass the stuff through Canada," replied Strong.

"That's a thought," said McGovney, as a list of potential destinations ran through his head.

He soon located the site of an old mine and got Willard on the radio.

"Willard—over!"

"I'm here," came the reply.

"I've got an old mine out near *Pearl Point*, which is right where their signal is coming from. You should be able to find a place to set down there."

"I'm on it," replied Willard.

Back in the tunnel, with the help of his flashlight, Travis found a passageway just inside the opening that branched off into an area that was loaded with all kinds of machinery. In their rush to get out of the tunnel earlier, they'd completely passed it by. "If only there was some light in here," he stated, talking to himself.

A fluttering noise overhead startled him. He lurched backward, directing his flashlight up, expecting bats—he was right. A cluster of the fury little creatures was hanging to the top of the mine just inside the opening. He kept an eye on them as he felt his way further into the open area. Suddenly he tripped, being thrown backward. As he caught himself, he realized he was leaning on a metal panel, and had triggered a switch, which lit up a series of lights—nothing like the lights in the other mine. These were dim, but adequate. They were balls of yellow glass, each in a small cage of steel, strung together, almost like Christmas lights, but spaced much further apart. "Look at all the machinery!" The stuff was old—looked like it hadn't been touched in years.

The metal panel had his interest. It sat at a slight angle and mounted right into a wall of rock. There were a series of switches, but no labels. There was obviously power to the panel, since that's how the lights had come on. He stood there facing it—wondering which switch had triggered the lights. Curiosity won—he flicked a switch. Something was moving—he wasn't sure what. Then he realized—it was he—*and* the panel in front of him—*and* the whole section of ground he was standing on!

It rotated him into a whole new shaft of the mine! The yellow lights continued for a distance, and then went straight down into a hole. He left the platform he'd been standing on to take a look. There was a ladder fastened along one side, running the entire depth of the hole, which dropped deep into the earth. It was like dropping into a manhole, only a lot deeper. "Where could it lead?" He had to see. Slowly he began climbing down the ladder.

He was waist deep into the hole when he could hear and feel another rumble. By the time he realized it was the platform moving, it was too late—he knew he was too far away—he'd never get there in time! He flew up the ladder and ran toward the opening, but it was a lost cause. The panel had rotated back to its original position. The side he was on was nothing but a wall of rock. He searched high and low for a way out. "There has to be switch, a secret lever, something!" He yelled for help, but it was hopeless. He'd been the only one in the mine, and it was doubtful he was being heard beyond the shaft he was trapped in.

Luckily the lights had stayed on. He had to see where the ladder led, so back he went—down into the hole. It was further down than it looked, but he did finally reach bottom. The lights continued to the end of the tunnel, where there were several pieces of equipment. This equipment *wasn't* old! *Could this be the project Harley referred to?* Then it dawned on him—they're tunneling under the bay! He had to find a way out and tell the others.

With the ferry out of view, Gary joined Wendy back near the landing. The two of them went back into the mine, spotting the lit area. There they located a couple of pallets, and a partial can of fuel. After lighting a fire out near the shore to signal the chopper, they went back into the mine to look for Travis. They figured Travis must have had something to do with the lights being on, but where was he now?

Remembering his earlier experience in the tunnel, Gary reached for the crystal. He grasped it firmly, and everything became clear. He could see that the mine continued beyond the wall of rock where the metal panel was located. "Travis is in there!" he said, pointing to the wall of rock.

Wendy came to where Gary was. "In where?"

"The mine continues beyond this panel. It's a false front, like the barricade at the other mine. One of these switches . . ." mid-sentence he tripped a large red switch—the ground below them began to move.

"There is *definitely* something to this crystal," he muttered.

"What did you say?" asked Wendy.

"Nothing," came the reply.

The crystal gave him an extraordinary sixth sense. He knew it was real—but unsure how to explain it, he kept it to himself.

Travis was almost back to the top of the ladder when he heard the familiar rumble. The platform was on the move. He hurried up the ladder and ran for the end of the shaft, arriving just as the rotation ended. There stood Gary and Wendy. Out of breath from the run, Travis panted, "*Don't move*," holding his arms out as if to block them from leaving the platform. Between breaths he continued, "Any minute now this platform is going to return to its original position, and I can't find the switch on this side."

They remained on the platform. Soon it rotated back.

Disappointed that he had missed out, Gary questioned, "What's in there?"

"A manhole that drops way down deep, and another tunnel," Travis replied. "I think it's the project Harley was referring to. Looks like they're tunneling right under the bay!"

Willard spotted the fire easily enough. Preparing to set the chopper down, he lit the place up looking for a landing site. A tall barb-topped chain link fence surrounded the area. The fence stretched right down to the water both east and west of the landing. The kids hadn't wandered far enough in either direction—they had no idea they were in a secured area.

Gary wanted to go back and see the tunnel for himself. Maybe the crystal would reveal something more—but the noise from a helicopter changed his mind. They quickly exited the mine and watched as the helicopter sat down.

Once in the air, Gary pointed the direction the ferry had gone hoping to get Agent Willard to check it out. Willard knew better than to pursue anything with civilians on board. Besides, he had orders to return the kids to headquarters at once.

Back at headquarters, Gary, Wendy, and Travis pled for mercy. They knew that if their folks got involved, it would be the end of life, as they knew it. McGovney was afraid for their safety. Their first encounter with the Underground had been innocent enough, but the irrational act of intentionally going back to *The Sedgwick* and stowing away in the back of the truck—was too much to ignore.

McGovney was going to have to get parents involved to keep these kids from getting themselves killed. If any of them got hurt and people later learned that the bureau was aware of The Island Gang's curiosity and hadn't warned the parents—that would cause big trouble for the bureau.

Gary begged, "If you have to call someone, call Mr. Grisham. He'll know what to do. We'll tell our parents when the time is right." Gary was quietly thinking that the time would be right when he was about *thirty*!

McGovney finally relented and in spite of the hour, called Grisham.

Grisham groggily answered the phone, "Hello."

"Hey Reg, sorry to call so late, it's McGovney."

Grisham was trying to read the clock on his night-stand, but sleep blurred his vision. Finally he made out the time—2:00 a.m. As his mind cleared from having been startled from a sound sleep, his first thought was that McGovney was playing a joke, trying to catch him still in bed. "You got me this time, you old geezer!"

"Grisham," McGovney said in a serious tone, "I'm not playing games."

Realizing from his tone that McGovney wasn't making a social call, Grisham asked, "What's up?"

McGovney laid out the evening's events, and told him that he had three of the kids downtown.

"Three?" asked Grisham.

"Gary, Travis, and Wendy," McGovney replied.

"Wendy?" Grisham questioned. "That surprises me. I thought she had better sense!"

McGovney told Reg of his intent to call their parents, but they had pled with him to call Reg instead. He expressed concern for the kids' lack of judgment. "Something's got to be done before they get hurt—or worse!"

McGovney's concerns were valid. Grisham agreed to head downtown for the kids. On the way, he determined to convince the kids of the danger they risked in going back to *The Sedgwick*. They had to understand that these were criminals, and would think nothing of—getting rid of them.

McGovney finished debriefing the kids while they waited for Grisham. The Island Gang told McGovney everything they could remember about the inside of the tunnel—names, layout, equipment, landing, etc. Gary also told McGovney about Streets and the encounter they had out at Raft Island a couple of months earlier, something he had withheld after the first mine incident. That really got McGovney's attention.

"I heard his voice, but never saw him again—till tonight. Streets said he rides his bike along Ray Nash several mornings a week," offered Gary.

Grisham arrived shortly after. While driving the kids back to the island, he tried reasoning with them, and was once again taken with their keen sense of right and wrong. They hadn't chosen to become involved in this drama—initially. But now that they were involved, they wanted to do all they could to quell evil. They couldn't leave it alone. They really believed they could make a difference.

Grisham tried to scare some sense into them. "There is a difference between innocently wandering into a situation and intentionally putting yourself in harm's way," he said. "Must be guardian angels watching over you! Do you have any idea what these guys would do if they caught you?"

Travis had a pretty good idea, but he couldn't let his friend go alone.

Wendy never had time to give the matter any thought. She'd followed the guys off the island having no idea what they were up to—until it was too late.

"It was all my idea," Gary confessed. "But I had to go! I knew I could help—I just knew it! Anyway, someone had to find the other end of the tunnel so they could get these guys. They have to be shut down—they're hurting too many people."

On one hand, Grisham wished there were more people in the world willing to take a stand, but on the other hand, " . . . How did you guys know about the tunnel anyway?" asked Grisham.

For a moment there was dead silence. Then Gary did the best he could to cover his tracks, "We were just trying to help catch these guys. Agent McGovney told us how glad he was that they now knew where the tunnel led."

Gary was becoming an artist at avoidance. He hadn't actually lied, but then he hadn't admitted to listening in on the conversation between Grisham and McGovney, either.

Grisham was a little suspicious, but agreed not to get their parents involved—yet—under the condition that they promise to stay clear of the Underground. The kids quietly made their way home and into bed.

19

Streets

With new information, the FBI was ready to set up a sting operation. Canadian officials were contacted and alerted of the smuggling operation. Both U.S. and Canadian agencies stationed undercover fishing boats in the waters outside the landing area where they could keep an eye on activity at *Pearl Point*. They soon learned the landing was more secure than the kids were able to see at night. Hidden by heavy vegetation was a cable drawn across the entry, secured by a lock.

Back at headquarters, Agent Strong had been cross-referencing current affairs and came across a report that made reference to a private investigator going by the name of *Streets*.

"Thought you might like to see this," said Strong, handing the article to McGovney. "If this 'Streets' is our 'Streets,' looks like we could have a vigilante with a bone to pick!"

The article spoke of a kid who had been run over by a vehicle suspected of fleeing the scene of a drug deal gone sour in the San Francisco Bay Area. The hit and run left the kid mortally wounded—he died days later. The kid apparently came from a prominent family. The kid's uncle was Streets. There was a picture of the family standing around a closed casket at the interment. They got the picture to Gary to see if he could ID Streets.

"That's him," affirmed Gary, "that's Streets alright! Just so you know—he's originally from Chicago, and he has the accent to prove it."

Having confirmed Streets' identity, they began asking some questions around San Francisco. They learned that Streets had come to the Bay Area from Chicago several years earlier, building a practice where he could be closer to family. He disappeared several months earlier. No one seemed to know where he was. Putting two and two together, they determined that Streets must have come across a tip leading him to the northwest. If they could only get to him, they'd have the insider they'd been hoping for. By now, Streets surely knew he wasn't going to take these guys down alone.

Agent Strong took the assignment to monitor the bike route Streets was known to frequent. Early the next morning, binoculars in hand, Strong was there—well disguised in an old white van the agency used for reconnaissance. Smoked windows front and back, no markings, it looked like a plain Jane vehicle parked on the side of the road.

It was an active morning. Bicyclists and runners were on both sides of the street. Strong hoped Streets would be alone. He wouldn't feel comfortable stopping him if he were in a group. Suddenly a bicyclist whose profile fit the bill was approaching. Strong studied the man closely. As he got closer, Strong could tell it was Streets! He was sure of it! He opened the car door, and called out, "Excuse me, are you from around here?"

Strong didn't want to spook him, so he thought he would take the nonchalant approach and try to catch Streets off guard. Strong, dressed in khaki slacks, a denim button-down shirt and lightweight flight jacket, looked like any other Joe in town.

"Can I help you?" offered Streets, as he stopped the bike, resting it between his legs.

Strong slowly opened his jacket revealing his FBI ID card that was clipped to his shirt pocket, and quickly stated, "Don't panic! You're not in any trouble. I know you're Streets, and that you're probably in over your head. Thanks to a mutual friend, *The Sedgwick* has been under surveillance for over a month. We also have a guy stationed in the waters between *Pearl Point* and *White Rock*, as well as surveillance near drop points at Lacey, Yakima, and Monroe."

Streets heard enough to know that Strong wasn't pulling his leg. "What do you mean by a mutual friend?"

"Remember a crazy kid named Gary—tried to heist your phone while you were crossing over to Raft Island a few months back?"

Now Streets was really puzzled. "You trying to tell me that kid works with the bureau?"

"Not exactly, but he does get around," replied Strong, as he let a smile cross his lips. "He and his friends have been inside the mines at both locations. *The Sedgwick* they sort of stumbled onto. *Pearl Point*," he said, chuckling and shaking his head, "they tried to play *Hardy Boys*. I have to admit, if it weren't for them, we wouldn't have much of a case."

"Sounds like this kid likes trouble!" replied Streets.

"Exactly—only he calls it adventure. We're trying to help him understand the difference between the two."

"How'd he know I was involved?"

Strong told Streets about the time the kids had tried to boat camp in Henderson Bay, and how they drifted—ending up near *The Sedgwick*. "The changing tide took them down by Olympia," explained Strong, "and by the time morning came, they were being pulled into the Narrows. They tied up to the pier there in front of *The Sedgwick* while they were getting their bearings. After watching the rail truck pull into the mine, they wandered up that way hoping to ask directions, but they were spooked by the secluded set up. In spite of that, three of them actually went inside!"

"They were *in The Sedgwick?*"

"They snooped around awhile and ended up over-hearing one of the other guys call you by name. Streets—it isn't all that common. They ended up exiting the mine through the top entrance and scaling the face of rock to get away."

"That was *Gary?*" exclaimed Streets, recalling the time they'd chased some kids away from the mine. "If it weren't for a passing train, those kids would have been in big trouble! We never knew they had actually been *inside* the mine!"

Changing the topic, Strong continued, "We came across an article from the Bay Area. We know why you're here. Working together, we can put these guys away."

Streets played the politician—listening, showing interest—yet deep down, he hadn't decided what he wanted. He'd thought of rigging a bomb to go off when all of the mukity muks were gathered for one of their meetings—that way he could bury them all right in the middle of their tidy little operation. "What ya got in mind?" Streets asked.

"Let us know when the time is right to get as many as possible in one place. We have the authorities in Canada involved; they'll take over across the border. We just want to catch as many as we can—dirty!"

"They're expanding," said Streets, shaking his head. "Their digging tunnels—at *Boundary Bay* and *The Sedgwick* . . ."

" . . . Tunnels?" questioned Strong.

"They've opened up more of *The Sedgwick*. They've been working on a tunnel for a year now that will take them out down by Chamber's Creek, giving them additional rail access. Word has it the old gravel quarry is closing, and they'll be ready. They're going to move right in. Mole will get the contract to clean the place up—just like he did the old mill near *Point Defiance*. They clean up, and at the same time they have production in high gear—right under people's noses. They either don't look, or don't want to see."

The Island Gang had mentioned Mole while telling of their encounter in the tunnel up north.

"Mole?" questioned Strong.

"Yeah. He's in charge, but he's invisible—I've never seen him. Keeps himself very aloof."

"Who's *they*?" asked Strong. "You said *they* don't look—or don't want to see. Who do you mean?"

"Inspectors," replied streets, "they mull around the old mill, and other projects—monitoring progress. I say they're on the take. Can't prove it—yet! Soon the supply line will be so covert you won't even know it's there."

"Oh?" questioned Strong. "How so?"

"Train cars, chip and gravel barges, tugs—you name it, they've got access!"

"It's not like this kind of people to let product out of their sight!" said Strong. "They usually deliver the goods and get their money on the spot."

"It's bigger than that," replied Streets, "they're well connected. When you traffic in an industry unaffected by the economy, it isn't all that hard to find partners. I'd like to visit further, but if I'm late, they'll be suspicious. It was difficult getting inside."

That's a story that interested Strong, but he knew it would have wait for another time. "How will I contact you?"

"See that fir up ahead," said Streets, pointing to an old growth fir just ahead of them.

Strong looked, "The one that splits near the base?"

"That's it. I often lean my bike up against that tree and wander back in the brush. Sometimes nature calls, and a guy has to see a man about a horse."

Strong got the idea.

Streets continued, "There's quite an exposed root

system where the bank drops off. I'll leave a note tucked in the roots day after tomorrow. I've got a couple of days off next week. I'll let you know where we can meet."

"Sounds good. I'll look for the note."

Streets went on his way. Strong got McGovney on the phone and told him of his luck in meeting up with Streets. They hoped Streets was sincere. They thought of hauling him in, but they didn't dare risk blowing his cover. If he showed in two days, they'd be in.

Two days went by—the note was there. "Tomorrow morning, 10:00 a.m., South Seattle train depot. Look for the bright yellow fleece-I'll be sitting on a bench out front."

He was there, just like he said he'd be. Strong took him to headquarters to visit with McGovney and the team.

20

Wedding Bells

The date for Grisham's wedding came quickly. The Island Gang didn't recall ever seeing a grandma bride, but they had to agree that Rose was beautiful.

There was a great turnout from the island, and lots of Grisham's FBI friends came. The Island Gang boys were decked out in white tuxes with tails, soft rose-colored shirts, and top hats. Rose had found the perfect dress for Wendy— it complimented the shirts perfectly. Wendy thought the boys were all very handsome, but one in particular had her eye—and her heart.

The actual ceremony would take place indoors. Friends from the island had decorated the hall. Reg and Rose enjoyed ballroom dancing and arranged for the *Island Band* to provide music appropriate for the evening. It wouldn't be what the younger set would choose, but then, this evening belonged to Reg and Rose.

The ceremony went off without a hitch. Wendy was the ring bearer, and the boys all stood in as best men. With The Island Gang all up front, Reg took the microphone in hand. "The last time we tried this we were interrupted by the disappearance of Tyler. We're happy to announce that he is present tonight."

There was a standing ovation! Tyler took a bow. He was funny that way. Sometimes he had no problem being the center of attention, but it had to be his idea.

Grisham continued, "I've always believed that individual character is strengthened when people with similar values band together. However, until these kids came along, I would have never guessed that a handful of kids could have such an influence on an old man. At the passing of my dear wife, I went into a dismal downward spiral. I was beginning to wonder when I would ever pull out. But this bright, determined, energetic bunch of youth came along and made all the difference. With their help, I left my self-pity behind, found new purpose in life, and became the person Rose could love. I will always be indebted to a special young girl and a group of boys who showed an old timer that he still had a reason to live."

People were listening—really listening. The sincerity of his remarks had caused most present to pause and take stock of their lives. Most were over programmed, which prevented opportunities for what had taken place between Grisham and The Island Gang. Life was running them, instead of visa versa.

Reg continued, "Thanks to my porch swing, I've learned that Wendy has a beautiful voice. Her love for singing has lifted my heart and my spirits more than once, sometimes without her even being aware."

Wendy squirmed a little as she remembered the time she'd overheard him sobbing.

"She doesn't know it, and most of you are probably unaware, but I also sing. I'd like to start the evening off by dedicating a song to The Island Gang. She hasn't been given any notice, but, Wendy, would you join me?"

Wendy was stunned. He was right! She had no idea Grisham sang. Questions were streaming through her head. What song had he chosen? *Was it one she knew? She'd never sung in front of a crowd this big—what if she choked?*

Hesitant, she nodded her acceptance, and walked toward Grisham. He pulled her close, whispered in her ear, turned, and gave a nod.

With the nod, Wendy expected the band to begin,

when suddenly she heard the sound of a familiar acoustic guitar. Wendy turned to see a big smile on her father's face as he looked intently at his guitar, studying the movement of his fingers on the strings. He picked his way through an extravagant intro, magically blending his way into a familiar melody.

Wendy watched her father with admiration. He loved the guitar, loved to perform, and she loved to watch him. The moment before Wendy and Grisham were to join in, Wendy's father paused—looked up, and sent a reassuring glance in her direction—mouthing the words, "It's just you and me."

She acknowledged with a wink, looked to Grisham, and the two of them harmonized beautifully to a tune that Grisham felt adequately bridged the generation gap, *You, Light Up My Life*. Following their song there was a lasting round of applause.

There were only brief pauses from the band for the next two hours. Wendy's father joined them on a couple of tunes, once again taking the opportunity to show his talent with the guitar. People danced, renewed acquaintances, and rehashed the events surrounding Tyler's disappearance two weeks prior.

The week after the wedding, it became clear to The Island Gang why there had been such a fuss over the crystals. They had been valued at nearly *four million dollars*! The fact that these were the diamonds of *Crystal Cove* had augmented their value significantly.

News of the discovery spread like wildfire. Collectors of First Nation items of antiquity from all over contacted The Island Gang, expressing interest in owning part of the collection. A northwest tribe up the peninsula was desirous of exhibiting some of the crystals in their museum. Another tribe from the islands of southeast Alaska was desirous to obtain some of the "*light stones*" that continue to be part of a legend told by their people.

The Island Gang insisted that the fortune be split seven ways, with Grisham receiving the seventh portion. Grisham was asked to manage all but a small portion of the funds, which were put into an account from which The Island Gang could draw as need be. Each member of The Island Gang identified a charity to which a generous contribution was made. Unbeknownst to Travis, a decision was made to give his father's handyman business some working capital so that the family would be stable enough to stay in their home. Grisham worked with the parents to establish college funds for each of the kids, and then saw that the remainder of the fortune was well invested, with monthly contributions going to charities and other worthy causes.

The Island Gang saw to it that seventy-three of the crystals were donated to the tribe in Alaska, the museum up the Peninsula, and to Skip for the museum his tribe was planning. They chose seventy-three as the numbers seven and three are significant in tribal culture. The museum up the peninsula responded by giving The Island Gang a 56-foot sailboat that had been willed to them the previous year. Curators of the museum had explored the possibility of making necessary repairs to the boat and obtaining permanent mooring, making it part of their museum, which sat near the waterfront. But red tape caused them to change their minds. They were looking into selling the vessel at the time the story of the crystals came to light. Learning of The Island Gang's plans to acquire a larger boat, and considering the generous donation of crystals, they felt compelled to return the gesture.

Grisham helped The Island Gang get the boat over to the Raft Island Marina, where they would have easy access to get her properly rigged for the following summer. They intended to take her into the San Juan Islands in search of new adventure.

Agencies from the U.S. and Canada worked on plans to shut down the Underground. Streets agreed to remain on the inside until enough intelligence had been gathered.

With the first day of school drawing near, The Island Gang gathered at Grisham's shed to reminisce on events of the summer. As they talked about the first time they had entered the shed—and all that had transpired since—they knew it had all been real, but it seemed more like a dream.

TATE PUBLISHING, LLC

Tate Publishing is committed to excellence in the publishing industry. Our staff of highly trained professionals—editors, graphic designers, and marketing personnel—work together to produce the very finest book products available. The company reflects in every aspect the philosophy established by the founders based on Psalms 68:11, "The Lord gave the word and great was the company of those who published it."

If you would like further information, please call
1.888.361.9473
or visit our website at
www.tatepublishing.com

Tate Publishing LLC
127 E. Trade Center Terrace
Mustang, Oklahoma 73064 USA